More Than Goodbye

Rox Blackburn

For Mat—Make your own damn sandwich

Chapter One

THERE'S AN OLD SAYING: IT'S ALWAYS DARKEST BEFORE dawn. This was something Harriet Cook knew to be true. The problem was, she had been waiting for the dawn for over a year and she still believed the darkness would last forever. The worst part? There was an odd comfort and familiarity in it, and the more she stayed the same, the less likely it was she would break the cycle.

As the summer sun rose higher into the crystal blue sky, the Scottish road, which Harriet was no stranger to, gave her a welcoming sense of warmth. She was heading to Ullapool in the northwest of Scotland. A place she had visited as a child and had been itching to go back to for some time. She had paced the floors of her once-happy home for several hours before she took the plunge and booked her getaway. If her anxious mind was going to continue to torment her at obscure hours of the day, she was at least going to do something productive with it. Before she knew it, she was on the road and by the time her common sense caught up with her, she had already crossed the Scottish border.

The feel of her car's steering wheel between her hands centred her and allowed her mind to wander—not too far, though. Just to the edge of her comfort zone. Anything beyond that was dangerous territory.

The soothing breeze blew in through the open window, bouncing her curly brown hair softly across her pale face. The music from her stereo was drowned out by the dull clatter of the changing road surface.

Harriet wondered how her mother might react when she saw the text she'd sent to tell her about her sudden departure. She could almost hear her voice as she imagined how the conversation would go. Overthinking was something Harriet had become an expert in over the past twelve months, and she scrunched her eyebrows together as she envisioned how this one would play out.

Some might find it odd that a twenty-eight-year-old had to explain her actions to her mother. But Harriet knew she had a courteous obligation, given how much she had leaned on her mother over the last year. She loved her dearly, and Harriet knew that without her watchful eye, she would have spiralled and lost herself completely.

As she passed Stirling Castle and William Wallace's Monument, the normal peacefulness Harriet felt when driving was replaced with a jittery feeling in her fingers, which worked its way up her arms. It put her entire body on high alert like something bad was about to happen. Existing in this state left her with a constant feeling of exhaustion, and Harriet knew if she ever wanted to change, she had to do something different.

She watched the colours in the sky change varying shades of blue as wisps of iridescent clouds danced on the horizon. Every time she rounded a corner and the light changed, everything looked different. Even with heavy eyes and a heavy heart, the changing Scottish landscape didn't fail to take her breath away. She tried to relax her shoulders and forced her chest to expand as the rhythm of her heart dropped to a steady beat in line with the soft music from the stereo.

She was home.

The last twelve months had brought so many unwelcome emotions, and Harriet had run out of ways to stop them overwhelming her. She took solace in the nostalgia of crooning nineties pop music and was grateful for something soft to take the edge off the constant bombardment of sharp thoughts that plagued her mind whether she was asleep or awake.

Marriages end all the time. Harriet knew the end of hers wasn't any more significant than the thousands that ended every year. The way it ended, though, was something else. Something she struggled to accept. The part she struggled with the most was there wasn't a thing she could have done to prevent it. She knew this. She had been told this. She had said it out loud a thousand times, yet her traumatised brain still fell into a state of shocked panic every time she got close to thinking about anything associated with it. As the first year by herself went on, she drifted into panic involuntarily, her subconscious being triggered by the most insignificant things, and when that feeling took hold, there was no way of fighting it. It consumed her.

It was just past Dunblane when her heart rate increased, and the tears started falling. A few moments later, the shaking in her hands took over and she had to pull over on the hard shoulder. She slammed the brakes of her car, bringing it to an abrupt halt. As she stumbled out of it towards the grass verge, her body was no longer able to keep the contents of her stomach where it was supposed to be, and she threw up everything she had eaten the night before.

"Just breathe through it," she could hear Julia, her therapist saying in her firm yet encouraging way.

Harriet tumbled to the floor on all fours, her breath short and shallow, getting stuck in her throat. With her last ounce of strength, she made herself sit up. Gripping her ankles, she forced the air in and out. Her sweat-soaked hair fell about her face as she dropped her head between her legs.

She gasped again, willing her body back to composure but all she managed was a pitiful cough before her stomach heaved again. Tears streamed down her face, stinging her eyes. Sweat poured from her brow, and the hazy world began spinning around her. She clenched her fists to her head, pulling her hair out of her face and squeezing her eyes tight, rocking back and forth, begging herself to stop.

"Just breathe through it," the familiar voice said again.

Eventually, after what felt like an eternity but was likely only a few minutes, her heart rate slowed, her vision came back, and she was able to regain control of her breathing. Concentrating hard, she squeezed her eyes shut just as she had been shown numerous times. Finally, the pounding in her chest, ears, and head subsided. She wiped the moisture from her hands down her jeans and the tears from her puffy cheeks as her shoulders slumped in a long, soothing sigh of relief.

She shook her head again and growled deep in the back of her already angry throat, cursing herself for not being more in control. Thankfully, a faint distant voice echoed in the back of her mind, and she remembered to forgive herself.

As quickly as her little episode had appeared, it didn't take long before it felt like it had never happened. She laughed to herself as she climbed back into her car. She mopped her brow and chased some cool water down her dry, aching throat and was back on her way.

The rest of the drive was, thankfully, uneventful. Aside from cussing at a couple of obnoxious lorry drivers hogging the middle lane on the motorway, nothing else happened. Harriet was relieved when she hit the highland roads.

When the road touching the south tip of Loch Broom and Ullapool came into sight, Harriet smiled and stuck her head out the window. The salty air filled her lungs, and her blue eyes glistened at the sight of the peaceful water. The driver behind her honked loudly as she dawdled her car around the harbour wall, shaking her back to reality. She put her foot down, and in no time at all arrived at the local supermarket.

"Good job, Bernard," she said, patting the top of her car before making her way inside.

She was in and out in no time and felt pleased with the haul of home comforts she had purchased for her stay. The feeling of accomplishment was short-lived as, when she returned to her car, something—someone—flashed in her peripheral vision, making her blood run cold.

Harriet did a double take. "You're not there," she said to herself under her breath, her heart rate picking up. She squeezed her eyes shut, reminding herself that no one knew where she was, and it was not possible for her ex-husband to be standing a few feet away from her. She closed her eyes tighter, making her forehead ache and, thankfully, when she reopened them, the car park was empty.

"You're tired. It's been a long drive," she uttered. "It's your mind playing tricks on you." Reaffirming this to herself over and over made her feel better, and she turned the ignition for the final part of her journey.

The north road out of Ullapool took her alongside the smokehouse, where they smoked fish, meat, and cheese. The smell of burning meat made her nose twitch and her tastebuds tingle. The tarmac stretched out before her, the incline taking her all the way up to the summit of a steep hill, and she thought how nice it would be to keep going in a straight line and disappear into the clouds.

Harriet steered her car carefully off the road to the right, following the single-track lane that snaked through large boulders. Sunshine poured into the car, bathing her soft features in a warm glow.

After passing a couple of newly whitewashed buildings tucked into the hillside, and what looked like a sign for a bed and breakfast, Harriet brought her car to a steady halt at the back of her cottage and breathed a sigh of relief.

The whitewashed two-storey building stood proud against the backdrop of the expansive bay. Dark wooden windows broke up the pebble-dashed walls which seemed to shine like the soft light of a full moon. A large wooden door at the top of three shallow steps welcomed Harriet, and the plaque above it read 'Taigh Air A' Bhagh'. Harriet later Googled it and found it meant 'House on the Bay'. She dropped her handbag on the steps, feeling she was in the right place. The gentle warm afternoon breeze ruffled Harriet's hair as she walked around the slate path to the front of the house. It was then that Ardmair Bay fully revealed itself.

Harriet walked straight past the cottage without

thought, totally immersed and captivated by the view. She recognised the mountains and the shape of the bay from the pictures online. She felt the pull of the past begging her to remember it all, but no matter how hard she tried, she struggled to bring her memory to life. As she made her way closer to the garden, the gravel crunched under her soft-soled trainers. Every sound was heightened and her senses came alive. She took a large step up onto the small garden wall through the rich purple heather, and to a large chair-like boulder that stuck out across the ridge. She inched closer to the edge of the thirty-foot drop below. Sharp rocks, nettles, branches, and bracken would break your fall—and every bone in your body.

Harriet stretched her arms into the air, reaching up as high as physically possible to undo the knots in her shoulders and back. She looked around, allowing the welcoming caress of the sun to coat her face.

Straight ahead, the bay bled into The Minch, and the tops of the Summer Isles graced the horizon. Isle Martin Nature Reserve sat snugly inside the bay, and Harriet could just make out a group of people in brightly-coloured canoes darting about on the water just beyond Ardmair Point. Ben Mór, part of the Coigach mountain range, rose up to the right at the edge of the water, standing tall and proud, showing off its terrain, illuminated by the afternoon sun.

The water was a brilliant shade of azure blue, dark in places and light in others, and the small ripples of the incoming tide created a shimmer. The contrasting cerulean sky was clear, save for a few wisps of cloud atop the mountain. The expanse seemed to go on and on; Harriet could see for miles in every direction. Her eyes followed the natural crescent-shaped curve of the shoreline to the tip of the pebbled beach, which stuck out into the water like the tail of a snake.

A tear formed in Harriet's eye as she felt a rush of emotions. A deep sadness etched so far into her face it ached all the way to her bones.

Why aren't you here?

She gulped the sea air deep into her lungs, which felt like it stung her from the inside out. She wiggled her fingers, the jolts of electricity dancing between her digits. A buzzing started in the back of her head and in her ears. She closed her eyes, expecting to be crippled by another panic attack. She stepped back from the rock to the soft mossy comfort of the walled garden and stood braced, suddenly aware of the unfamiliarity of her surroundings. But nothing came.

Confused, she looked around as the swell of buzzing rolled down the hillside behind her. Her eyes darted back and forth as it echoed between the rocks and the thick undergrowth. It wasn't a sinister noise but something curious. It had Harriet temporarily vexed as she tried to determine its source. Still puzzled, she returned to the front door of the cottage and rotated the dials on the lock safe to collect the key. The sound of it bouncing against the solid stone step as it fell to the ground made her jump.

Harriet stepped inside, taking in the details of her temporary home. The thing that hit her first was the empty silence that seemed to mirror her own. The utility room boasted everything she would need: a washer, dryer, and an array of camping equipment. The kitchen was spacious. Pine cupboards hung from two of the back walls. A small window above the sink to the right overlooked the conservatory.

A cabinet full of pamphlets, books, and games sat snugly against the opposite wall. A four-seater dining table was pushed under the long window that flooded the room with light. Harriet chuckled as fond memories of family board game night jumped to the front of her mind. How she would sit with her parents, brother, and older sister — who she used to idolise — and fall out over Monopoly.

Harriet knew the frosty relationship with her sister needed to thaw. For the time being, Louise was being sensitive and kind, but she knew it was only a matter of time before they would be at loggerheads again. Or perhaps they'd just stop talking completely.

The entire downstairs was hardwood floors with strategically placed rugs to dampen the thuds that inevitably rattled through them when the cottage was full. But it wasn't. She was alone.

A twin double bedroom and a small shower room were off to the left of the kitchen. The stairs stuck out into the middle of the living room, which had a log-burning stove and a floor-to-ceiling window. The front porch housed fishing gear, and when Harriet opened the glass door, she was greeted by the smell of oil and diesel, which appeared to be coming from a small boat motor on the floor in the corner. Up the stairs were two further bedrooms. One on the left appeared to be a children's room with colourful bedspreads and stuffed toys stacked in the corner.

The master bedroom was enormous. The dormer windows stuck out of the front of the house, and she could once again see the entire bay below her. The window on the other wall looked up across the hillside, and Harriet could make out the veranda of a neighbouring property, which was bustling with activity.

Suddenly, a draught blew across her cheek, which made her gasp and turn around. The air in the cottage was warm and still when she first entered, but this was ice cold and lingered ominously. She looked around to see if a window had been left ajar but couldn't spot anything.

Her stomach growled, interrupting her search for the source of the draught, and gripping hunger was suddenly all she could think of.

Chapter Two

SCURRYING BACK DOWN THE STAIRS, SHE DECIDED TO put off her habit of unpacking the second she got somewhere new and ventured back into Ullapool for a meal. It wasn't long before she was seated in the conservatory of The Seaforth Bar on the harbour front, tucking into fish and chips and enjoying a glass of the local brew.

Her food went down too quickly; Harriet hadn't realised how ravenous she was until a cheery waitress came to collect her empty plate. The girl had a petite, slender frame, shoulder-length mousy brown hair, high cheekbones, and turquoise eyes. Her name badge was half covered by a black towel draped over the shoulder of her white blouse.

"Thank you," Harriet said, gazing at her as she reached over and took her plate away. The soft scent of lemons mixed with cooking oil drifted from her.

"Pleasure," replied the girl, smiling. "Will there be anything else?"

"Maybe in a minute," Harriet replied, struggling to make eye contact.

Looking someone in the eyes made Harriet feel vulnerable, and she swiftly cast her gaze back out across the water. The waitress didn't linger. The restaurant was bustling, and Harriet looked back to see her darting around like a busy bee.

Harriet turned her attention back to the boats bobbing around on the ripples. She enjoyed watching the people walking by and the steady hum of evening activity in the quaint town.

A childhood memory returned. She recalled being in the same restaurant with her family. She surmised she must have been about ten. Her parents argued over the difference between haddock and cod, and her little brother had dumped an entire bowl of ice cream in his lap.

She laughed to herself again. For the second time that day, something had made her smile. She let the warmth of the memory wrap around her, enjoying the comfort of a simpler time before her sister, Louise, had moved away and, more recently, her world had fallen apart.

The icy nervousness she had been holding onto melted a fraction, and she felt quite content in her surroundings. Harriet knew she was in the right place to begin her healing. *Baby steps.*

She looked back out across the water as it turned different shades of silvery grey and bottle green under the dimming light. She steadied her mind and her heart rate by depositing the remains of her drink down her throat but was pulled from her stroll down memory lane by a chair screeching across the cobbled floor.

"Do you mind if I sit here?"

Harriet froze. Her eyes were drawn to a tall, broad-shouldered man who thudded into the chair opposite her. He had short but rich light brown hair shaped meticulously

12

around his ears with a slight wave on the top. He had a perfectly square face but a rounded chin, with a strong jawline, adorned with just the right amount of stubble, and a light dusting of freckles speckled across his nose.

Harriet shocked herself, surprised at how much detail she had taken in from a swift glimpse. She glanced again, noticing his blue denim jacket was rolled up to his elbows, with a maroon hoodie underneath it. He leaned on the table, frowning at his phone, which he held in his shaking hands.

After a moment, he put his phone down with a frustrated clunk and ran the palm of his hand across his mouth. His agitation was palpable as he looked around the room. It was then he caught Harriet looking at him, and their eyes met. His deep hazel eyes with tiny flecks of gold lingered on her for a moment. Immediately, Harriet looked away, her heart pounding in her throat.

"Sorry for disturbing you," he said softly. "I'm waiting on some friends. They appear to be running late and I fancied a beer." Harriet's heart rate quickened as he continued to talk. He huffed and looked around again. "Is there anyone serving today?" He raised his hand to get the waitress's attention.

Harriet feigned a smile, trying to hide how blindsided she was by his company. But even she couldn't deny she was strangely intrigued by him, and she stole another sideways glance.

"Thanks for letting me sit here," he continued without looking up. His phone buzzed again, and his attention was drawn back to whatever was making him unsettled.

"What can I get you?" the waitress asked, notepad and pen in hand.

He vigorously typed a reply before setting his phone

back down.

"You look like you're having a rough day," the waitress said. "Yeah." He laughed. "Just a bit." He rubbed the back of his neck and rolled his eyes. He looked up at her, and Harriet noticed a familiarity between them. "Oh, hey, Kathryn. I didn't realise it was you." He attempted to smile up at her. That smile may have graced his almost white lips, but it never reached his eyes.

Stop staring.

Harriet wondered what was wrong with him. Tension radiated from him.

"Hey yourself," she replied, smiling and revealing her braces between her thin, rosy lips.

"A pint of Coast to Coast please," he said quickly. "And a.... whatever my friend over here wants," he continued, motioning towards Harriet.

"Oh, it's okay," she replied, panic-stricken. "I can get my own."

"Not at all. It's the least I can do for your hospitality." His gaze met hers, and she felt a strange sensation in the pit of her stomach as those hazel eyes locked onto hers.

She hesitated for a moment, flustered, but not really sure why. Maybe because it had been so long since someone bought her a drink. Maybe she was floored by his unexpected kindness, or perhaps she was unable to think of an excuse to say no. "I'll have the same," she replied with an awkward shake in her voice.

The waitress nodded and went over to the bar. He glanced around, obviously looking for his friends, and leaned back against the solid restraint of the dark wooden chair when he concluded they weren't there.

"Thank you," she said, her voice barely above a whisper. "You didn't have to do that."

"Not at all." He smiled before turning his attention back to his phone, which had started ringing.

Harriet looked away, trying hard not to listen to his conversation. She had intentionally not pulled her phone from her bag whilst she ate. She wasn't quite ready to explain herself to her mother, even if the guilt was starting to gnaw at her.

"Oh, come on. What do you mean you aren't coming?" he said to the person at the other end of the phone. It was hard to make out what the other voice was saying, but she could tell by the tone they were in the middle of an argument. After a few moments, he sagged back in his chair and muttered, "Fine. I'll meet you later." He hung up, a deep frown cut into his brow.

Harriet was doing her best to give the appearance of being in a world of her own. Her eyes glazed over as she concentrated on staring out across the water, but she could feel his gaze burrowing into her.

The tension was interrupted by the arrival of their drinks. Kathryn lingered a moment at the end of the table, looking at the man, clearly wanting to chat, but the sound of the kitchen bell ringing soon pulled her away.

"Cheers," he said, lifting the glass and downing a third of the drink in one go. The sweet nectar seemed to soothe him as he rolled his shoulders and relaxed his elbows on the table.

Harriet glanced sideways again, catching his eye and a glimmer of a soft smile. Curiosity got the best of her. "Is everything all right?" She tucked her hair behind her ears and dipped her eyes.

"Yeah." He half laughed, pulling his glass to his lips and taking another gulp. "It's daft," he said in a rich southern English accent.

Harriet nodded and raised her eyebrows, grinning. "Well, you're gonna have to tell me now."

He frowned at her in a curious, almost playful way and bit his lip. "My friend and I sort of had an argument," he began as he glanced down at his phone and then back at her.

He paused, tilting his head to the side as Harriet's expression urged him to continue.

He dropped his head. "We're in a band and we're having some... conflicting views on a couple of things." Harriet nodded to show him she was listening. "And we said a bunch of jerk stuff to each other and, um, I left to clear my head, thinking he was going to meet me here and now he isn't."

Harriet giggled involuntarily, pulling a balled fist to her mouth. "Oh, dear." She tried to muster up some sympathy, but all she could think about was a time in college when two of her friends had been playing an open mic night and had fallen out over something trivial. It had gotten them all kicked out of a bar that barely held fifty people.

"Yeah, it's silly. I know." He laughed. "Two grown men fighting like kids."

"It is a bit, but still, fighting with your friend sucks." She reached her slender fingers around the glass, pulling it to her lips. The way he watched her made her a little uneasy at first. But there was kindness in his eyes, and Harriet found it quite endearing.

"Yeah, it does. We never fight normally."

A natural silence fell between them.

"So, why are *you* sitting here by yourself?" he asked.

Harriet's stomach turned over in panic. She tried to scrabble for an answer that kept herself hidden but didn't come across as brash. She told herself that this man didn't know her or what had happened to her, that she was quite capable of holding a friendly conversation with a pleasant stranger.

"I'm on holiday," she mumbled hesitantly. Her heart was beating so fast it felt like it might jump out of her chest.

He eyed her with a puzzled frown.

"I'm sorry, I have to go," she garbled, standing abruptly and inching her way past the table. "I hope you work things out with your friend."

Clutching her handbag for safety, she approached the waitress station, paid her bill, and exited at a rapid pace. She walked by the windows with her head dipped and her hair covering her face.

It was a few minutes before Harriet realised her feet had pounded her the entire length of the harbour front. The warm summer air had turned to a brisk evening bite as it hit her face. She willed herself not to throw up the meal she had just spent her money on. The motion of her pace and the sound of her feet hitting the tarmac seemed to quell the nausea, and by the time she reached the edge of the promenade, it had gone completely. She kept walking, kept breathing, just as Julia had taught her to.

She was a little embarrassed by her fumbled departure, and part of her wanted to go running back and apologise. But her legs kept moving. Harriet had slowly learned to speak kindlier to herself and she reminded her inner monologue that people were generally good, and it was normal for them to want to interact. Light, harmless conversations with a stranger over a beer were a million miles away from the conversations she'd been having with people back at home. There was always someone trying to fix her or make her relive the memories she was trying to forget.

Once Ullapool's seafront ended, it rounded a bend and turned north, opening up into the most spectacular and dramatic landscape. The open water disappeared between the rolling hills on the horizon. Working her way along the unfamiliar roads, Harriet was relieved to find a much-welcomed bench and sat down to take in the dusky air.

She closed her eyes and crossed her legs underneath her, enjoying the melodies of her surroundings. Water gently hitting the rocks, and the humming of boats on the water. The soft rhythm made her feel calm and safe. Leaning back into the bench and zipping her coat up, Harriet took a moment to appreciate how much she liked the stillness.

Her mind drifted to pleasant places; the king-sized bed back at the cottage and the plush purple heather swaying in the breeze. She knew she would never tire of the way she felt when the light hit the mountains and the clouds cast shadows over the sea. Harriet sighed deeply, sitting in blissful quietness. The light faded further, and it wasn't long before she was surrounded by darkness.

Losing track of time was nothing new, but it wasn't until Harriet opened her eyes again and she had to adjust to the dark that she realised how long she had been sitting. She glanced around, trying to determine the way back to her car, but something on the footpath caught her attention. She squinted to focus her tired eyes. A figure was walking on the opposite side of the road.

Harriet dropped her head to hide her face, a self-preserving habit she had gotten into, but she was also curious about who might be walking the quiet streets after dark. So she waited, sitting perfectly still as the figure got closer.

A small white speedboat spluttered on the water, its

lights bouncing off the ripples, distracting her momentarily. It bunny-hopped on the surface before taking off into the distance. Harriet followed it until it was out of sight.

When she looked back over her shoulder, the figure was gone. She wondered if she was going mad and if anyone had been there at all. She pulled her jelly legs out from under herself to stand up.

As her feet pushed into the soft grass, she was joined by the guy in the blue denim jacket. He parked himself next to her with such stealth and speed it took a moment to register it was him.

"You left pretty quickly," he said, pulling his collar up, shielding himself against the night's chill.

Harriet gasped, raising her brows as her mouth fell open. Her pulse quickened in her throat, and she felt a little lightheaded.

"Did you follow me?" she blurted out, more out of shock than anything.

"No, of course not," he replied. "I'm meeting my friend for a lift." He had a hint of urgency in his voice as if he was hurrying to explain himself. "What are you doing up here?"

"Nothing," she replied, softening her tone. "Just sitting."

She could feel him looking at her, studying her, and although it made her a little uncomfortable, she didn't mind.

"Are you all right?" he asked in a surprisingly warm way.

"I'm fine." Harriet took in a sharp breath to try and calm her racing pulse. "Honestly, I'm fine," she muttered, pushing her lips into a smile.

She turned to look at him, watching the dim yet persistent hue of the weathered streetlight cast lines of gold down his nose and chin. He looked puzzled and swayed a little, making Harriet wonder just how many pints of Coast to Coast he'd drank whilst waiting for his friend.

"I guess your friend didn't show up." Engaging in conversation forced her out of her comfort zone, and she felt her outer shell crack.

"He did not," he replied, half laughing. His eyes scanned the water and his hands rubbed against each other. "You know that was two hours ago, right?"

"Oh," she replied. "I guess I lost track of time." Her racing heart slowed a little as she rolled her shoulders, realising how unhinged she appeared.

"Well, I can see you're fine, so I'll be on my way," he said, attempting to stand up.

"I'm sorry I left so quickly," Harriet said as he towered above her.

He fell back onto the bench, blinking slowly and smiling. The orange shimmer showered him again, accenting his strong jawline and kind, albeit slightly inebriated eyes.

"I... I..." She tried to say something else, but the cold air captured her breath, and it stuck in the back of her throat. He didn't notice. All his concentration looked to be taken up with sitting still and not swaying.

"I'm Harriet," she eventually blurted out.

"Owen."

She caught him looking her up and down. She didn't dare imagine what he thought of her or why he was still talking to her.

"Did you work things out with your friend?" she asked.

"Yeah, for now," he replied. "I'm heading back so we can pick practise back up."

"Oh, yeah. You said you were in a band. What do you play?"

"A bit of all sorts, but mostly drums. I also do backing vocals, and I'm often tour manager, referee, and general dogsbody."

Harriet knew she was hard to read, but this guy was an open book. He wore his giddy emotions all over his face, and she could tell he knew it too by the way he blushed. She wished she had something in her life that lit her up the way Owen lit up as he spoke about his band.

"What's the band called?"

"Whelven."

"Whelven?"

"Yes, Whelven."

"What does that mean?"

He rubbed his fingertips across his chin and pursed his lips. "To turn things upside down."

Before Harriet had a chance to think, she started laughing, which made Owen laugh, albeit with a puzzled look on his face. She thought it ironic that the band name perfectly summed up everything that had happened to her. Any overlapping tension following her abrupt departure dissipated into the night air.

"Do you like it?" Harriet went on as she regained her composure, her conversation skills improving the more she spoke.

"Most of the time," he replied, hiccupping and holding his -chest.

"I'm glad you worked things out."

"We'll see." He rubbed his hands again. "Here's Ricky now," Owen said as he stood and smoothed his jeans.

The bright lights of the approaching car stopped a few paces away from where he stood. Harriet stood too, her eyes fixed on him. She couldn't look away; she had never met someone so tall. She came in at a respectable five foot seven, but he was a good half a foot taller than her.

"It was nice to meet you, Harriet," he said, slightly slurring his words.

"You too, Owen,"

"Are you going to be all right getting back to wherever you're going?" Owen asked.

Harriet paused, wondering if, in fact, she would ever get back to where she was going. She felt a million miles away from who she was and what she thought she knew.

"Thanks. I'll be fine."

Owen stuffed his hands in his pockets and looked at the ground. "I guess I'll see you."

Harriet's cheeks flushed. "I'll see you," she replied, turning on her heel and heading in the direction of where she thought she had parked her car.

Once back inside the comfort of her lodgings, Harriet donned her lilac cotton pyjamas and succumbed to the call of the king-sized bed.

It was only when she pulled the covers up to her chin and closed her eyes, she noticed she could still hear that strange buzzing sound from earlier.

She threw the covers off, leapt out of bed, and stomped to the window, pulling back the curtain. Her eyes were drawn to the house up the hill that was fully illuminated and bursting with life. She scoffed at the noise, cursing her too-close-for-comfort neighbours and hoped it wouldn't become a nightly thing.

Harriet shut the curtains and dropped into the crisp white linen of the bed, pulling the pillow around her head to block out the noise. She closed her eyes, and her body sank into the mattress. Thankfully, it wasn't long before she drifted into a deep sleep.

Chapter Three

Harriet dreamed of boats and water, of unfamiliar children splashing on a pebble beach. A boy and girl no older than six. Their matching brilliant white hair dazzled in the sun, and their infectious laughter rose like a song, drifting carelessly along with the sea breeze. The image was intermittent; flashes of a door opening and closing interrupted her happiness. Harriet saw herself standing on the threshold, frustration building as the door bounced back and forth on its hinges.

She was powerless to stop it. She tried to grab the handle, but it moved away too quickly. The vision of the children flashed in and out of the scene, interrupting the image of the door, making Harriet dizzy. She was determined to grab it and pull it closed once and for all. But as the images swirled and blurred, her resolve wavered, and she knew she was losing.

Beneath the sheets, Harriet tossed and turned, tangling herself up in a tighter knot. Sweat dripped from every pore of her body. She tried to scream for help, for the door to stop, but no matter how hard she tried, her voice got stuck, and she crumbled to the floor, helplessly watching the door swing. A flash of red filled her vision, jolting her awake. She sat bolt upright, panting for breath, her hair sticking to her face.

She pushed her hands into the soft fabric beneath her as she came to realising she wasn't sitting on the tiled floor of her kitchen back home but was safe in the centre of a duvet with only darkness staring back at her. There was no door, no children, and no pebble beaches, only darkness and a thin sliver of light shooting straight across the floor from the gap in the curtains.

She tied her hair in a bun on her head, shaking herself to awaken her muscles. The buzzing noise that was there when she had fallen asleep was even louder. Harriet untangled the sheets and pillows, almost falling to the floor as she got out of bed. Padding to the bathroom, she washed the perspiration from her face and neck before returning to the bedroom.

She peeked out through the curtains and saw the house up the hill was still lit up; there were people in the garden, and the large patio doors onto the veranda were wide open. Real music, not a CD or a random playlist blasted out into the night. The clear sound of a guitar and voices howling at the moon drifted down the embankment and straight into her window. She looked at the digital clock on the bed side table; it read 03:15 in bold red.

Harriet was furious with the noise spilling down the hillside and decided she was not putting up with it for the next nine and a half nights. Without a second thought, she pulled on her walking boots—neglecting her socks— and threw her arms into a long olive-green cardigan to pay her unruly neighbours a visit.

She locked the door, phone and torch in hand, and

crunched across the gravel and up the hill. Taking a left at the bend, the wind whipped around her, making her shudder, but tunnel vision kept her mind on the task at hand. She continued to march with purpose until she met the porch of the house hidden in the hillside. It was at that point Harriet asked herself what exactly she was doing.

The pointed roof of the porch was lit by a solitary bulb hanging a few centimetres from the peak. The blue panelled door with four frosted windows rattled as she banged it hard with her fist. No one answered. Her stomach churned. She banged again with the base of her hand, but still no reply. The voices in the garden were climbing louder and louder, and the music was barely audible above their raucous shouting and singing.

She walked the length of the deck, her arms folded as she rounded the corner at the back of the house. Trepidation crept in as she took the final few steps to the open veranda and garden that sloped down the valley. Then she saw them; three very drunk men standing on the grass below the decking.

One was tall with bleached blonde hair that flopped to one side of his face. He had the loudest voice and was belting out notes like his life depended on it. The fact he was out of tune didn't seem to bother him. He threw his head back, made a fist, and scrunched his eyes shut as he hit a note only dogs could hear. The sound of his voice lifted into the night sky, the natural landscape the perfect amphitheatre. He wasn't alone. He had two companions egging him on, whooping and cheering and attempting to sing along. The lawn was strewn with empty beer cans, indicating they were having a hell of a night.

Harriet imagined at some point they may have been in harmony, but not now. One stood sideways, and she could

25

just about make out a familiar-looking band logo on his t-shirt. The third man's face was shadowed at first, but when he stepped into the light, the outline of a chin full of beard and what looked like a beanie hat came into view. He looked as if he had fallen out of an early nineties grunge video. Harriet's arrival caught his attention, and he nudged the blonde guy in the ribs and nodded in her direction.

"We have an audience!" shouted the blonde guy as he looked at Harriet. He stumbled a little as he walked up the steps towards her, a drunken grin on his face.

Harriet laughed a little bit. His goofy face eased her nerves, melting away the uneasiness she initially felt. The environment was certainly not hostile.

"Howdy, neighbour," she said as the other two ran up beside him and caught him under his arms before he knocked into her.

"I'm so sorry," the one with the beanie hat said as they pulled him back to sit on a bench.

Harriet laughed again. He really was quite a sight. The two men froze at his side.

"What can we do for you, love?" asked the drunk blonde guy as he relaxed back into the cushions, spreading his legs and stretching his arms to cover the entire seat. He tried to pour more beer into his mouth, but the dregs of the can only found their way down his white T-shirt.

"Well," said Harriet as she took a step forward, "I was..."

"WOULD YOU GUYS KNOCK IT OFF ALREADY?" came a coarse, angry voice bellowing from somewhere inside the house. Harriet heard footsteps stomping down the wooden stairs then moving swiftly across the internal floor and out onto the veranda. She tried to peek inside to see who they belonged to, but her gaze fixed on the form of another person laid out across the sofa, feet crossed, arms folded, and eyes shut tight. Before she had a chance to guess what was happening, she was met with a shocked yet familiar face.

"Harriet?" Owen asked. His eyes looked like they might pop out of his head as his mouth fell open in shock and his broad shoulders tensed with embarrassment.

"Owen!" Her weary eyes widened as she pressed her hands to her chest and her face filled with a light flush. Rubbing the sleeves of her sweater down her cheeks, she hoped she had done enough to conceal her surprise.

"Get him inside, would you?" Owen commanded in such a tone the other two had no choice but to comply.

Harriet stood and watched as they once again picked up their drunken friend and carried him back into the house.

"Ach, he weighs a ton," one of them groaned.

"Just shut up and get him inside," the other man replied as they manoeuvred his dead weight across the threshold. Before his body hit the empty chair, he was already snoring.

Owen watched them intently with his hands on his hips, pulling his white T-shirt snug across his rigid chest. Harriet noticed a tattoo on his forearm but couldn't make out what it was in the shallow light. She guessed he had been trying to sleep as he wasn't wearing any shoes.

Owen turned to Harriet, his face scarlet beneath the freckles. He looked tired. Dark circles hung beneath his eyes, and his hair was more than a little out of place. His appearance was very different from when they had met earlier.

"I'm so sorry. I've been asking them for hours to knock it off." He spoke between pursed lips and slightly gritted teeth.

"Yeah, they are a bit loud. I could hear them all the way

down the hill," she replied, pointing in the direction of her cottage.

Owen rubbed his face with his hands and blinked repeatedly. "The joy of being a drummer is that I always have earplugs on hand." He smiled, shoving his hands into his pockets, proudly brandishing the items for Harriet to see. He was somewhat coy, and Harriet couldn't deny how endearing he was.

"Well, if you have a spare pair, send them my way." She laughed, making Owen chuckle too.

"I'll see you," she said, turning slightly and wrapping her cardigan around herself.

"Nice to see you again," he replied, half whispering.

"Not at three in the morning it isn't."

His two companions had joined him and were now repeating everything he had said back to him in a mocking manner. As Harriet walked back down the road, she heard laughter, then a couple of doors bang. Before she had made it back to her own door, the house above was in darkness.

Harriet quickly scrambled into the house, locking the door behind her. In a sleepy daze, she fell back into bed as the hauntingly familiar scent of leather boots and Lynx lingered in the air. She was too tired to question it. She acknowledged it before drifting into a deep dreamless sleep.

IT WAS LATE THE NEXT MORNING—CLOSE TO NOON— before Harriet woke. The sweet sound of the birds and the quiet drone of passing cars pulled her tenderly from her sleep. The sun was high in the air and the thin beige curtains did little to keep it out.

Harriet almost skipped out of bed. Despite the

interruption, she could not remember the last time she had slept so well. She showered quickly and sat on the bed deciding what her day may look like when her senses were overcome by the same smell of leather and Lynx. Her body shuddered, sending an ice-cold chill up her spine.

"Stop it!" she commanded, quickly standing, trying to push the lingering memory from her mind. She pulled on a long-sleeved white cotton top, a pair of blue jeans, and unravelled her hair from the towel.

Once down the stairs, she brewed her coffee and stood in the conservatory, nursing the cup of liquid gold as she admired her surroundings. She ran her hand across the soft wooden windowsill, letting her eyes drift out across the bay. A modest, almost happy sigh escaped her rosy lips, and she acknowledged her moment of peace.

Coffee cup in hand, she wandered the house, admiring the furniture and casually inspecting the leaflets of local attractions. Her eyes were drawn to the back door, where a white envelope had been pushed through the letterbox. Puzzled, she ripped it open.

Really sorry again about last night.

We're playing at the Macphail Centre tonight. Here's a ticket on us by way of an apology.

Hope to see you there.

Owen

HARRIET PULLED OUT A TICKET, WHICH READ:

WHELVEN PLUS SUPPORT
   7.30 p.m. doors
   - Macphail Centre, Mill Street, Ullapool

. . .

SHE SMILED, A GENUINE HAPPINESS WARMING HER from within. Harriet couldn't remember the last time she had been to see a live band. At one point in her life, there wasn't a week that went by when she wasn't crammed into a pokey club watching her friends make prats of themselves at open mic nights. Her heart ached for those times when she had felt most alive. The urge to reject the invite was strong, but the urge to feel normal again was stronger, and she decided she would go.

Her phone vibrated in her pocket. She knew who it was and that she could no longer avoid speaking to her mother.

"Hi, Mum," Harriet mumbled, sucking a breath between her teeth as she pulled the phone to her ear and rested the coffee cup on the table.

Not wasting any time, her mother launched straight into the inquisition. "Have you really taken off to the northwest of Scotland, or am I about to knock on your door and find you standing there?" Her Mum's tone was jagged and thorny; Harriet could tell she wasn't going to accept anything besides the truth.

"No, Mum. I am most definitely not at home," Harriet replied, rolling her eyes.

Silence. Harriet braced herself for impact. She knew that once Pauline Sanderson had her sights locked on you, the only thing you could do was hold on tight. The inevitable dressing down coming was like a freight train with no brakes. "This is something, even for you, Harriet. What on earth were you thinking?"

"I needed to get away." Harriet shrugged. "I'm fed up with staring at those four walls."

"You can't just up and leave in the middle of the night."

"I'm a grown woman, Mum. I think you'll find I can." Harriet's hands began to shake as adrenalin beat through her.

"Not in your state, you can't."

"And what state is that?" Harriet bit back. "Fragile, broken Harriet, who everyone tiptoes around and doesn't know what to say to anymore? Poor Harriet, all on her own in that big house. Oh, whatever is she going to do now? I'm fed up with it. If someone else looks at me with that pitiful look one more time, I'm going to lose my mind."

Pauline fell silent. Harriet hoped she knew there was some truth in her words, even if the delivery of them wasn't her best work.

"Harriet, I...."

"You what, Mum? You what?"

How was it possible for there to be so much tension with someone who was hundreds of miles away? The urge to backtrack and apologise stung her gut, but Harriet fought it and huffed her cheeks out, holding her breath.

"Have a nice time. Call me when you get home." The phone beeped, and the line cut off. Her mother had hung up.

Feeling even more guilty, Harriet tossed her phone into the fruit bowl on the kitchen table and pushed her palms into her eyes so tight she thought she might pop them. Upsetting her mother was the last thing she wanted to do, and she understood how difficult it was for her to take a step back. Going over the conversation in her mind made her temples ache, and she imagined her mother was doing the same. Hopefully, they would both arrive at the same conclusion; that Harriet was right. It wasn't just Harriet who needed a break. Her mother did too.

About to tackle drying her hair with the seventies-looking dryer she had spotted in the bathroom, Harriet's phone lit up again.

She looked at the name on the incoming caller photo and a fresh rush of adrenaline swept through her. "Not today, Wendy!" Harriet let it ring out.

There was such a finality referring to Wendy as her ex-mother-in-law, but in essence, that was what she was. The thought of describing to her as such made the hairs on the back of Harriet's arms stand up. She hadn't hugely warmed to Wendy—which she concluded was fairly standard when it came to in-laws—but she had never hated her. She had simply gotten used to her the same way she had gotten used to the crack in the corner of her phone screen. It didn't really do any harm, she just accepted it was there. Eventually, she knew she would have to speak to Wendy, but for the time being, it felt easier to avoid her.

Less than an hour later, Harriet was walking casually along the harbour wall in Ullapool, watching the sailboats dip up and down on the gentle ripples of Loch Broom. Her hair was pulled back in a messy ponytail, thick black sunglasses perched on the end of her nose, and her handbag swung carelessly off her shoulder.

Harriet spent the day doing all the things she wanted to do in Ullapool. A trip round the local fishing museum, followed by a walk around the churchyard sated her need to explore the Scotland of days gone by.

Harriet continued walking the soft grass, noticing some of the graves she passed were worn and weathered and barely legible. She found herself stopping by most of them, pausing for a moment and giving into her imagination as she visualised the vast, vivid lives of those who lay underneath her feet. It was oddly consoling. The air was still and soft; she felt protected by the souls resting underneath her, quietly succumbing to the peaceful bliss of oblivion, undisturbed, unwavering, and completely at peace. It wasn't that Harriet wanted to join them, but she did envy them a little.

Upon leaving the churchyard, she pulled out her phone and text her Mum.

I'm sorry about earlier. Please don't be mad at me. I promise I'm ok and I'll speak to you soon. Love you. x

She wasn't sure she would get a reply, but at least she felt a little better for saying it. Even though she needed a break, Harriet missed her parents.

The day was rounded off with a spot of lunch at a local café, followed by a visit to the local candle store, where she spent more money than was necessary on candles that smelled like heather and looked like the sunset over Ardmair Bay.

Unable to resist a quick look in the local bookstore, Harriet made swift work of her haul before returning to her car. The smell of old books filled the air. A combination of cooking oil, coffee, talcum powder, stale cigarettes, and a hint of sherry-soaked pine, like an old whiskey barrel. Her day had passed in a heartbeat and a delicate smile pulled the corner of her lips up as she drove back to her cottage. Yes, she was alone, but for the first time in months she didn't feel lonely.

Chapter Four

Finally settling on what to wear to go and see Whelven, Harriet nervously made her way to the car. The crunch of the gravel under her feet was the only sound she could hear, aside from the faint ripple of the ocean below her. The sunset hadn't yet begun, but the hints of its arrival showed on the horizon— the Summer Isles had a white line around them, and the water began to darken as the light gently faded.

She pulled her leather jacket together, covering the white V-neck vest that hugged her ample chest and thin waist. It sat snugly on top of a pair of high-waisted black jeans, finished off with a pair of blocky lace-up ankle boots. She had pulled her fingers through her waist-length locks and even managed a hint of makeup. Though she was loath to admit it, the mascara and eyeliner made her blue eyes seem even bigger. Concluding she looked acceptable didn't do a great deal to calm her nerves.

She climbed into her car and tossed her brown suede

handbag onto the passenger seat, taking a moment to glance in her rear-view mirror. Shock overcame her, and she gasped. Her breath hitched and lodged in her throat. A familiar but impossible reflection filled the mirror.

Her heart raced like a runaway horse beneath her ribcage. Harriet squeezed her eyes shut for a second, then turned around, looking over her left shoulder to the back seat. It was empty. *Of course it is.* Attempting to compose herself, she focused forward. She closed her eyes tight again, dropping her head and puffing long breaths out through her gritted teeth. Her grip on the steering wheel tightened, fingernails digging into the pads of her thumbs. Harriet pleaded with her mind to stop playing these tricks on her.

"You're not really there," she whispered to herself. "You're not there." Her hands were shaking as she released her grip, the steering wheel damp with the sweat from her palms. Inhaling deeply, the air filled her lungs and her chest expanded. She was determined to banish the familiar feeling of a panic attack building inside her. She relaxed her tongue to the bottom of her mouth and counted to five as she inhaled, and again as she exhaled.

"Not now," she said, pleading with herself not to crumble.

After a few moments of intense concentration, she worked up the courage to check her mirror again, which thankfully only showed the ocean and cliff faces. She slumped, relieved, into her seat, blinking away the tears brimming in her eyes.

Let go.

She stretched her fingers and released the steering wheel. The world settled again. Harriet growled in frustration. She was so tired of this cycle. She'd had enough of feeling fragile and weak. Defiantly, she tossed her curly hair over her left shoulder and turned the ignition.

She drove along the gravel track, and although her mind could not shake the reflection, she was more determined than ever to put it out of her mind. It was difficult. Everything about it was so clear; the square jawline, green deep-set eyes, and thick black hair that was swept neatly to the left. She knew exactly who was staring back at her. He felt so close, and it unsettled every fibre of her.

Oh, how exhausting it was to be constantly at war with herself.

It was a simple drive down the main road from Ardmair to Ullapool seafront. For a small fishing town, Ullapool was always brimming with life. It was a main stop on the North Coast 500 route, the five-hundred-mile coastal route that took visitors around the most coastal and beautiful route of northern Scotland.

The sound of snarling motorbikes made up the background noise of the evening. The weather was particularly pleasant, and as she pulled her car into a tight space on the seafront, she saw the line of local taverns fit to pop with locals and tourists enjoying the pleasant summer night.

She began walking to the venue. The warm highland air whipped up smells of boat oil, seafood, and peat as she meandered slowly around the corner onto Mill Street. As she passed the front of the building where the gig was to be held, she heard raised voices coming from inside.

Harriet headed toward the line of people queuing down the street in the opposite direction. Surely, she wasn't the only one who heard the commotion? Perhaps Harriet, with her heightened senses, was more in tune with chaos. The bystanders continued their conversations, faint shrills of laughter lifting above them as they enjoyed the sea air and familiar company.

Abruptly, the heavy wooden doors of the stone building flung open. They crashed against the wall, making her jump. The drunk blonde guy from the night before came thudding out. He stomped right past her, hands stuffed in the pockets of his white trousers. His black coat was pulled up around his chin and sunglasses covered his eyes. He didn't acknowledge her, which didn't surprise Harriet given they had only met briefly the night before. He muttered under his breath as he passed her and walked off into the distance.

She paused for a moment, wondering if someone would follow him. She even debated going after him herself. But then she remembered something her best friend, Jessica, had said on the phone the day before she left. *"You have enough going on right now. Don't be taking on other people's problems."* It reminded her how important Jessica was to her. She always had her back, just like a sister would.

Thinking about Jessica made her think of her real sister over in Lossiemouth. Perhaps now was the time to make amends. As uncomfortable as she felt around Louise, she also knew that the rift couldn't go on forever. When Louise had left her family to enrol in the RAF, Harriet hadn't always been as supportive as she could have been, and if the last year had taught her anything, it was that life was too short to stay mad at someone you cared about.

As she approached the line, Owen appeared at the front step of the building, looking flustered. He was scanning the street, clearly looking for his friend. A pair of drumsticks protruded from the back pocket of his black jeans. Harriet saw him first and her stomach did a back flip. She looked away, pretending to admire the old buildings across the road, but it took only a second for him to realise it was her. When he did, he jogged towards her, red-faced, with beads of sweat along his hairline.

"Have you seen Ricky?" he asked, his wild eyes darting back and forth as he bounced from one foot to the other.

Harriet pointed along the road. "He went down there towards the church."

Owen bounced away. Harriet was impressed by his stride and the speed he took off at, not to mention the way his faded black jeans hugged him in all the right places.

Where did that thought come from? She laughed to herself.

Harriet was delighted to find a wall to rest against whilst she waited. There was quite a crowd assembling around her. Some older people, and some who couldn't have been any older than fourteen.

She kept her head down, mindlessly scrolling through her phone, trying to keep to herself. Harriet wondered why Ricky had stormed off in a huff. Her thoughts were interrupted by a group of girls joining the line behind her. She glanced up, recognising one of them as the waitress from The Seaforth.

She cleared her throat quietly, but unbeknownst to her, the sound had captured the attention of the group.

"Hi," said the girl from The Seaforth.

Harriet shook her head briefly and made eye contact with the girl who had spoken.

"You were in The Seaforth last night," she went on in a friendly and quirky tone. Her accent was strange, Glaswegian mixed with somewhere in the south of England. Harriet had been trying not to draw attention to herself and it hadn't worked, but she was determined to push through her awkwardness and engage in conversation.

"Yes," replied Harriet. "I was." She smiled before returning to her phone. She knew she had heard the girl's name, but embarrassingly, she struggled to bring it to her mind.

The girl turned away, but out of the corner of her eye, Harriet could see her looking back. The other girls chatted amongst themselves in an excitable tone. They were amped up for the gig and looked like they had enjoyed a couple of tipples to get their night going. They laughed loudly, shouted over each other, and passed around a half-drunk bottle of wine.

Harriet smiled at their infectious energy and envied them not having a care in the world. She listened as they talked about who was better looking in the band and which song was their favourite, and the time one of them had a beer with the bass player. Harriet fondly remembered her days following bands around the country, and she felt a warm sensation in her stomach as she listened to them exchange stories.

"You're not from around here, are you?" the girl said, smiling warmly at Harriet.

Harriet shook her head. "What gives me away?"

"The accent more than anything."

Harriet laughed, something that had happened more in her first two days in Ullapool than in the last year. She felt an instant connection to the fresh-faced girl who had brought it out of her.

"I'm on holiday," she replied once she had regained poise and stuffed her phone in her back pocket, not wanting to appear rude.

"Oh, nice. Are you having a good time?"

"Yes, I am," Harriet lied. At least she thought she lied.

Truth be told, she wasn't sure what sort of time she was having. It wasn't bad, though, so she ran with it.

"I'm Kathryn," said the girl, reaching out her hand.

"Harriet," she replied, taking the girl's hand and squeezing it firmly.

"Great to meet you."

"You too."

"So, how long are you staying for?" Kathryn went on, seeming determined to lock into conversation with someone outside of her group. Harriet had forgotten how wonderfully welcoming highlanders were.

"I'm not sure yet. I guess we'll see how the week unfolds."

"That must be lovely," replied Kathryn. "Not being on the clock."

Harriet coughed out a half laugh into her hand and chuckled a little. "It's taking some getting used to."

Their conversation was interrupted by one of Kathryn's friends playfully leaning in between them and shouting at Harriet, "What's your favourite song?"

Harriet tried to respond, but the girl spoke so quickly it was hard to get a word out.

"Whelven. What's your favourite song?" the drunk girl repeated even louder than before.

The girl hung off Kathryn, barely able to stand. Her long, straight brown hair fell across her face as she gripped her friend's shoulder tighter to keep her balance.

"I think you've had enough already, Bex," said Kathryn as she put her arm around the girl's waist. Her cheeks flushed a little under the weight of her friend and the awkwardness of her behaviour.

In an instant, Bex seemed to forget she had asked Harriet a question and she turned back to her friends, raising her empty wine bottle into the air. Harriet took a moment to admire the girl's outfit and physique. A perfectly shaped Barbie doll from behind. Her hourglass figure was hugged by a knee-length dark blue dress that accentuated her curves. Another twang of jealousy hit. The last year had not afforded Harriet the proper amount of self-care a figure like that demanded.

"Just ignore her," said Kathryn. "I'll be pouring her into a taxi before the support band has finished."

Harriet laughed again, enjoying the normality.

"So, what *is* your favourite song?" she asked.

"Okay," Harriet began, speaking very quietly and inching a little closer to make sure she wasn't overheard. "I don't actually know any of the songs."

Half expecting to be chased down the road with a pitchfork, Harriet was most surprised with Kathryn's tender reply.

"That's cool. You're in for a treat. These guys are so good. My brother is friends with Owen, the drummer. You met him in the bar last night."

Having overheard the conversation between the group, Harriet wasn't sure if Kathryn was telling the truth about knowing Owen or hitting her up for information about him. She had seen the familiarity between them, but still wasn't sure how far it went.

Harriet thought it best not to divulge too much information about her recent interactions with Owen. The conversation he'd had the previous night seemed sensitive, and she didn't want to give away what she knew.

"Oh, was it?" she replied, shrugging. "We didn't talk much, to be honest. He bought me a drink to apologise for the intrusion and was on his phone with his friend after that."

"Was he okay? He seemed a little flustered." Kathryn asked, looking off into the distance, a puzzled look on her face. She looked around to check on her friends and then manoeuvred herself to sit on the wall next to Harriet. The closeness of another human being, although a little alien, wasn't entirely unwelcome. "Was he arguing with Ricky again?"

"Oh, erm, I don't know," Harriet replied hesitantly, the look on her face accidentally giving away that he was.

"That's interesting," Kathryn went on as she swayed a little as she sat next to Harriet. She took a moment to smooth her green chiffon skirt down and adjust her handbag strap over her shoulder.

"What do you mean?" asked Harriet.

"Well, between you and me, Elliott told me there has been some, I don't know, tension between Eric and Ricky."

"Who's Elliott?"

"My brother."

"And who's Eric?"

"He plays keyboards."

"Okay, got it."

"My brother and Owen talk all the time. Every day. They are really close, and Owen is basically playing referee between Ricky and Eric. Eric's brother, Adam, plays lead guitar in the band, and Ricky is getting pissed off with Eric."

"Why?"

"Because he isn't committed. He's always late, he doesn't practise, and he never brings any new ideas to the table." Harriet leaned in closer, not normally one to entertain idle gossip, but she found herself intrigued.

"I don't know if you've met Ricky, but he's a star. He just oozes it, you know? And he has big ideas." She paused for a moment to take a chug out of a hip flask she had pulled from her handbag.

Harriet was in awe of how quickly and quietly Kathryn spoke and how infrequently she needed to come up for air.

"You want some?" she asked.

"Oh, no thanks," replied Harriet and watched as Kathryn tilted her head back, her auburn hair shimmering in the evening sun. Her skin was perfect and looked so smooth and well cared for without a blemish in sight.

"In a year," she went on, "these guys are going to be huge if they do things right. But Eric's laziness is causing problems and Ricky wants him out."

The crowd began to stir, and Harriet glanced around to see if the line was moving. She caught a glimpse of Owen and Ricky as they went through the front door, then turned back to Kathryn to hear the end of the story.

"So, as far as I know, Ricky has been scoping out someone to replace Eric and Adam has hit the roof. Owen is stuck in the middle of Eric and Ricky arguing, and Adam has been none the wiser 'til now."

"Wow. That's pretty intense!"

"And the thing is, these guys are building quite a big following as you can see. This is kind of like a warm-up show. They're supposed to be doing a tour in a few months and have a new album coming out in a few weeks. So, it kinda needs sorting out quickly."

Harriet shifted her weight to her other leg and adjusted her bag on her shoulder. "So, how do you replace a band member right before you go on tour?" Harriet asked.

"That's a very good question. I wouldn't be surprised if Ricky has been meeting with someone behind everyone's back, helping them learn the material for when the time comes."

Harriet processed what Kathryn had said. She couldn't stop herself feeling bad for Owen, even though she had only met him a couple of times. He had seemed quite aggravated in the bar the previous evening. As much as she had tried hard not to listen to his conversation, she had got a sense of how upset he was about falling out with Ricky.

"Poor Owen. He must be feeling pretty rubbish about it all."

"Oh, he is, bless him. He doesn't know what to do. I think part of him agrees with Ricky, but at the same time, he feels some sort of loyalty to Eric and Adam."

"He seems like a nice guy."

"Owen is a sweetheart. Elliott has known him for years, and like I said, they speak every day."

"And you?" Harriet asked, raising her eyebrow in a way girlfriends do when they ask each other a question about who they have a crush on.

"What, Owen? No way. He's my brother's friend, that's all. I just hear the tail end of their conversations and Elliot fills me in on the rest."

"I see."

"I'll take the overly dramatic singer any day." Kathryn nudged Harriet in the ribs, making them both giggle. "Owen did spend a lot of time up here a couple of years ago after that two-timing bitch broke his heart, but I was away at uni and Elliot hasn't seen him for ages." She paused, taking another swig from her hip flask. The aroma of single malt danced on the air, making Harriet think of her father. He always enjoyed a small tipple when the time called for it.

"They've been recording the album and stuff, and I think he got a place in London, but I'm not sure."

Kathryn was cut short of telling the rest of the story as

the line began to move and people started pouring into the building.

"Come find me for a drink," Kathryn said as they were separated in the entrance foyer by her friends bustling her into the event hall.

Chapter Five

HARRIET PAUSED AT THE ENTRANCE TO THE DARKENED room. At the far end of the room was a stage that rose three feet from the laminate floor. The performance area was lit from above by brilliant white lights pointing in the direction of where the band would be playing later. The rims of the drum kit glistened behind four microphone stands that stood tall and proud at the front of the stage. Thick black curtains framed the space and people had begun to congregate in groups around the room.

To her right, she spotted the dimly lit bar and the silhouette of a single server darting back and forth between patrons. The bar was already bursting with people who had flocked in. Harriet stood patiently in the shadows to the left-hand side of the room, close to the door she entered through.

A strange odour drifted through the air—a peculiar mix of stale beer, cigarettes wafting in from outside, and sweat, intertwined with a hint of floral perfume. To most, it may have seemed quite unpleasant, but for Harriet, it was all too familiar. She had spent most of her university evenings in dark underground bars watching her friends play music.

Harriet spotted Kathryn and the other girls near the front of the stage, and the large security guard lingered around them, watching Bex make quite the spectacle of herself. Realising she was being watched, she quietened and regained her composure.

Harriet's phone buzzed in her bag, and she fumbled in the darkness to retrieve it. Wendy again; she had called twice now. Harriet could not bring herself to answer it. She knew exactly what Wendy wanted to talk about, but she just couldn't bring herself to do it.

Although she felt guilty about abandoning Wendy when she needed her, she still didn't want to face her, even on the phone. She would likely be incoherent from whatever cocktail of drink and pills she had consumed throughout the day. Wondering if her mother had told Wendy about the impromptu holiday, Harriet didn't want to find out and continued to stare at her phone until it finally stopped.

All that aside, Harriet was beginning to enjoy being in Ullapool. The sense of security had given her time to breathe, and watching flocks of people going about their everyday lives made her realise the world kept turning and life went on. Harriet let herself think about what she might do when she got home. Perhaps she would retrain, having quit her job at the local council. Maybe she would sell the house and move somewhere completely new.

Seeing her opening, she squeezed into a gap between two sets of couples at the bar and ordered a pint of the same local ale she had drunk in The Seaforth the night before. Owen's smile flashed in her mind as she collected her drink and returned to her quiet corner.

Through her long lashes, she spotted Kathryn making a beeline for her, and she smiled.

"How's your friend?" Harriet asked, taking a long sip of her drink.

"Annoying and ridiculous," huffed Kathryn. "I've ordered her a taxi and I'm shipping her home. The security guard has been over to her twice and she's sitting in a chair by the stage almost falling asleep."

Harriet struggled to contain an impromptu giggle. "How very high school of her."

"I know, it's ridiculous," replied Kathryn as she chugged down an entire bottle in one gulp. "You're welcome to come stand with us if you like."

Harriet hesitated for a moment. Being surrounded by a group of people made her nerve endings tingle and her stomach bunny hop. But she found herself incapable of saying no to Kathryn's charming grin, and reluctantly nodded in acceptance. It had been a long time since someone had extended the hand of friendship and she wasn't about to let that pass by.

"Guys, this is my new friend, Harriet," she said, reaching out her arm and introducing the rest of her chums. "This is Lucy, Amy, Violet, and you already met Bex over there." She pointed to the girl slumped in a chair.

"We'd better get her outside before the band starts," said Amy to Violet, and they hoisted her out of the chair. Taking an arm each, they practically dragged her from the room.

As the girls returned, the lights dimmed, and the stage turned from white to a brilliant blue hue shrouded in fake smoke. Harriet was quietly relieved she didn't have to make small talk with the rest of the group and watched attentively as three guys and one girl took the stage. The first echo of feedback sent a shrill reverberation around the room, the type of sound that pierced your ears and resonated deep in your chest, knocking the wind out of you. After a couple of seconds of wire adjusting, the sound subsided, and the support band, Dunnahue, broke into their first number. They played several lively folk ditties about maidens in the mist, searching for true love and lonely rivers; each song sounded remarkably like the other.

It wasn't to Harriet's taste, but she appreciated the effort and rocked her head politely, softly clapping between numbers. After six songs, Harriet wasn't hugely disappointed when they departed the stage.

"Well, they sucked," said Violet loudly as the sound of the guitars faded and it was quiet enough to hold a conversation.

Harriet tried to ignore the comments people made about them and found her fingers twitching and her stomach roiling in anticipation of Whelven taking the stage. The crowd drew in closer, filling the room to the brim as a tension-building buzz boomed around her.

She gasped as the lights dimmed again and the crescendo of a guitar lifted into the air. Harriet's heart skipped a beat. Five guys sprang onto the stage and launched into a crunchy, bass-filled song, full of chomp and layers.

Harriet looked up at them in complete awe. Within a few seconds of Ricky opening his mouth to sing, she knew what Kathryn meant about him being a star. An enigmatic confidence radiated from him. He nailed every note, every beat, and popped his head to flick his hair back in ways only true rockstars know how to do. The rest of the band followed his lead as he guided them through their repertoire.

Harriet marvelled at how perfectly harmonised, tight,

and together they were; like a well-oiled machine. Their style was solid, smart, and appealed to everyone, and their lyrics were full of wit and ingenuity. Kathryn nudged Harriet, but she didn't flinch. Her eyes glistened as she stood in amazement.

Ricky introduced the band and launched into a harrowing ballad about going to war, writing letters to your love, and not knowing if you would ever see them again. It brought a physical lump to Harriet's throat; she closed her mouth and swallowed deeply.

Owen bounced out of his drum stool and scanned the room. He met Harriet's gaze, flipping her stomach.

"Hi," he mouthed subtly at her. Smiling coyly, she looked down at her shoes as her cheeks warmed. When she looked back up, he was still looking at her, sniggering.

Eric, who stood behind the keyboard, hadn't smiled once, and kept his head down, focusing on his keys. Ricky looked over at him a couple of times, a fleeting frown pulling at his brow before he shook it off and resumed his stance centre stage.

The girls around Harriet danced and threw their hair around, singing along to every song. Harriet took a couple of steps backwards to avoid being caught in their wake. Whenever Ricky spoke between songs, Violet and Amy shouted back at him, and he laughed along with them, but by the end, it was clear he had grown annoyed by it.

After the final song, the band joined arms on stage and took a bow, waving at the packed room and people they knew in the crowd. It was heart-warming watching them take the time to acknowledge everyone who was supporting them. During the set, Ricky mentioned the tour and the new album, and as they left the stage, the girls in the group were already planning how many gigs they might attend.

Before Owen left the stage, he motioned Harriet towards him, crouching at the edge. She glanced around, not quite registering he was trying to get her attention. He dropped his head and laughed before saying, "Yes, you." He waved his hand again. She moved between the crowd and looked up as he leaned over.

"Thank you for coming," he said and handed her his setlist before jumping to his feet and running off the stage to his bandmates, who were waiting in the shadows.

Harriet looked down at the handwritten sheet, repositioning it towards the light. It had the names of all the songs they had performed, when guitars would be changed, and various other prompts. Harriet was delighted with it and folded it quickly, securing it safely in her bag. She didn't plan to stay once the band had finished playing, but Kathryn had insisted on her staying for another drink.

Harriet agreed, even more taken with Kathryn after watching her immersed in the show. She ordered them a final drink after Kathryn excused herself to the ladies' room.

Violet and Amy accosted Ricky as he not-so-subtly tried to make his exit and were pawing all over him indiscreetly. Harriet watched them as she leaned on the bar, waiting for Kathryn to return.

As she waited, Owen emerged from the stage door with a white towel around his neck. He made a beeline for the bar and asked for two bottles of water, which he polished off in a matter of seconds. His face was flushed, and his black shirt appeared to be stuck to his athletic frame. His tight black jeans made Harriet wonder how he managed to sit comfortably on a drum stool, and a pair of half-laced black boots completed his look. He was captivating, and Harriet couldn't look away.

He sighed, catching his breath as he swept away beads

of sweat hanging from his brow and stubble, but once he removed the towel from his face, he looked refreshed.

"Great set," she said.

"Oh, thank you." He smiled widely. "And thank you again for coming."

He looked different from the man she met the day before. His eyes were wide and wild, he stood taller, and his energy was coarse, disjointed, and overflowing.

"I loved it. You guys are really good."

"We're trying," he said, taking a deep breath.

A strained silence fell between them. Harriet shuffled on the spot as she caught Owen's side-eyed glance.

"I really am sorry about last night. We honestly lost track of time and didn't realise we had someone staying so close by."

"Don't worry about it, honestly. It's fine. It was actually kind of nice to get a sneak preview of the show." Harriet grinned as she craned her neck to look at him properly. "Is Ricky okay? He looked a bit upset earlier."

"Yeah, he's fine. He was being a dick, but we're cool now."

"How so?"

"Some of the drama from last night spilled over to today, and he stomped off in a huff."

"That's annoying."

"That's front men for you."

Harriet laughed, and they both leaned over the bar, discussing the best local ales and where they were brewed. Owen was a font of knowledge about the beer fermenting process, having shared how he watched his dad brew his own when he was little.

Harriet found herself very much enjoying their

conversation, which flowed with playfulness and ease. She liked the way he leaned in a little closer when he was about to say something funny. Goosebumps appeared when he accidentally brushed his hand against hers as he reached for a beer mat.

He teased the top of his glass with his fingers and leaned in, overwhelming Harriet with his closeness, his scent, and those piercing eyes that captured hers and refused to let go. He dropped his head playfully and smiled, showing all his teeth, and suddenly stood upright.

"What?" she said, trying to meet his eyeline, but he immediately looked away.

"You never mentioned you were married," he said, glancing back at her outstretched hand out of the corner of his eye. He took half a step back, chewing his lip.

Harriet followed his eye line and remembered she was still wearing her wedding ring. She'd debated taking it off for some time but hadn't built up the courage to do so. She pulled her right hand over her left to try and hide it.

"It's complicated," she replied hastily.

Owen paused for a moment. Harriet could feel the awkwardness and the rising tension between them. She was scared about what he might say next.

"It's cool, it's just..."

"Just what?"

"You don't give off the vibe of someone who is married."

The words Harriet had been dreading to hear out loud were spoken so simply yet felt so brutal. They cut through her like an arrow. She bit her lip to stifle its quivering.

"So, what vibe do I give off?" she asked with a forced grin, wondering if she could keep it together long enough to make it through the conversation unscathed. Curiosity and shock kept her knees locked and her feet firmly planted rather than fleeing for the door like her mind was screaming for her to do.

Harriet could feel Owen's post-gig energy oozing off him, like most performers when they came off stage. He was restless, like a firework about to go off. But his eyes remained locked on hers, making her feel naked and vulnerable. And for reasons unknown, she still couldn't look away.

He stepped forward, bending his knees to look at her at eye level as the cheeky smirk on his lips made its way up to his raised his eyebrows. "Not married," he replied as he winked at her.

Her stomach lurched forward like she had gone over the apex of a rollercoaster. Heat rose from her toes up to her scalp, and tension filled her entire body, twisting its fingertips uncomfortably into every nerve in her spine.

She gulped down her beer and forcefully placed her glass on the wooden bar. She had to leave.

Harriet gritted her teeth, her muscles tightening as her heart almost burst out of her chest. She hadn't paused once to think what she might look like eating alone, staying in a big house alone, attending a gig alone. Putting herself in Owen's shoes, she could almost understand how he had arrived at that conclusion.

If only he knew the unnerving effect he was having on her; The way her mind sprinted to find an answer that didn't give away the truth. She wasn't ready to tell anyone who didn't already know. She felt like the walls were closing in and her head throbbed like it might explode. It was an innocent enough remark but the crippling reality of it made her wish she could click her fingers and stop time.

"You should get back to your, erm, friends." Harriet motioned towards Ricky and his entourage as she threw her bag on her shoulder.

"Why?"

"You seem so different from the guy I met yesterday." Harriet narrowed her eyes, looking for a quick escape.

"Really? I can assure you I'm not," Owen bit back defensively, taking a step back from her.

Harriet could feel herself bubbling, her fight or flight mode kicking in.

"Yes, you are," Harriet replied, her bottom lip still shaking as she glanced over his shoulder, spying the exit. Refusing to say any more through fear of bursting into tears, she pulled her lips into a tight line and slowly breathed out through her nose.

Silently, Owen retreated, scanning the room, a pained expression pulling his features together. Harriet couldn't tell if it was judgment or confusion that scrunched his face up, but she was sure that if it wasn't for the laughter of Ricky and his congregation, she could have heard Owen's cogs turning.

"You know what, forget it. I'm sorry. I should go," Harriet conceded. She tried to walk away, but Owen reached for her arm, pulling her back.

"You don't have to."

Harriet shrugged him off.

Owen released her, his attention captured by the laughter coming from across the room. His eyes darted between Harriet and his frontman in the middle of the crowd of girls. He chewed his lip as a new bead of sweat dripped down his temple.

Harriet was shaking from head to toe, jumping to the

conclusion he was comparing her to the flock of females hanging off Ricky. "I am nothing like those girls." She fumbled in her bag for her keys, tilting her head in the direction of Ricky and the growing number of female companions hanging off his every word. Relieved, she grasped her hand tightly around the familiar feel of her pompom keychain.

"I never said you were," Owen retorted, taking a step towards her.

His gaze locked onto hers again, his jaw clenched. Harriet pulled her hand to her mouth to stop her lip from shaking and tears built silently in the corners of her eyes.

"I should go."

Not giving him a chance to respond, Harriet bolted for the door as the drops escaped her eyes and fell onto her flushed cheeks.

"Harriet," she heard him faintly say as she heaved the door open, and once she was sure she was well out of his eyeline, she let out a pitiful sob as streams of relentless tears slipped down her face onto her jacket. There was no stopping them, no hope in controlling them. All she could do was walk slowly and cry quietly; much was the story of the last year of her life.

She wished she'd had the chance to say farewell to Kathryn properly and thank her for being so kind, but she surmised it wasn't likely she would see her or her friends again. *Why would anyone want to see you again?*

The keys fell from her shaking hands, bouncing off the pavement. As she bent down to retrieve them, she realised just how closed off, unapproachable, and borderline rude she had been. Kathryn had been nothing but lovely since the moment they met, and there she was telling herself she wasn't bothered if she saw her again. People she cared about had left her, so why waste time caring about someone new?

A set of hurried footsteps behind her grew louder, and as she was about to open the car door, Owen caught up with her.

Harriet didn't want to face him. She stood with her hands on the cold roof of her car as the tears continued to spill down her face and fear gnawed her deep inside. She dreaded what he might say to her. Perhaps he would tell her off, or maybe he would take pity and forgive her for running off again.

Lifting her head, she briefly accepted their eyes were going to meet. His hardened expression immediately softened when he realised she was crying.

"I'm sorry," she said through the tears. "I shouldn't have spoken like that and run away." Harriet let her delicate frame slump against the car, knowing any attempt to hinder her sobs would be futile. Since the moment she had laid eyes on Owen, she had wanted to pour her heart out to him, and the way he looked at her made her feel so exposed. It terrified her.

Harriet could sense his hesitation and his eyes digging into her. She wished she knew what he was thinking. For a split second, she prayed for the ground beneath her to open up and swallow her. Feeling fraught and fragile took the wind out of her sails, but a tiny voice of reason whispered for her to be brave and face him.

He stepped carefully towards her, gently placing his hand on her shoulder. The shock of his touch made her body jerk, but she let him pull her towards him. She searched his face for reassurance, and once this was granted in the form of a reassuring smile, she buried her head in his chest as fresh tears began to fall.

His arms wrapped around her, and he rested his head on top of hers, squeezing her tightly against him. She could hear his heartbeat beneath his chest, slightly raised but somewhat comforting, and she managed to steady her breath in time with the beat of his heart.

Harriet felt comfort in his arms as they stood in silence. She optimistically wondered if a tight squeeze would force her broken pieces back together. The despair she had been holding onto evaporated, and her tears eventually dried.

Harriet lifted her head and pulled away from him.

"You want to talk about it?" he asked softly, releasing his grip but not letting go. His hands fell to her waist.

Harriet reached into the pocket of her jeans and retrieved a tissue to dry her face. She puffed out a big breath and looked up at Owen. His expression was delicate and concerned, if a little confused.

She took a deep breath and bravely uttered, "He died. My husband died."

Owen turned a grey shade of pale and gasped, taking a step back as if he had been punched in the gut.

"Oh, Harriet. I'm so sorry."

His brow furrowed, and he wiped his face with his hand. Harriet hung her head, staring at her shoes. Shame and sadness had become her blanket and her prison. She had been so concerned with keeping her guard up she was blindsided when Owen, who was none the wiser, had said what he did.

"What happened? When did he die?"

"About a year ago," she replied, sniffing up into the back of her nose. "In a car accident."

Owen moved forward again and wrapped his arms around her. Harriet closed her eyes. He wasn't to know the things he said would trigger her. Her inability to handle her own thoughts and emotions was hardly his fault.

They stood a few minutes longer. Harriet welcomed his warm arms and the security they gave her, but she also felt a stab of guilt on top of everything because it was the first time since Joe, her late husband, had died, that she had found comfort in the arms of another man.

Chapter Six

Owen had a restless night. He lay in bed thinking about Harriet and what she had told him. He found himself wondering what Joe was like, what happened the night he died, and how Harriet felt when she got the news. His heart ached at the thought of her world falling apart. He wondered how she had coped, who had looked after her in the wake of such a tragedy, and why she was now hiding away in the northwest of Scotland where she didn't know anyone.

Harriet's night was plagued with vivid dreams, memories, and visions of Joe. They flooded her mind in a myriad of beautiful colours, tones, and sounds. Twice she woke in the night, trying to reach out for him, feeling like she could touch him. She had been sensing him around her since she arrived and had been ignoring the fact she could hear him, smell him, and see him. Julia had told her it was normal to see those lost, but that Harriet must consciously remind herself that they were merely shadows.

Harriet knew the physical and psychological effects of her grief took a terrible toll, and she had already prepared for the emotional hangover from hell by laying out fresh clothes and food for the following day.

The next morning, she thanked her past self for the foresight as she slipped into her clean, comfy tracksuit bottoms and cosy jumper. Wrapped in a blanket, coffee cup in hand, she slid into the armchair where her reading glasses and a stack of comfort films awaited her. She kept the curtains drawn, the doors were locked, and as the opening credits of the film loaded, she thought of Owen.

Having declined his offer to ride home with her, Harriet found herself going over the previous night in painstaking detail. He was the first new person she had spoken to about Joe's death outside of the people who knew him. Closing her eyes, she pictured the look of disbelief on his face as he stood before her with his kind yet confused eyes piercing into her.

Without warning, she was overcome with conflicting feelings of grief, guilt, and unrelenting sadness. Harriet gave in, letting it all flow through her. It proved she could run as far away as she liked, but one way or another, things would always find a way of catching up with her. She was frustrated with herself for still not being able to cope with conversations about Joe, even though it had been over a year since his death. She sometimes felt like she would never be able to let go and move on, but something about Owen had stirred the tiniest fleck of hope left in her, and she wondered if she was finally in a place to move forward.

After spending the morning on a phone call with Julia and clearing the air with her mother, Harriet felt a little better. She had fed herself and given herself lots of time and patience to complete the simple tasks required to function. By the time she wrapped herself back up to watch the sunset, she knew she wouldn't be able to rest her head that night until she had returned Wendy's phone call. So, she braced herself and swiped right.

"Harriet, thank God. We've been worried sick," came the shrill yet fragile voice down the line. It was nice of Wendy to say she had been worried, but Harriet already knew she wasn't really worried about her. It was more likely she had obligated her to do something Joe-related and was now throwing out the guilt line to lure her into doing it.

"Hi, Wendy. How are you?" Harriet replied.

"Where on earth are you? I've been trying to reach you for days."

"I took a little holiday. Julia thought it was a good idea if I got away for a while." Harriet wiped her brow as sweat began to pool on her eyelids.

"That bloody woman would do well to remember you have things to deal with here before sending you off somewhere." Her tone was as sharp as knives, unrelenting and cold.

"What exactly do I have to deal with?" Harriet pushed back.

"Well, for starters, you have to come and see us," Wendy replied with a venomous bite.

"What for?" Harriet sucked her breath in. "So we can all sit in a room and be sad together? What's the point?"

A long silence fell across the line. Her cheeks flushed and her hands shook with bubbling frustration. Wendy's breath drifted down the phone like a haunting wind.

"Did you want something, Wendy , or did you just call to give me a hard time again?"

"Well." She coughed, clearly having spent the day chain-smoking as usual. "Some of Joe's cousins are in town, and with it being a year since he died, I thought you should come and see them while they're here."

Harriet stood up, the blanket fell to the floor, and she replied firmly and clearly. "No. I do not want to do that."

Julia had told her she needed to stop taking on the burden of grief that others carried for Joe and focus on dealing with her own. Harriet had agreed, for although they had all lost him, they all carried it in different ways. His family, particularly Wendy, had not coped well. His parents were not dealing with it together, pulling each other through. They were offloading it on to Harriet, and she was carrying it for all of them.

"What do you mean you don't want to? You have to."

"As I've said, Wendy, I don't. You need to deal with it, and you need to get some help. I can't fix it, and you need to stop thinking I can."

Wendy started to cry. The sort of cry that a child forces when they don't get their own way, but it was enough for a lump to form in Harriet's throat. The pitiful sound just made her more determined to keep it together. She did not want to drift back into her old ways, and she didn't want to lose another day cocooned in sadness like a depressed caterpillar who couldn't find the energy to catalyst itself out of the veil.

"We'll talk again when I get back, but please, just leave me alone for a while." Before Wendy had a chance to reply, Harriet hung up, turned her phone off, and let more silent tears fall whilst she watched the sunset across the bay. She rested her head on her hand and wiped at her face as the sky turned the most dazzling shades of yellow, gold, and orange. She watched until the sun descended through the

63

clouds, and a line of soft yellow sky spread across the horizon just as the sun appeared to burst like a firework in the sky before melting into the ocean.

At that moment, Harriet wasn't sure where the earth ended and heaven began. As the fiery glow dimmed like the dying embers of an open fire, she knew she had to start working through things. It was time to start having the difficult conversations, not just with her mother-in-law, but with herself. She knew things needed to change and she needed to move forward; it was what Joe would have wanted.

But she couldn't shake the feeling that the reason she wasn't able to move forward was because there was something she had missed. A piece of the puzzle that didn't quite fit. Surely something was holding her back, but what?

Harriet woke early the next morning. The summer sun oozed through the window and rested softly on her face. She stirred, turned over and fluttered her eyes open to greet the morning haze.

She looked at the clock: 6.15 a.m. Her mother had always said that once you were awake, you should get up and start your day because a morning spent wishing yourself back to sleep made you grumpier than an old dog. Harriet rolled out of bed, her vest top riding up above her belly button, and she pulled it down as she stood gazing out the window across the bay, so vast and beautiful. She tried to etch the image deeper into her mind so she would never forget it.

The sun hit the ripples of the bay and scattered a million beams of light across the sea as if someone had emptied glitter across the water. The mountain in the distance was well illuminated, and the morning sun hit in such a way that Harriet could see every crevice of the rocks.

She wasn't surprised she had woken early. Drained and exhausted, she had turned in just after the sun had set. After her conversation with Wendy, Harriet had expected to awaken feeling sluggish and still nursing her fragile mind and body, but when she stirred, feeling fresh and lively, she delighted at herself practically bouncing out of bed.

As she pulled her hair into a messy bun on the top of her head, she caught a glimpse of herself in the mirror. Harriet was stunned at the freshness in her face. Her dark circles had shrunk, and she carried a slight summer radiance in her cheeks. She also felt a sense of relief, but at the same time, there was a niggling sense of weakness for letting herself go so much in front of Owen. Although used to battling conflicting emotions, these were different. Her shoulders were less tense, but the dull ache of guilt knotted her stomach, making her bloat.

All that aside, even though her delivery wasn't ideal, it was right to tell him, and lifted a load she hadn't acknowledged she was still carrying. Everyone back home knew her and her story, but she had never been in a position where the decision to tell someone was entirely hers.

Pouring warm coffee into a cup and gently stirring the milk in, she smiled just a little bit. She concluded that anyone who wanted to get to know her deserved the opportunity to understand who she was. Hiding away from her past didn't make it go away, it only complicated things. In that moment with Owen, under the friendly gleam of the streetlight, she made the decision to tell him. Not to excuse her behaviour, but to see if she could talk about it and to give someone a chance to understand her. She felt empowered knowing she had been brave enough to share her story, even if it had scared him.

She let her playlist shuffle through and began singing along to a song she knew but couldn't place. Where had she heard it?

"And I know I shouldn't feel this way, can't beg, or borrow or steal you away. I'm longing for a better day when you don't cross my mind."

She pulled her phone from her pocket and glanced down. To her surprise, her streaming service had recommended *Yesterday* by Whelven.

Harriet laughed, thinking back to a conversation she'd had with her best friend, Jessica, about her phone listening to her. She turned up the volume and bopped her head, once again looking out at the bay as the light grew brighter around her.

The cottage was full of light by nine o'clock. Floor-to-ceiling windows in the conservatory meant it held the heat, and opening the door let it pour out into the rest of the house.

She sat down at the pine dining table underneath the kitchen window, watching the heather dance in the early morning breeze. No midges were out yet, but as the day unfolded, the garden would be swarming with them by lunchtime. Losing track of time intently, was something Harriet had committed to doing on holiday. Not like when she was back home and days would pass by under a fog of loneliness and grief. Sitting in her comfy clothes, sipping the most perfectly brewed coffee, watching the world come to life around her, she felt a fleeting pulse of serenity.

Thoughts of Joe fluttered into her mind. Memories from one of their previous Scotland road-trips clouded her vision. They had been somewhere on the east coast, close to John

O'Groats, and had stopped at a little seafood café for lunch. She could remember, with crystal clarity, the look on his happy, sated face as he chewed on what he called the most perfect plate of calamari he'd ever had in his life.

It wasn't memories of Joe that were difficult to house, it was the aftershock that surged through her body when she had to remind herself that's what he now was—a memory.

She closed her eyes and put her hands over her ears, as she could hear the remnants of his laugh echo around her. Her palms clammed up and her pulse started to race.

"You're not here," she said at a volume a little higher than her normal speaking voice. "Not now, please," she begged quietly.

She could feel it building. Breath coming and going. Her heart rate increased. Her head became fuzzy.

"NO!" she shouted, slamming her balled-up fists onto the table. It shuddered, knocking her coffee cup off the coaster. She gritted her teeth, face going bright red and veins popping out of her neck. Anger built to the point she thought she might burst.

"NO!" she said again, standing up and throwing her chair back so hard it knocked the cabinet behind her, and a pot of pens spilled onto the floor.

She panted, held her breath for a second, then blew it out. And after doing this a few times, she pulled her stomach tight, growled, and screamed at the top of her lungs into the empty house. It was so loud she swore the campers in the bay could hear her. The sound echoed in every nook and cranny of the stone walls and bounced back into her ears.

When she was out of breath and no more sound could come out, she opened her eyes. They stung with tears her body forced out when she screamed. The ringing lingered in initially but subsided after a few seconds. She looked around as silence and calm returned, and slowly, her body was restored to its normal state.

Taking a couple of deeper breaths to steady her shaking hands, she began to tidy the items that had been caught in her wake. The tap at the sink frustratingly stuck a little at first, but soon, clear, cool water was flowing. She washed her hands and splashed her face before replenishing the water in the kettle and rinsing her cup, ready for another coffee.

Her addiction to caffeine had grown at an alarming rate over the last few months. She justified that it was one of her last remaining pleasures, but she knew deep down it was a habit she needed to kick.

Returning to the dining table feeling more composed, she began to plan her day. Determined to spend another day in Ullapool, she meticulously plotted her route. She would park at the back of the supermarket and take a long walk through the park, over the wooden footbridges, and back around the seafront. Then she'd venture up to the candle shop again and finally to the Royal Hotel for a spot of lunch.

As she rinsed her dishes, her mind yo-yoed back to Owen, and she sighed.

Poor Owen.

She had spewed out quite a lot to him, not all of it very nice. Even though they had made peace, she still covered her eyes, cringing at herself for how she behaved. Had the world really made her so closed off? Or was she using what had happened as a defence tactic to stop people getting close again. Either way, there was no justification for being like that. Owen didn't deserve to be spoken to the way she had. He also hadn't needed to wrap her in his arms when she fell apart, but he had.

The feeling of his arms around her brought comfort and, whether she wanted to admit it or not, a flutter in her stomach; a flutter which returned when she thought about it. She wasn't quite able to put her finger on how Owen made her feel, but she could certainly determine how he did *not* make her feel. He didn't make her feel stupid or pathetic or pitiful. He made her feel something entirely different, but what remained a mystery.

There was no denying the urge to stop by and apologise for dumping all her issues on him. She would have to drive by the house the band was staying in on her way to the main road; it wasn't too far out of her way. Julia had told her she needed to own how she felt and own up to any mistakes she made because of it. She'd also said people would cut Harriet some slack because of what happened to Joe, but even those closest to her would only put up with it for a certain amount of time. Grief is not an excuse to treat people badly, especially those who care about you.

Once again, Harriet was lost, gazing out over the open water, but the sound of the kettle boiling accompanied by a rattle at the door jolted her from her daydream.

Confused and suddenly self-conscious, she opened the door to find Owen looking up at her.

Harriet froze.

There he was, the man she had just been thinking about, was at her house, standing in front of her. His arrival threw her off balance and her mind went blank. She looked him up and down, taking a moment to consider if beige jeans looked good on anyone. But even she had to admit, they looked alright with the black Converse trainers and blue denim jacket. The morning light hit the side of his face, accenting the perfect spread of freckles across his nose.

She smiled softly, and he awkwardly shuffled, his hands in his pockets.

"Morning," he said, looking up at her.

"Good morning," she replied, trying to sound cheerful.

"I hope this isn't weird, but..." He dropped his head, averting his eyes away from her briefly before they darted back to her face.

"I just wanted to check if you were okay."

Harriet's heart melted a little. She folded her arms and leaned against the wooden door frame, feeling the flush rise up her neck and into her cheeks. She was scared she wouldn't be able to look at him, but in a split second, he locked her gaze in and she managed to find the courage.

"I'm so sorry, Owen. I really am." This time she made no attempt to pull her eyes away from him. "I'm a bit of a mess sometimes and I feel awful dumping on you."

Owen relaxed his shoulders.

"It's all right. I didn't think before I spoke. I shouldn't have jumped to the wrong conclusion. I'm sorry too. I really didn't mean to upset you."

A momentary hush fell comfortably between them. Owen's kind eyes, accompanied by the head tilt and cheeky smile, indicated there was nothing to forgive.

"So, we're good?" he asked.

"We're good." Harriet smiled.

Owen rocked back and forth, switching his weight between his legs.

"I've got some coffee on. Do you want one?" Harriet asked, beckoning him inside.

"Yeah, go on then." He leapt up the steps without hesitation and through the front door, where he crossed the threshold next to her. For a split second, she felt the heat radiating from him as he passed.

The churn of self-consciousness grew, and Harriet paused and took a step back into the utility room to look herself up and down. Acutely aware she was still in her pyjamas and her hair was messy, she figured she would just have to own it and work with what she had. When she was satisfied her top wasn't see-through and she didn't have terrible morning breath, she joined him in the kitchen.

He had made his way through the galley and into the conservatory and was admiring the view. He still had his hands in his pockets, like a shy teenage boy. Harriet rattling the cupboard door made him jump a little, and he came back through and leaned against the countertop as Harriet poured fresh cups.

"No milk for me, thanks," he volunteered, obligingly accepting the cup Harriet offered him.

She motioned to the table, inviting him to take a seat. He took the spot next to the window and she sat opposite.

"Your view is better than ours," he commented. "You can't see round the corner of the bay from up there. It's blocked by a huge tree."

Harriet nodded as she gulped down a bigger-than-intended slurp of her sweet, warm nectar.

"How long have you guys been staying up here?" she asked.

"We've been here a couple of weeks, trying to work through things and prepare for the tour. Ricky grew up around here, so he knows some club owners. We have another warm-up gig in Inverness tomorrow."

She watched him keenly. The pensive, slightly melancholy look he wore made it hard to look away.

"Then we have another week before it's back to London for final rehearsals."

"Oh, that's right," replied Harriet. "You're heading out on the road soon. Are you excited?"

"Honestly? No, not really."

"That's a shame."

Owen looked longingly down into his cup and groaned a deep, forlorn sigh.

"Everything okay?" Harriet asked.

"I don't know." Owen chewed on one of his fingernails. "Ricky and Eric got into it again last night when we got back." He sighed again. "If I'm not around, they're going to murder each other."

Harriet said nothing; she simply let him speak.

"Eric got blind drunk and passed out after they argued, and Ricky has woken up this morning seething. I told him to go for a run or a swim or something to get him away from the house for a while."

Owen stroked his chin, then his hair, and ran both hands down over his face, rubbing his eyes.

"I just..." he started speaking and stopped himself.

Harriet reached over and gently rested her hand on his, encouraging him to keep talking, trying to reassure him she was listening.

"I just don't want it all to fall apart, you know?" His cheeks puffed out as he blew out a long, drawn-out breath. "Ricky is my best friend in the entire world. I'd die for that dude.

That sounds intense, I know, but I had a real hard time a couple of years back and he pretty much rescued me. He always has. We've rescued each other several times over the years, both literally and figuratively."

He drained the last drops out of his cup and moved it softly to one side.

Harriet smiled at him speaking so lovingly about his friend. It made her miss Jessica.

"It's like I'm holding onto something that's broken, and if I let my hands slip, it's going to shatter."

"That's a lot of pressure to put on yourself," Harriet replied.

"I know. I can't help it. But this band, it's everything. If I don't have it, I... I don't have anything."

"What do you mean?"

Owen paused again, this time for longer, and Harriet wondered if she had overstepped the line with her question. She wished she hadn't asked. Hoping she wasn't prying too much, she ran her finger around the top of her cup, awaiting a response.

"Okay," he said, breathing in. "There was a girl. There's always a girl, right? Anyway, we were together, and she did something... something terrible, and I left. I had nowhere to go, but Ricky took me in, and to stop me from spiralling, we threw ourselves into this. We wrote and practised, then we toured every dingy club in London, and I felt so much better when we were playing, and this band... it got me through it." He pursed his rosy lips, his face a little pink.

"And I *cannot* let it fall apart."

He sighed again. "Maybe I jump to conclusions too much. Over think things. You know?" His eyes widened. Harriet nodded, unable to look away. Her fear of saying the wrong thing and getting under his skin touched a nerve. "The band thing makes me anxious and maybe, I don't know, a different version of myself, and I forget to be the real me."

Harriet could see his hand on the table, clenched into a tight fist. It was as if he was physically holding it all together in the palm of his hand. She reached over and moved her fingers under his, separating his nails from his palm. He relaxed a little and looked up at her, their eyes meeting. Owen squeezed her hand gently and smiled, letting their touching skin linger a moment before they parted at the same time.

"If you don't mind me asking... why are Ricky and Eric at each other all the time?"

"Eric is lazy. He always has been. But it's grating on Ricky something chronic, so he wants him out."

He shook his head.

"I'm sorry. I came over here to check you're okay and you end up listening to my sad little story." He laughed, half amused and half sincere.

Harriet chuckled too. The ease she felt with him made her relax back into her chair and study him further. She watched him spin a coaster on its corner and grin, glancing occasionally off into the distance. She leaned forward over the table and spoke quietly. "We sort of have that effect on each other."

He nodded in agreement, giving her a half smile before looking down and then back up. Harriet couldn't tell if he was being coy or if she was having the same effect on him that he was having on her. Either way, he couldn't seem to stop looking at her, nor she at him.

"There was also something else I wanted to ask you," he said, a slight quiver of hesitation in his voice.

"Ricky wants to ditch Eric for the day and take a drive out to Polbain to see his aunt. He and Mike want to go bodyboarding and take a day away from it all." He paused. "Do you want to come?"

Chapter Seven

Harriet immediately accepted Owen's offer, and after he left, wasted no time dressing for the day ahead. She could barely contain herself as she trudged up the hill to where she had arranged to meet him. The mid-morning sun shone bright and glaring so she was glad of her sunglasses and sun cream. Her hair was half tied up, the loose strands round her face jostling in the breeze. She pulled at the straps of her backpack, inching it off her shoulders where the fabric of her white linen shirt was bunching.

As she approached the crest of the hill, Harriet spotted a white minibus with slightly tinted windows waiting for her with the engine running. Owen leaned against it, arms folded, sunglasses hiding his eyes. He was every bit an enigmatic mystery in that moment. Harriet smiled to herself. His denim shorts and loud, yellow, floral-print shirt worn over a plain vest tickled her. His choice of clothes was brave if nothing else. But she quickly saw beyond it because when he lowered his glasses and their eyes met, she felt his eyes look all the way into her soul.

Her mood had shifted. Every second spent in her

beautiful hideaway had felt like a step back to her old self. Owen's invitation had given her a revived sense of confidence, and she felt sure enough about herself to wear a tight, soft pink vest top; denim shorts; and a white linen shirt. Before leaving the house, she had sprayed just the right amount of her favourite coconut perfume, making sure it clung to her collar and hair. When she brushed closely by Owen, he turned his head away and pulled his eyes shut, indicating the scent had had the desired effect.

"Can I sit by the window?" Harriet asked playfully, watching him smirk.

"You can sit where you want," he replied, seemingly hiding in the shadow of the door. He held out his hand to help her up the large step into the side of the van. She took it, grasping his fingers—tighter than 'thank you', but less than 'don't let go'. Their touch lingered a split second longer than Harriet intended, and she pulled her hand away once she was safely inside the vehicle.

"Morning," Ricky sang out from the driver's seat, his blonde hair pulled back with a headband.

"He's driving so he can play DJ," chimed a voice from deep inside the vehicle.

"Shush, you." Ricky laughed, plugging his phone into the stereo. The interior of the minibus had two sets of forward-facing seats on either side of a central aisle. It reminded Harriet of the small bus she had rode to school, except for the tinted windows that reduced the glare from the blazing sun.

The large boot space behind the seats was mostly empty aside from three bodyboards and a pile of rucksacks on top of them. Harriet imagined the Tetris-like precision it must take to get all their gigging equipment in the back of it.

She shuffled between the seats, tossing her bag

underneath the seat. Thudding into the solid chair, she pulled her knees to her chest to let Owen past once he had slammed the sliding door shut.

He stood awkwardly in the aisle, his hands resting on the headrests at either side.

"Sit down already," said a gruff voice from the opposite seat. Harriet vaguely recognised it as belonging to the guy with the beard and the bass guitar, but other than that knew nothing about him. He introduced himself as Mike and grimaced in an attempt at a smile. It was obvious to Harriet he was an introvert, much like her younger brother. He didn't make eye contact, shielded his body under crossed arms, and made no attempt at small talk. He returned to his headphones and book without hesitation.

Harriet patted the seat next to her. "Come sit next to me. I haven't been down these roads before. You can be my tour guide." Her attempt at flirting felt awkward but seemed to work as Owen grinned, spun on the spot, and sat next to her.

"How are you liking Ullapool?" asked Ricky from the front seat as he put the bus in gear and spun the steering wheel.

"Oh, it's great. I love it here," replied Harriet. And it was true—she did love it.

Conversation with Ricky flowed easier than she expected. They talked like old friends about Scotland and music. She liked that they had that in common. More than that, she liked that Ricky didn't pry or ask intrusive questions.

Harriet wondered if Owen had someone to talk to outside of the walls of the band. The way he had poured his heart out earlier that morning made her think he didn't.

The vehicle paused as Ricky let some horse riders by,

and he turned round to give Owen a peculiar, all-knowing glance—the type exchanged between friends who have known each other a long time and can speak without saying a word. The type of look that says, 'I like her, but don't air our dirty laundry'. Harriet recognised the energy and connection between them. They were, at their core, a family. A dysfunctional one, but a family, nonetheless.

She smiled reassuringly at Ricky, trying to convey that their secrets were safe with her. It was difficult to do without letting on that she knew in the first place. Luckily, he quickly turned his attention back to the road.

Until a couple of days ago, Harriet had no idea who the band was and had never heard a single note from a song. She barely knew them and certainly wasn't about to start gossiping about a situation she knew very little about.

Once outside of Ardmair, Harriet caught Owen smiling softly at her, looking relaxed and wide-eyed. His quiet, reserved energy was infectious, and Harriet matched his posture, resting her head back on the headrest.

"Are you sure your aunt won't mind me tagging along?" Harriet asked Ricky, raising her voice above the sound of the engine. She wasn't necessarily nervous about meeting Ricky's aunt, more that she was arriving uninvited. She wished she had thought to bring a gift to show her appreciation. If nothing else, she surmised she could earn her keep and offer to do the dishes.

"Nah," he replied. "She's used to us bringing friends up here."

Harriet smiled, enjoying the warmth of being called their friend; she was ready to have some new people in her life. Looking out of the window, she had to stop herself wondering how many 'friends' Owen had brought along over the years.

Unexpectedly, he stretched his arm out across the seat, drawing her attention back to him. He leaned over, pointing out the different mountains and lochs along the winding road. He told her the names, and Ricky laughed when he didn't pronounce them properly. They went on to regale her with stories of the times they got lost off the trail or caught in the rain. His breath was warm against her cheek and the brief touch of his arm against hers set off a surge of electricity through her. She tried not to tense when the sensation took hold, but she couldn't always control the way her body reacted. Owen pulled away, making Harriet think her reaction had scared him off.

"What about that one?" she said, leaning in closer to him to correct herself. She pointed into the distance as a small nub she'd first noticed on the horizon several miles back now towered above them to the right of the road.

"Stac Pollaidh," said Mike, craning his neck to look up. "We've been up there a dozen times."

"I bet the view from the top is amazing," Harriet mused.

Mike nodded and lifted his head even further, the sun lighting the delicate curls of his beard.

Suddenly, the brakes screeched, and the bus came to an alarming halt. Harriet grabbed Owen's hand, digging her nails into his soft flesh. Ricky was shouting out of his window at a couple in a campervan. The couple waved and gesticulated while Ricky seethed and bellowed back at them. Harriet's heart pounded beneath her chest and she quietly closed her eyes, gripping onto Owen with all her might.

A few minutes later, they were moving again, the bottleneck of campervans on the single-track road having cleared.

"Bloody tourists," Ricky grumbled as he threw the

steering wheel around the next corner and carried on as if nothing had happened.

Harriet's pulse was still racing, thudding in her throat and her head. The usual sensations of a panic attack bubbled beneath the surface.

"Hey," said Owen softly. His voice ripped her out of her spiral. "You're okay." His tender voice cut through the chaos of her thoughts and her body reacted to his command. He had reassured her, and surprisingly, she had believed him.

"Can I have my hand back?" he whispered. She looked down at her white knuckles, and tensed rigid fingers which had his hand gripped like a vice.

"Oh, sorry," she replied and instantly let go. He flexed his hand and wiggled his fingers before returning his outstretched arm and leaning into her, just a little closer than before. This time, she didn't pull away or tense up. She revelled in the warmth that radiated from him and listened as he spoke softly of nothing in particular for the remainder of their journey. He had seen her demeanour shift from relaxed and playful to tense and frightened in a split second, yet he hadn't faltered. Harriet was impressed.

The dirt track road to the Summer Isles reached a fork as the horizon opened up. It was there, on what felt like the edge of oblivion, that a lump formed in her throat. All she could see for miles was water that sparkled like a million suns. Crags and rocks were dotted around, and above it all, miles and miles of endless sky. Just like that, she thought of Joe and how much he would have loved it. She wished she could give him her eyes so he could see it all too.

"Beautiful, isn't it?" Owen said, pulling her from her thoughts. "It never fails to take my breath away." He sighed. "But on days like this, when the sky is clear and the sun is warm, it feels just a little bit magic."

More Than Goodbye

Harriet turned to face him. His hazel eyes with their flecks of gold lit up, and she fell deeper into them. She clenched her jaw a little, worrying she wore her internal conflict all over her face. She blinked her thick lashes over her grey-blue eyes and held his attention to the point where everything around them fell away.

———

POLBAIN HAD EXACTLY SEVEN HOUSES SCATTERED about the hillside, a cattle grid and not much else except for the spectacular view of the ocean and sky with Tanera Mòr, the island rising up from the middle of the bay.

Aunt Ellen's cottage was one of those seven dwellings and faced east. A large bay window with a pitched roof took up most of the front aspect of the house. An enclosed garden to the side was filled with flowers and happy, little bees humming away. The front garden was a lawn that sloped towards the stone wall. It looked like it might fall over the second the wind blew the wrong way.

Ricky pulled the van into the driveway and the crunch of the handbrake brought the vehicle to a sudden stop. He and Mike were out in a flash, closely followed by Owen. Harriet hung back a couple of paces to get her bearings. A slender, grey-haired lady with her hair pulled back in a bun was halfway across the lawn before the van had come to a standstill.

Ricky bounded towards her like an excitable puppy and scooped her into his arms, spinning her around. He said something inaudible as he put her down and she tapped his shoulder. "Ack, go on with ye, laddie," she said as Mike went in for an equally warm embrace. "Good to see ye, Mike. How's yer ma?"

Mike reassured her his mum was well and that she sent her love, before tailing after Ricky through the side gate.

Harriet watched Owen lovingly fall into the old lady's arms. She stood on her tiptoes and tried to wrap them around him but only made it as far as his shoulders. When they stepped back, she held his face with her worn hands and smiled. "Ye look better than last I saw ye." Her accent was rich and thick, sending waves of nostalgia through Harriet.

"Aunt Ellen, this is my friend, Harriet," Owen said, motioning her towards them.

"Och, aren't ye a bonnie thing?" Aunt Ellen's open arms stretched out again and she grasped Harriet's hands firmly. She looked at her, surveying her and taking her in. Harriet froze, finding it just a little intrusive, but after Aunt Ellen concluded her findings with an approving nod, she felt more at ease. "Ricky said ye were comin' and you're very welcome, hen."

"Thank you," replied Harriet. "Your home is beautiful."

"Och, you're too kind." Aunt Ellen linked her arm with Harriet's and led her slowly round the lawn. "It's in need of a bit of lovin'. That was our Billy's job, but since he passed, it's no' as easy to keep up wi' all the work."

Harriet felt an instant connection with the rugged, somewhat frail old lady who clung to her arm. "It must be difficult," Harriet said, trying to work out why Ellen stayed in such a remote corner of the world and wondered if she, too, would end up running away to bury herself in her loss.

"It gets easier," Ellen continued, squeezing Harriet's hand. "Your grief weighs heavy on ye, lassie," she remarked, an observation rather than a question.

"Sometimes," Harriet defeatedly agreed, trying to work out how the old lady knew.

Aunt Ellen led her through the gate and wrapped an arm around her, pinning her tight against her. "You'll be all right, hen. Ye carry it well."

Harriet watched her climb the back steps into the kitchen. She was mesmerised at how this woman could read her the way she did. There was no way she could have known what had happened to Joe, how Harriet felt, or what she carried, but after five minutes of being in her company, Aunt Ellen could read Harriet cover to cover.

Old Scottish stories sprung to mind again; tales of folklore, ancient healers, clairvoyants, and even witches. The Witches of Mull was one of her favourite fables; she recalled her grandma telling the story over supper when she was about eight years old. Harriet always assumed them to be children's stories that had become blurred through the echoes of time—used to make sure children brushed their teeth or ate their vegetables— but she was sure that if Aunt Ellen had been around in the 1700s, she would have been burned at the stake.

Harriet was the last to enter the kitchen as the three boys jostled over a boiling pot. They dipped their fingers consecutively in the creamy, buttery sauce that steamed on the back burner of the dated fifties stove.

Mussels in butter, fresh baked bread and piles of warm crab meat drenched in more butter were laid out on the table. The smells had Harriet salivating before she hit the chair and they all quickly dug into the feast Ellen had lovingly prepared.

Conversation rolled easily and the atmosphere was light and comfortable, even when Ricky spoke about the troubles they'd had with Eric and the upcoming tour. The other band-related matters seemed to fly over Harriet's head. Ricky brushed most of it off, pulling up his frontman façade from time to time, but Harriet could see how much it affected Owen as he tensed in his seat. Unable to stop herself, she reached out under the table to squeeze his shaking hand.

Once the food had been annihilated and the dishes cleared, Harriet took a moment to admire the house some more. It was full to the brim of nick-nacks, photos, paintings— decades of memories, each with a place of their own and some undisturbed for what looked like years.

Harriet had spent many nights lying awake, wondering what would happen to all of her and Joe's things— their memories. She hadn't even been through his belongings properly. She was terrified of turning into a bitter old woman, resigned to the life of a grieving widow clinging to photos and random things to remember him by. It's said time is a healer, but Harriet did not agree. Every waking second, her soul learned a little bit more how to live without him.

"It'll get easier," came the gruff, croaky voice from behind. Harriet was standing, staring at a weathered black and white photo of Ellen and Billy on their wedding day. "It feels heavy for a time, but eventually, grief fades t' memory."

"When?" Harriet asked with more desperation than she intended.

"When ye finally make peace with th' fact that he didn't just die, he also lived."

"You sound like you know what you're talking about." Harriet sighed, searching Ellen's wise eyes for answers she herself was so desperately seeking.

"It's been four years since our Billy left us, and it gets a bit easier every day. One day ye wake up and realise ye don't feel the same sadness anymore." Aunt Ellen pulled a photo off the shelf and brushed her finger across the dusty glass. Harriet imagined a million memories flashing in front of Ellen's eyes before she returned it to its home and smiled.

"I'm scared that if I don't feel sad, I won't feel anything," Harriet uttered, wrapping her arms around herself and feigning a smile. Her eyes drifted back over the old photographs with envy, each one capturing a perfect moment in time. Harriet's loss felt deeper than ever. Her longing for moments like the ones in the images felt like it would cripple her.

The sounds of the boys jostling outside caught her eye, and she saw Ricky's blonde hair and toothy grin as he playfully nudged his friends. She was sure they were talking about her as Owen appeared red-faced and had dipped his head. Harriet resumed her visual search of the dresser, looking into Ellen's memories of the past that she clearly held dear.

"Do you ever..." Harriet began but trailed off, catching herself before another honest thought fell out of her mouth.

Aunt Ellen raised her eyebrows and nodded, encouraging her to continue.

She opened her mouth, sighed a little, and finished. "I don't know. Do you ever feel like he's still around? Like you can sense him or smell him?"

"Ach, yes. All th' time," she said, brushing the dust from another frame. "Something happens— maybe I'll drop a plate, or a book will fall from the shelf— and I'll ask, *Billy, is that you?*"

Aunt Ellen drifted off again, and Harriet watched her intently, studying the lines on her face. The gruelling evidence of a life well lived, and a body well loved.

"Oh, he had a happy life, lassie. Don't be frettin' that. " Aunt Ellen pulled a tissue from her apron pocket and passed it to Harriet, who had tears brimming in her eyes. "He's in a better place now." She paused, wistfully looking beyond the photos and trinkets. "No more pain or illness. Yes, I think he pops in to say hello every now and then, but he's gone. He's at peace."

Harriet gently placed her hand on Ellen's. "I'm sorry for your loss," she said softly, feeling a kinship with the first person who had understood her in months.

"And I you, hen. Tell me, what happened to yer man?"

Harriet took in a big breath. "He died in a car accident a little over a year ago."

"Oh, lassie." Aunt Ellen took Harriet's hands, sandwiching them between her own. "That's awful sad. Taken so young."

Harriet nodded, unable to speak for a moment. They stood in solitude for a while as Harriet regained her composure.

"I see him and hear him all the time, and at the most random moments." She paused, debating if what she was about to say next would make her sound like she was losing her mind. "Part of me thinks Joe isn't at peace. That I've missed something, and he isn't able to rest."

"Aye, I'm not surprised," Ellen replied, much to Harriet's comfort. "Taken so young and so suddenly is a shock, and it's hard to imagine him at peace when ye feel so at war. But my mother once told me that some people touch our hearts in such a beautiful way their echoes linger long after they've gone."

"What a lovely way to put it," Harriet said, attempting to smile.

"I've had longer than you to get used to it, lassie, but ye will. I promise. You just have to be gentle with yourself until ye get there. You can't change the cards, but you can choose how you play them. And darlin', you want him to be at peace."

Harriet turned to look at her. Aunt Ellen took her hands firmly in hers and they locked eyes— the wisdom of a thousand lifetimes in one set, the fragile longing of youth in the other, but Harriet felt sure they shared a connection few ever would.

"Do you think I'll ever be happy again, ever feel love again?" Harriet asked. "I don't want to be on my own forever."

Ellen pulled her close and wrapped her arms around her. She stroked Harriet's hair, just like her grandma used to. "Aye, you will. It'll feel a bit different, but it'll be a safe and warm love that fills all the dark corners inside of ye."

Harriet clung to Ellen like her life depended on it, scrunching the soft fabric of her cotton dress in her fingers. Aunt Ellen squeezed back with shaky might, as if she was trying to force all of Harriet's broken pieces back together.

"But you have to want it too, and ye have to be open to it. Even at your lowest, darkest hours, ye have to hold on to the belief that ye *will* get through it. Give yerself a fighting chance." She pulled back and held her hands to Harriet's face, wiping the tears that had escaped her eyes. "Promise me ye will give yerself a fighting chance."

Harriet nodded, dipping her head and sniffing heavily. "I promise."

She hugged Aunt Ellen again, the steady beat of her aged heart thudding strong beneath her chest.

"I guess if it hadn't happened, I wouldn't be here right now with my new friends, eating the best seafood I've ever had in my life."

Aunt Ellen chuckled and they both relaxed and wandered back into the kitchen to watch the boys in the back garden. They were singing and tapping away, laughing and joking. Aunt Ellen pulled her hands to her chest, her eyes full of pride and love.

"Ach, those boys," she said, opening the back door. The midday heat overwhelmed them instantly. "We were never blessed with children of our own. When my sister had Ricky and he brought those fellas into our lives, we fell in love with them all instantly."

Harriet smiled when she caught Owen's eye as he crooned into the midday sun.

"I can see why."

Aunt Ellen raised an inquisitive eyebrow and nudged Harriet in the ribs with her elbow, encouraging her out of the door to join the group. Owen made room for her at the table and his face lit up when she approached. The boys basked happily under the summer sun, and Harriet glanced back over her shoulder to see Aunt Ellen's face beaming. Everyone was relaxed. Harriet could see how grateful they were for having somewhere safe they could come back to. A deep sense of ease settled in as she finally felt her soul catch up.

A short time later, once the singing had stopped and the stomachs had settled, Ricky and Mike went inside to check the tide times. They were hoping to catch the swell at the beach that afternoon. This left Harriet and Owen in the garden, leaning over the waist-high picket fence overlooking the ocean.

"It suits you, this place," Owen said, inching closer to her. "You seem at peace."

Harriet looked up at him and shielded her eyes with her hand from the sun beating down on them.

"Oh, yeah?" she replied, flicking her hair as he looked her up and down. "I don't know about that."

He pushed back from the fence and fidgeted awkwardly, unsure where to look. Harriet ruffled her dark hair, that was turning more golden and copper in the sun, letting it roll off her shoulder. It was a fidgety habit she fell into when she became anxious. She'd started hiding behind her hair when she was a teenager. Her best friend had always pointed out when she did it. To Harriet, it was a nervous quirk, but to others, it had been seen as flirtatious.

"You guys are easy to be around, you know? Maybe you have that effect on me," she replied, pulling her fingers softly through her curls.

"Us and all our chaos and noise?" He couldn't hide the faint flush still clung to his cheeks.

"I said maybe *you* have that effect on me."

Owen blushed even more and had to look away. He cleared his throat and Harriet watched the muscles in his jaw tense and ease once, twice, and a third time. Eventually, he wiggled his nose and relaxed his mouth into a soft smile.

"Are you guys okay?" she asked. Having tried to find the answers on his face throughout the day, she tried to figure out where things were with them.

"Ricky is better when he's here. Aunt Ellen is a calming influence."

"And what about you?" she went on, forcing him to look at her, unwavering in her determination to have him open up. "You carry it all and they have no idea."

"I've got you to talk to." He raised one eyebrow, trying to be playful. "And you're easy to talk to." He paused and sighed. "Perhaps too easy." He smirked and faked a cough. "You have no idea," he concluded, shaking his head and lifting his hand slowly to the back of his neck.

Harriet's heart thumped in her chest as she entertained the idea of him perhaps reaching out and touching her.

The effect they had on each other was strange and evolving. Not only was she fighting the urge to blurt out every small secret and thought she had ever had, but she also now found herself practically craving his touch. All she could think about was the way he had wrapped his arms around her outside the gig and how she suddenly wanted nothing more than to be right back in them.

Harriet had caught Aunt Ellen studying them from the kitchen window and it came as no surprise that she wanted to speak with Owen before they left. She walked behind them as they all made their way back to the bus.

"You're no right, laddie," she croaked as they walked steadily. "Actually, you're a bit right and a bit not right. I canna get a read on ye."

"I'm okay, Aunt Ellen," he replied.

Harriet knew he was lying. She wasn't sure where to put herself. She didn't want to eavesdrop, but they were standing in front of the door, and she thought it rude to move them. There was no choice but to stand awkwardly and try not to listen.

Aunt Ellen took a moment to study Owen, taking his face in her delicate hands and squeezing his cheeks with her thumbs.

"You're as fragile as she is," she concluded as she met Harriet's inquisitive eye. "What is our Ricky doin' to ye?"

"It's not just him," Owen replied gingerly. "The stuff with Eric is getting a bit messy. I guess I feel like I'm stuck in the middle."

"Aye, I see that, but there's something else." She was so matter-of-fact and correct in her observation, it only took one glance between Owen and Harriet for her to blurt out, "Ahhh, a woman's got ye vexed." She and Owen laughed, and Harriet turned a deep shade of scarlet. "That one will no cause you any trouble, lad. She doesn't know how."

Owen pursed his lips, snickering at Harriet as she tried to hide behind her hands.

"Be steady, my boy." She cupped his face in her overly familiar way and reached out her arm to bring Harriet into the embrace. "Be patient with her, with them, and with yerself. It's not your job to fix everyone." Aunt Ellen released them and looked at them standing side-by-side.

Owen chuckled, making his strong shoulders shake. His infectious laugh made Harriet giggle too. "Yes, Aunt Ellen," he replied, giving her a peck on the cheek. He extended his hand to Harriet. She took it firmly and locked her eyes on his as she stepped up into the bus, feeling him closely behind her.

Aunt Ellen waved them off. Harriet was grateful for her wisdom and hospitality and hoped she was able to rest peacefully that afternoon, surrounded by the warm memories of her beloved departed.

Chapter Eight

THE DRIVE TO ACHNAHAIRD BEACH TOOK TWELVE minutes from Aunt Ellen's house, and the boys were buzzing to see the swell of the incoming tide. During that twelve minutes, Owen and Harriet said nothing to each other, but their silence spoke volumes as they exchanged knowing looks and coy smiles.

Harriet felt conflicted but hopeful. Her growing feelings towards Owen were natural and easy, and she finally believed she was in a position where she could lean into them. The way Owen looked at her sneakily yet tenderly out of the corner of his eye made her think he was leaning into them a little too.

Once parked at the top of a small hill, Ricky and Mike hurried out of the bus, followed by Owen. Harriet was the last to let her feet hit the floor, but when she did, her legs felt like jelly, and she had to sit back down. The air was fresh and salty and her belly was full, making her feel sluggish. She watched the boys jostling around, poking fun at each other and laughing heartily. It gave her a moment to pause, collect her thoughts, and bask in the vastness of her surroundings.

After a few minutes, Harriet walked to the edge of the gravel and looked out across the grey-blue crystal mass of water that stretched out to her left and entwined itself in the safety of the rocks to her right. The endless sky seemed to go on forever on a sheer pallet of dazzling blue. The horizon was flat, a perfectly straight line, except for the mountains of the Coigach Peninsula, which stood tall and proud. Perfectly formed mounds of grey contrasted against the skyline. The water swelled against the rocks, tossing up white foam. The colours penetrated her eyes and lit her up from the inside out.

Harriet couldn't pull her eyes away from Owen, who was halfway to collecting his wetsuit and bodyboard when he stopped in his tracks. She watched him look out at the ocean and then back to the bus, then at her.

"What?" Harriet asked, smirking.

"Maybe I won't go bodyboarding today," he replied, throwing his wetsuit back into the bus. "I've done it plenty of times." His hands drifted back into his pockets. "Besides, who's going to make sure you don't fall in a rock pool?" He chuckled, kicking a stone.

Harriet didn't protest. She was glad she would have his company and smiled softly. The butterflies in her stomach flickered and a warm flush raced from her stomach up to her cheeks.

Ricky and Mike were making a commotion at the back of the bus as they wrestled their wetsuits on. As warm as the day was, the water was likely freezing cold. They waited patiently for Owen, but when they realised he was stalling, Ricky tossed him the keys and rolled his eyes.

Harriet stood up, indicating she was ready to go, and

when she moved, Owen moved. When he moved, the others followed.

They made their way through a pointless gate at the edge of the car park and walked across the grass hillocks to the sandy bay.

"We're paddling out, right?" Ricky said to Mike as he beckoned him to finish pulling up the zip on the back of his wetsuit. "We can catch the swell if we head out to the right past the rocks." He pointed out into the vastness of the raging blue and white folds of the incoming tide.

Harriet looked in the direction he was pointing and squinted. From where she stood, everything below her looked tiny. She tried to comprehend how far out into the watery vastness they were intending to go.

The dynamic between the three was interesting to watch. Harriet walked a couple of paces behind them, listening to them talk. She thought she might better be able to understand their conflicts if she took a minute to watch them together. Ricky was tactile, constantly jostling, ruffling his friends' hair, and touching their arms when he spoke to them. Physical touch was his love language, and he oozed it.

Ricky commanded attention, and his friends were happy to give it to him. They laughed as he joked about the potential aftermath of too much seafood and ribbed him when he recalled a misstep from a previous gig that had almost landed him in the arms of the folks in the front row. When Owen mentioned his parents, he shut him down dismissively, and when Mike attempted to bring Eric up, he sneered and pulled his hair back out of his face.

"Have you ever bodyboarded?" Ricky asked Harriet, cleverly diverting the conversation.

"Me? Absolutely not. No way."

The thought of squashing herself into a wetsuit made

her skin crawl. She could swim but wasn't strong or brave enough to tackle the incoming tide. In the time it had taken them to get down to the beach, the swell had moved further inland but had not yet reached the rocks.

"I'm going down to the rock pools to search for sea glass," she said before any further discussion could take place.

As she made her way towards the rock pools, Mike and Ricky darted off across the beach and splashed into the waves. They paddled so far out, that even when she squinted, she wasn't able to see them anymore.

It took a few moments before she noticed she was on her own. Holding up her hand to shield her eyes from the afternoon sun, she scanned the beach, wondering where Owen had gone. When a passing cloud temporarily blocked the sun, she spotted him at the edge of the sand with his phone out, taking a photo. Her eyes were glued to him. He walked towards her, and she struggled to even blink without blushing. Whatever thread of self-restraint Harriet still had, was hanging by a thread.

When Owen realised she was watching him, he immediately jogged towards her, his ridiculously loud shirt billowing out behind him. Fear and excitement gripped her to the point where she had to stop herself from jumping into his arms when he got close.

It took a few deep breaths for her nerves to calm and for the conversation to start flowing. They ambled down towards the crags. Harriet swung her shoes at her side. She spotted Ricky and Mike on their boards, bobbing up and down on the swell near the cliff face at the far side of the bay.

"Don't worry about them," Owen said. "They know what they're doing." Every time he spoke, another piece of her icy core melted. He shifted his eyes, and she watched the sparkle in them grow. He seemed to know what she was thinking and the right thing to say.

Harriet didn't know where to look. Between Owen and the enchanting views, she was stunned and had to remind herself to breathe. The drifting clouds made the sea change colour rapidly from sapphire to turquoise and all the tones in between. It sparkled like a million stars. The sea foam touched the edges of the rocks and folded in on itself, pushing a perfect crescent shape into the water as it brought in the afternoon tide.

Once they reached the point where the golden sand met the jagged rocks, Harriet darted between the rock pools. Owen wandered off into the taller structures, obviously knowing the bay very well. She'd bend down, grab handfuls of sand and stones, inspect them thoroughly, and then toss the remains aside. She was having something almost resembling fun and had lost herself staring at little pool dwellers. She was particularly careful not to disturb anything she thought might be living or hiding.

Moving with caution and respect, she was delighted to have found a few bits of coloured sea glass which she had safely stuffed into the small pouch of her handbag. She had discarded it a few feet away from her, above the waterline of the tide. She had attempted to climb over a large boulder covered in dry seaweed but soon realised it was too big for her to navigate. Now she was stuck, unsure what to do. If she moved away from her seated position, she would be up to her waist in sea water on one side, and the drop was bigger than she realised on the other. She laughed at herself as she straddled the top like she was riding a horse and was relieved when Owen came back. He instantly cracked up when he saw her stranded.

"What are you doing?" he asked, peering over the crest of the rock. His chin was almost touching her knee, and his breath danced delicately across her skin. Their eyes met.

She surveyed the situation, debated jumping down, yet she hesitated. She brushed the water and sand down her sleeves and dusted herself off. "I'm not sure yet. I was trying to reach that sandy spot under the water over there." She pointed towards the little inlet of water. "But I appear to be stuck." She laughed, throwing her head back.

Owen laughed too, holding his belly. She was aiming for the look of a Gaelic goddess sitting atop of the rock as the summer air whipped her hair about. But she thought she looked more like a stranded hobbit who needed rescuing from a situation that could have been easily avoided. He reached his hand up and she took it, swinging herself around. She managed to land more gracefully than she expected but still knee-deep in seawater. The splash she made bounced up and soaked them both, which made them simultaneously erupt with laughter.

Owen reached down under the water next to the seaweed-covered rock, dropped his arms beneath the waves, and scooped up a handful of the soft sand. Holding perfectly still, he presented a mass of sand, pebbles, stones, and shells for her to look at. The rising water was above their knees, but Harriet bounced with joy when he held his hands out to her. She loved searching for treasure. It reminded her of digging up the garden with her sister looking for Roman coins when they were younger.

Her hand held his steady and her fingertips lightly brushed away at the pile, spilling the sand out of his hands and returning it to the beach. He stifled a gasp and held his breath when she touched his wrist. She felt him tense, and his jaw locked as he closed his eyes.

"Nothing in that lot after all that." She sighed. "Thank you, though." Smiling softly, she looked into his eyes, permitting herself to get momentarily lost in them as he shook the sand off his hands. "And thank you for rescuing me." The swirling in her stomach had her in knots. She appreciated his tentative approach, and the last thing she wanted was to scare him off, but all the time, every cell in her body was pining for him.

"Have we had enough rock pool diving?" Owen laughed as they made their way back to dry land. Harriet nodded, still grinning. The warm sun quickly dried her legs, and she followed Owen's lead as he directed them across the beach.

At the crest of the crescent bay, Owen took the weight off his feet and sat with his legs stretched out. Harriet, not waiting for an invite, sat beside him, and they sat a while in silence listening to the waves lap the shore.

"Are you okay?" Owen asked, shuffling to move the sand beneath him.

"I'm okay, I guess," Harriet replied, leaning her head against her shoulder. She peeked at him with one eye open as the sun beat down on her. Looking at him made her nervous. not just because he was under her skin, but because she felt there was no point trying hide herself from him.

"You know, one of the reasons I came here was to give myself some space." She paused, pulling her hair off her face and scooping it back between her thumb and finger. "Does that make sense?" Owen nodded, and she continued. "I need to understand myself better. Regain a bit of control."

"How's that going?" Owen smiled softly. He leaned back on his elbows, arching his back in a stretch that made his bones crack. "Sorry. All those years hunched over a drum kit take their toll."

Harriet agreed that it felt good to have a satisfying stretch in the warmth of the sun and raised her arms into the sky, pulling the muscles in her back and shoulders. He fiddled a shell between his fingers, his eyes fixed on her. She shrugged and shook her head. "Tell me what you're thinking," he asked softly.

The warm tones of his voice seeped into her, and she raised her eyebrows. "You really want to know what's going through my head?"

He nodded and sat upright as he tossed the shell away. Inching closer, she felt his warmth, and this time, she didn't flinch. His breath gently brushed against her cheek, making her feel at ease. She stopped fighting the urge to shut down and began unravelling some of her thoughts.

"I'm starting to think you're only granted a certain amount of happiness in your lifetime. So, everyone has an allocated amount, and once you've used it up, the happiness has to stop. You've had your fill and you're not allowed anymore." She realised how cynical it sounded, but since he wanted to know, she kept going. "It makes me feel like I shouldn't have let myself to be so happy because it ran out, and if I'd been less happy, it would have lasted longer."

She shook her head, wishing somehow that doing so would help her thoughts settle, like the snow inside a snow globe when it's stopped moving around.

"Huh, maybe," he replied, linking his fingers together as he rocked back and forth a little. "Perhaps two people in the same situation feel their happiness differently. Happiness isn't the same for everyone."

"I get that too. I sometimes think I've talked myself into thinking I was happier than I actually was, and Joe was happier than he was too. And because he's gone, I'm not in a position where I can openly admit that things were less than perfect."

Owen nodded. "Sounds exhausting."

"It is. I can't speak honestly about him around his family. They'd chase me out of the village with pitchforks." She laughed. "I still can't shake the feeling something wasn't right."

"It's hard for people to imagine that someone is unhappy," Owen said. Harriet caught him closing his eyes as he sighed. "It's even harder to think that you may have been the cause of it. Before you know it, someone you thought you were close to feels so far away and you're broken, confused... empty." Owen's eyes glistened, filling with moisture and glazing over. Harriet watched his hands shake as he pushed his thumb into the corner of his eye.

She felt the sadness pouring from him, and as much as she wanted to reach out and touch him, she could tell he wasn't finished.

"You shut yourself down and don't let anyone in, and it turns into this deep, harrowing loneliness that no amount of music, practise, or being around people ever seems to fill. It's like being stuck in a dark cave, and you're fumbling around, trying to find an exit with no compass, light with no matches, nothing. You slowly lose hope of ever finding a way back to yourself."

The tears escaped his eyes, sliding down his cheek before evaporating in the sun. He looked in the opposite direction, shielding himself from Harriet's eye line.

She cautiously reached out, her hand shaking as it landed on his arm, and she lightly ran her fingertips along the muscle of his forearm. Goosebumps covered his skin, and he locked her fingers into his. He turned to face her, his lips pulled together in a thin line.

"That person sounds like they need someone to help them remember that they are the light," Harriet said. He smiled at her. The deep appreciation in his eyes made her stomach flip again. He sniffed, clearing his airways, squeezing her hand a little tighter.

"Do you miss her?" Harriet asked.

"Not anymore."

"Do you know where she is?"

"Not a clue."

"You must really hate her."

"You would think that, but to be honest, I don't. I feel very little for her these days. I don't think about her often, but I sometimes think about what she did and what she left."

"Which was?"

"A bad taste and a mountain of debt." Owen laughed, breaking the tension. "You wanna know what happened?" he asked, raising an eyebrow.

"Only if you want to tell me." Harriet clung to his hand. She found herself wanting to know all his stories, all his secrets, everything about him.

Owen adjusted his position and crossed his legs but kept Harriet's hand firmly locked in his. She relaxed her elbow on his thigh, hoping her demeanour calmed him enough to open up.

"Here goes. I had been on and off the road for about six months. Some weeks, I only made it home for a night, maybe two at a push. When the band wasn't on the road, we were writing, rehearsing, recording." He leaned in a little and whispered, "In case you hadn't noticed, Ricky is a bit of a machine."

Harriet laughed.

"Anyway, Tess and I had a place in Bournemouth. It's where we met and where our families live, but it was a good four-hour round trip into London and back. So, when we were working, I would stay with Ricky, Adam, and Eric.

"I was always honest about my band and my music, and I still am. It's the most important thing in the world to me. I came from not much of anything, and I have worked my arse off and poured my heart and soul into it. When I met Ricky, it was like the planets aligned, and I knew from the second I met him that we could do great things. I don't mean that to sound big-headed but sometimes..."

"You just know," Harriet said, intuitively finishing his sentence.

"You just know," he concurred, nodding gently.

Harriet nodded too, beckoning him to continue, giving his hand another reassuring squeeze.

"So, anyway, I'd spent a month solid in London, and I went home a few days before her birthday. I'd planned to take a week off, properly stop and celebrate and spend time together. When I got home, she was sick, and I mean, dog sick, for days. She couldn't keep anything down.

"After what should have been her birthday weekend, she was no better. I insisted she went to the doctor, but she flatly refused and somehow, we ended up in a fight. I was beside myself with worry. She hadn't slept, and I didn't dare sleep in case she passed out or got worse. I waited on her, sitting in the doorway of our bathroom, and just watched helplessly as she hugged the toilet bowl.

"In the end, I called my mum, who's a staff nurse at the hospital. Keep in mind I never call Mum for anything. She's utterly hopeless at being a mum, but even so, I was so worried about Tess. I practically begged her to come take a look at her. She did, and after one glance, she dragged me into another room and said, 'That girl isn't sick, she's pregnant.'

"Mum had to push my mouth closed. I went into the bathroom and sat next to Tess. She lifted her matted head off the toilet seat and looked at me. I asked her if she was pregnant, and she only had the energy to nod. And then I asked how far along she was. In her sleep deprived, dehydrated state, she said she was only a few weeks gone.

"I remember scooting back across the floor and jumping to my feet. I could feel her eyes following me as I paced the bathroom and when I caught her eye she mouthed, 'I'm so sorry.'"

Harriet gasped, covering her mouth with her palm. "It wasn't yours."

"No. It wasn't physically possible for it to be mine. I had been home maybe three nights in two months, and we hadn't slept together in twice that long. Mum saw it all go down and just shook her head, calling her a silly girl and asking what she had done. Tess sobbed all over Mum, but I grabbed my jacket, wallet, and phone, and I walked out. I left everything I owned in that apartment and got a train back to Ricky's."

"My God, that's horrendous."

"I didn't know what to do. On the train, I did all the logistical stuff. Took my name off the bills and drained my savings account. There was no way she was getting her hands on the money I was saving for a house, for our future." He paused and sighed, grunting a little. Harriet's heart ached.

"I didn't even send for my things, not that a struggling musician has a lot, but I just left it."

Harriet couldn't hide her shock. In her mind, she could

vividly see all of it happening. Imagining Owen's face when he found out and trying to conjure up what she thought Tess might look like made her head hurt.

"Perhaps I wanted her to be constantly reminded of me." Owen paused, rolling his neck. "And how shit she was. I stayed with Ricky, he lived on his own then and I think was grateful for the company. But after a while, I felt suffocated. As I said, he's a bit intense, and I was so angry at everything that in the end, I left his too."

"Wow." Harriet could feel how hard it was for him to talk about what had happened. He looked off into the distance and closed his eyes as the memories washed over him.

"What did you do after that?" The thought of Owen having no one to turn to, not even his parents, gave her a new appreciation for her own.

"I came up here and stayed with Elliott, our buddy from uni. He had moved back with his parents and started working on the wind turbines when his sister had a breakdown. You met her, actually."

"Oh, you mean Kathryn?"

"Yeah, that's her. Nice girl. Scatty. A bit of a mess."

Harriet playfully tapped his shoulder and laughed. "You and I are in no position to be passing judgement on people who are a mess."

He laughed along with her. Harriet could feel how synchronised they were.

"Yeah, I know," he replied and raised his eyebrow again. "But you have to admit, she *is* a bit scatty."

"Endearingly scatty," Harriet replied.

"Exactly."

"So, you came up here to hide?"

"Isn't that what people do? Run away to the lonely highlands and hide?"

Harriet's back tensed. "I'm not hiding. I'm regrouping."

"Same thing," he said with a smirk.

"Shush, you. I'll have you know that running away is an emotional and reactive response, whereas regrouping is a mindful choice."

"I'll take your word for that," he said, bringing her hand back into his. She liked the way it felt and didn't attempt to fight the pull towards him.

"I was back and forth between here and Ricky's for a while, but once Ricky got a bigger place, Mike and I moved in with him, as did Eric and Adam. It's much easier now."

Owen's shoulders relaxed. Harriet could tell the weight of his story sat heavy with him, and once he'd let it out, he seemed lighter. The colour returned to his face and the corners of his eyes pulled together when he smiled.

"It was my idea to come up here to work the band stuff out," he said, batting a couple of midges away. "And I really, *really* need them to work it out. It was the only thing that kept me together these last couple of years, and I..." He trailed off, biting his lip.

"Just can't bear losing anyone else," Harriet replied, knowing what he was going to say and how he was feeling. "Why didn't you ever have it out with her?" she asked, making sure to maintain eye contact so he knew she was with him.

"Because I couldn't cope with what she might say."

"What did you think that would be?"

"That I wasn't enough."

Harriet moved closer to him and rested her head on his shoulder, squeezing his hand tighter. She felt like she would never get enough of the feeling of being that close to him. A peaceful stillness washed over her when he held on to her, holding her hand like he would never let go. Harriet rubbed her cheek against his and uttered, "I struggle to believe we live in a world where you are ever not enough."

He melted, leaning his head back against her. "I struggle to believe that you've used up your lifetime supply of happiness," he whispered softly as they both settled into a comfortable silence and let time tick by.

"COME ON. LET'S GO CALL THOSE GUYS IN AND WE CAN hit the road," Owen said, jumping to his feet.

Harriet followed his lead, and without thinking, took his hand as they walked in the shallows of the rising tide. They joked, laughed, and talked, and as they approached the rocks on the far side of the beach, Owen jerked his hand away. He wrapped his arms around her waist from behind and lifted her clean off the ground.

"What are you doing?" she squealed, wriggling to free herself from his strong grip.

He stepped back and put her down, keeping his arms firmly locked around her. "Jellyfish." He nodded towards a translucent mass of moving parts. The sight of it turned Harriet's stomach, but before she knew it, she was laughing again.

She rested her hands on the firm muscles of his forearms, pulling them against her. She leaned back against his chest, his arms closing in around her. His breath danced on her skin as he nuzzled into her flowing hair at the nape of her neck. It was nice to be held by someone who felt something for her besides pity. What that something was, she didn't yet know, but what she did know was that Owen was safe, and when he held her, everything else seemed to trickle away.

She didn't want him to let go.

THE DRIVE BACK WAS QUIET. CONVERSATION BETWEEN the boys was minimal and shrouded in peaceful weariness. Owen stretched his arm across the back of the chair and Harriet leaned in close. Resting her head on his chest, she closed her eyes and drifted into a light doze, listening to the steady rhythm of his heart.

The quiet hum was intermittently interrupted by the boys bursting into beautiful three-part harmonies. Ricky always took the lead, Owen a little higher, and Mike a little lower. Harriet watched them laugh, forget the lyrics, and every now and then, perfectly nail a trill. She hadn't heard Tom Petty's *Free Fallin'* or *Brother* by Need to Breathe sung in such a way before and it filled her heart with joy.

Once back at Ardmair, Ricky and Mike argued over who would be the first to use the shower and whose turn it was to cook. The atmosphere between them was much calmer than it was when they left. Harriet hoped they found some peace away from their struggles and could now face them with a new sense of clarity.

Harriet jumped out of the bus and readjusted herself. She was soon in Owen's eye line as he leaned against the bus, wearing a smile from ear to ear. The soft glow of the beckoning sunset settled over the hillside as she moved closer to him. She stood on her tiptoes and left a soft peck on his cheek.

"Thank you," she whispered. "I had a lovely day."

Intently, she lingered a second longer than needed, enjoying the warmth and scent of his skin.

There had been many words exchanged throughout the day, and Harriet was glad of a moment's quiet. She was always appreciative of silence in a world where people never stopped talking. Sometimes, she knew, you didn't need words, and hopefully, he would feel her lips against his cheek for hours.

Harriet grinned to herself as she locked the door of the cottage and kicked her shoes off. The fresh salty air sat in her lungs and her head felt weary yet clear. It was only a few minutes before she was wrapped in the covers of her bed, reliving the perfect day she'd had.

Chapter Nine

Harriet slept soundly, her body full of the rich sea air and her heart brimming with affection for her neighbours, especially Owen. Hours drifted by as she lay perfectly still, engulfed in peaceful slumber. She was surprised to wake in darkness as her body jolted awake to answer nature's call.

She hadn't drawn the curtains, and the soft light of the stars and crescent moon drifted across her room as she made her way to the bathroom. Although she hadn't been at the cottage for long, she was familiar enough to walk around in the dark.

She washed her hands and splashed her face with cool water, feeling more and more awake as the moments drifted by. Gripping the banister, she descended the stairs, the feel of the cool, smooth pine drifting across her palm.

Entering the kitchen, she looked out over the bay, noticing a couple of small campfires had been lit on the beach. She imagined who might be down there and what fun they could be having splashing in the ripples that lapped the pebble beach.

She paced softly throughout the house, turning lamps on as she passed, all the while admiring bits of driftwood, colourful stones, and pebbles. All of them no doubt collected from the shoreline and used to decorate the house. Throughout the house, paintings hung on every wall, but the one that grabbed her attention was the one depicting the rugged rock formation to the left of the cottage. The landscape was blanketed in a soft covering of pure white snow. There was a stag at the crest of the hill, standing proud, looking directly at her. She hadn't seen anything other than a pine marten since she arrived, and she wondered if the stag had really been there or if the artist had simply imagined it.

Harriet enjoyed looking at the interpretations of the landscape and how different artists saw it in different ways and in different lights.

The ink-like vastness of the bay pulled her attention, and she remembered Kathryn had told her that on a clear night she should lie in the heather and look up at the Milky Way. Kathryn had tried to describe the sensation of seeing more stars than her eyes could take in and, excited, Harriet grabbed some blankets and a camping lantern and made her way outside, turning the lamps off first.

She followed the gravel path around the front of the cottage, taking care as she stepped up onto the garden wall and waded through the thick stalks of bracken and heather. The bristles that tickled her ankles greeted her like long lost friends. She treaded carefully, checking each step afforded her firm ground to put her weight on.

She made her way over to the rock that jutted out over the embankment. The one that sat up like a reclining chair, at just the right angle so she could comfortably lean against it. Nestling in, Harriet pulled the blankets around her shoulders, over her knees, and under her chin. It wasn't too cold, but neither was it particularly warm. She wanted to make sure she was comfortable so that when she turned her torch off, she could stay outside for as long as possible and take in the sky that was about to unfold above her.

She was slightly nervous, and in true Harriet style, was worried it wouldn't be as magnificent as she expected. After a long pause, she rested her head back and opened her eyes. At first, she didn't see anything, but slowly, as her eyes adjusted, the sky came to life. She tried to recognise some of the constellations she knew, but she couldn't spot them because they were shrouded with other stars.

She opened her eyes wider, trying to see everything at once. Her mouth fell open as she noticed a mass of stars and clouds stretching from north to south. The Milky Way was right there. She could see it. She felt like if she stretched enough, she could reach up and touch it. When she focused on one star, all the stars around it clumped together. Her eyes darted back and forth, glistening as she watched the magnificence reveal itself over and over again.

She gasped and laughed, all the while scanning the cosmos as another glimmer, sparkle, or movement caught her eye. She saw a streak of white shoot across the mass of stars and she laughed again. She had never seen a shooting star in her life, and as she thought it, another caught the corner of her eye as it disappeared into the sky to the west. Harriet relaxed a little more and ruffled her hair between her fingers, incredibly gratified by her solitary piece of cosmos heaven.

Her mind drifted to Joe and how he had always wanted to see the stars properly. She closed her eyes and smiled, accepting for just a brief second that she felt him there with her. *I see it*, a voice in her mind whispered. Feelings of familiarity intertwined with hints of sadness swelled inside her, but briefly, it felt like Joe was by her side.

———

MEANWHILE, AT THE TOP OF THE HILL, IN THEIR cottage above the rocks, Owen had been pacing his room, unable to sleep. His mind was racing over his day at the beach. He had been replaying his conversation with Harriet, debating if he had revealed too much too fast and hoping he hadn't scared her off with his stories of his past. She had enough to contend with without the burdens of his broken heart and band drama. On the other hand, she was good at listening. He found her very easy to talk to. Perhaps a little too easy, and he liked that she didn't offer solutions or try to fix any part of him. She just listened. He was beginning to realise how much he needed someone to do just that.

For a long time, Owen had felt indebted to Ricky, and he was constantly trying to repay him for helping him in the past. He didn't have as close a relationship with the rest of the band as he did with Ricky, and being so far away from home all the time made it very difficult for him to reach out to his family for someone to talk to. He mused how much he had distanced himself from people since he left Tess, and perhaps he did need to open up more. But the thought of doing so scared him witless, which made him question his recent actions even more.

Frustrated and restless, he stood at his window, looking out over the bay. The endless midnight black of the water stared back, speaking to him in a way that echoed his loneliness, but it wasn't long before the light coming from the rocks at the edge of the hill caught his attention. He stood puzzled for a moment, watching a small beam moving back and forth before coming to a halt in the thick of the heather. His stomach flipped a little when he thought it might be Harriet. Then an even more curious thought entered his mind as to what she was doing wandering around in the dark.

He decided to investigate, for no other reason than to check she was all right. At least, that was what he told himself. He pulled on his denim jacket and black leather boots and quietly made his way downstairs. Eric was passed out on the couch, and the room stank of stale beer. He wasn't quiet about leaving. He thudded around slamming doors, part of him hoping he might wake Eric up so he could give him a good dressing down over his behaviour the last couple of days. Unfortunately, he had no such luck. He shook his head as he left the room and turned the lights off as he snuck out the patio doors that led to the veranda at the front of the house.

His footsteps were light against the wood, and he swiftly jumped down the steps and down the pitch-black single-track road towards Harriet's cottage. The soft soles of his shoes didn't disturb the pebble driveway, and he reached the wall before Harriet noticed he was there.

"Can I join you?" he asked, his stomach aflutter.

"Owen! Yes, of course," she replied, patting the ground next to her.

"Sorry. I didn't mean to scare you." Owen plonked himself onto the blanket next to her. "I saw lights moving around and I came to check..."

"That I wasn't throwing myself off the edge of the rocks?" Harriet laughed and then caught herself. "Sorry. That was in bad taste."

Owen laughed as Harriet offered him one of her blankets to pull over his knees. He lay back against the rock next to her and asked what she was looking at. With excitement in her eyes, she went into great detail about all the things she had seen since she had been out there. He listened without interruption, and his eyes drifted all over her as she became more animated in recalling her night's adventures. The more she talked, the more he smiled, and the more he smiled, the more she felt the connection growing between them.

Once she had finished regaling him with shooting stars and campfires, they fell into a comfortable silence as she moved a little closer. She pressed her shoulder against his and let her head fall back. Her heart was beating like a kick drum. Strong, loud, and persistent. She felt like a thousand volts were passing between them, but all she could do was look up and watch the sky's midnight dance.

Harriet turned to Owen, just about able to make out the features of his face. He turned to face her too; she wanted to look into those big hazel eyes. He leaned forward and turned the campfire light's adjustable brightness, casting a warm, candlelight shimmer over them both.

"Owen, I had such a great day. Thank you so much," Harriet said, keeping her eyes locked on his.

"Me too," Owen replied, moving his head further into the light, showing off all the shadows and curves of his jawline.

"How were things when you got back?"

Owen sighed and leaned back, placing his hands under his head and looking directly upwards. "Pretty much the same. Eric is still passed out in the front room, and Ricky stormed off to bed and hasn't left his room since. The other guys went into town and haven't come back."

He sighed again. This time, he held his breath before puffing it out and closing his eyes. "I hate to say it, but I think Ricky is right. Eric has to go."

"Oh, Owen. I'm so sorry," Harriet said, gently placing her hand instinctively on his.

A short gasp fell from Owen's lips. Harriet jolted as goosebumps pebbled up her arm. She had felt a spark earlier when Owen had picked her up around the waist and pulled her out of the way of the jellyfish. This felt different, more intense, like magnets pulling together.

"It's not good for the band members to constantly be at war with each other," Owen said, pressing his fingers in between Harriet's.

"What are you going to do?"

"We have to get through these tour dates, and then we'll have to make the call."

"When does the tour start?"

"In four weeks. I just hope Eric and Ricky can call a truce before we get there and somehow we can make it through it."

Owen almost growled through his last breath. "God, it just shouldn't be like this right now. We're supposed to be touring. The new album is ready to go and..." he trailed off, biting his lip and turning his head away.

Perhaps he hadn't meant to get worked up again. She watched him chew his thumb and his body tensed once more. A soft squeeze and reassuring nudge brought his attention back to her and he raised his eyes back to hers.

"I say this with as much modesty as I can muster," Owen went on, "but this album is something else. If we can get ourselves together, it could be the start of something really big for us."

Harriet smiled as sympathetically as she knew how, and he met her gaze once more.

"I don't want anything to wreck it."

Harriet understood him completely. Although their situations were different, in some respects, they were the same. She knew what it was like trying to hold on to something that was broken. She understood the balance required to grasp something fragile, to hold it with a soft touch through fear of squeezing it too hard, but the light touch also makes you feel like you will drop it. Either way, you live in a constant state of anxiety and fear and nothing you do seems to fix what is broken.

"I understand," she said softly, taking a moment to glance at him out of the corner of her eye.

Owen hardened his position again and seemed to regain immediate composure.

"Can I ask you something?" he asked. "We spoke a lot today about what happened and life before now, but let me ask you this." He looked at her and raised his eyebrow. "What's next?"

Harriet scrunched her nose a little and pursed her lips.

"If you could do anything in the world, what would it be?"

She pondered a moment, and she retraced her thoughts from earlier. "I keep coming back to the idea of selling my house," she replied. "I can't live there anymore; it's suffocating. I need a change of scenery." Harriet knew the reality of selling her house was a lot different from the notion of it. Her parents would likely kick up a stink, Wendy would have something to say as she always did, and then there were the practicalities of where she would go.

"That already sounds like the start of a plan," replied Owen.

"Trust me, it isn't. But that's okay. I think that's what I want right now. No plan. Just to be able to drift a little, see which way the wind carries me."

"That's brave."

Owen's smile, without judgement or contradiction, felt encouraging. There was no protest, no listing of reasons for her not to, but a sentiment of acceptance.

"I don't know if brave is the word. But I do know that drifting along hasn't got me anywhere and trying to have a plan hasn't got me anywhere, so maybe it's time I try something else."

She spread her hands and pulled her hair out of her face, stretching her forehead and releasing the tension behind her eyes. She turned to him, letting her curls fall back around her face.

"Everyone has a plan for me, and no one has asked me what I want. So, I'm shaking it all off, and they will just have to suck it up."

Owen was beaming. If Harriet didn't know better, she would have thought him impressed.

"You are quite remarkable, do you know that?" he asked as he reached out and tucked a wisp of hair behind her ear, sending goosebumps tingling down the back of her neck and into her spine.

In that moment, Harriet felt so sure about her decision not to make a decision that it afforded her a sense of satisfaction she had forgotten existed.

"What about you?" she asked as she shuffled lower, almost lying down. "If you could do anything in the world, what would it be?" Her eyes fixed on a small cluster of white and orange dots on the horizon that captivated her more than anything else she had seen.

Moments passed before she realised Owen hadn't replied. She sensed a little tension grow between them again, and when she turned to look at him, he was sitting perfectly upright and still. She felt trepidation, but she could see his chest rising and falling rapidly under his coat.

Slowly, she sat up, and he turned his head towards her; his hazel eyes glistened against the cosy shine of the lamp.

"I think I want to kiss you," he replied, his voice trembling a little as he deliberately fixed his eyes deep into hers.

The kick drum in Harriet's chest upped its tempo and echoed up through her throat into her ears. She looked back at him, his eyes pleading with her to agree. In unison, they both gave in, and their lips came together faster than the rush of blood to Harriet's cheeks.

He gently cradled her face. She pressed her body against his, her arms under his shoulders as she pulled him against her. His hand moved from her jaw, slowly down over her shoulder, onto her waist, pulling her even tighter against him. All the while, the need for air built, but the need to keep their lips together was stronger. Desire surged inside her as he held her firm again against his strong chest, but she reluctantly pulled away. Gasping and panting to bring air back into her lungs, his eyes bore into her. Once her oxygen necessity had been sated, she leaned in and, once again, their lips met as her burning need for him erupted to the surface. Without realising, Harriet had all but laid down against the cool rock beneath them.

Owen rested his forehead against hers, and she delicately stroked her fingers against the grains of stubble on his chin. He kissed her again, slowly and deeply. She could feel his zipper becoming tight against the swell inside his jeans as she pressed her hips against his thigh and kissed his neck.

"Do you want to come inside?" she whispered into the nape of his neck.

He closed his eyes, almost purring. She couldn't pull her hands or lips away from him, and the way he responded to her touch made her sure he was as swept up as she was.

"Are you sure?" he asked courteously, looking down at her, his full weight bearing down on her soft form, which moulded against him like putty.

"Very sure," she replied, pressing her nose to his and breathing him in. She stood quickly, watching him rub his fingers across his swollen lips.

She paused for a moment, gulping in a couple of breaths of cool Scottish air. Scared he might change his mind, Harriet reached out her shaking hand to him. Relieved when he took it, she led them across the gravel and up the steps into the house.

Chapter Ten

Harriet stood, nervous with anticipation, looking out her bedroom window over the bay. The light from the hallway dimmed as the bedroom door closed. Just a small sliver remained and the room descended to a couple of shades above darkness. Her mind was empty and her heart was pounding; the anticipation was palpable as she quietly waited for him to come closer.

She felt like all the air had been sucked out of the room. The time it took for him to cross the distance felt like an eternity, but as soon as his body was against her back and his hands rested gently on her hips, the tension melted away. He slowly let a warm breath drift across her shoulder. She closed her eyes, letting her nerves dissolve.

She turned her head slightly, letting the tip of her nose touch his cheek.

"I'm nervous," she admitted, her voice shaking.

"It's okay. We don't have to do anything if you don't want to." His caramel voice washed over her. He breathed out again, making the hairs on her neck stand to attention.

"It's not that." She hesitated, unsure how to phrase what she was thinking. "I haven't done this in a while."

His hands tightened on her waist, and he pushed his hips into hers. Bringing her close with just a little bit of force stirred butterflies in her stomach, and she found herself wanting him more than anything. She had never been with a man who took control like that; it incited a deep, animalistic desire she had never experienced before.

Reaching her hand to his jaw, she stroked her fingertips across his stubbled, perfectly angled chin. The chin that had been driving her nuts since she first laid eyes on it. She felt a thrill listening to him purr and melt beneath her touch.

"You're already better at this than you think you are," Owen whispered before lightly kissing her neck and spreading his hands across her stomach. She pushed herself back into him, feeling his heat and his heartbeat thudding in his chest. She almost pulled away. Apprehension about enjoying the closeness to someone was something she didn't know she was missing, and in a split second, she allowed guilt to drift into, and then quickly out of, her mind.

They stood quietly. Harriet lightly stroked Owen's face as his soft lips caressed her skin. She enjoyed the way he let her weave her fingers into his hair, pulling him closer. Her body ached, begging for more, and he spun her around to face him, pressing his lips against hers. They moved, soft and rhythmic, as he dug his hands into the waves of her hair that cascaded over her shoulders, falling gently against her cheeks.

In the secret corners of her mind throughout the day, she had imagined what it might feel like to have him bury his hands in her hair, to pull her lips to his. Now it was happening, she had to open her eyes for a second to check it was real. She cradled his face with her hands, barely able to breathe and unwilling to part their lips. Every part of her craved him. His lips, his touch, and when his hand moved slowly down her spine and into the small of her back, she melted into him like warm butter.

He gently laid her down on top of the covers and hovered over her. Their eyes met in the darkness and Harriet gave him a smile indicating she wanted more. She reached under Owen's white shirt and slipped it up and over his shoulders, tossing it to the floor. Harriet took a moment to admire his trim body. The enticing tufts of curly brown hair on his chest and the way his trousers hung desperately to his protruding hip bones.

She curled her arms underneath him, pulling his body against her, exploring every inch of his back with her fingers. She moaned when his kisses landed on her neck, collarbone, and behind her ear. He felt so new, so different, so firm, so warm, and she ached for more.

Owen moved his mouth slowly down to her hips and kissed her stomach. She was scared she would freak out and pull away at any moment. Her body tensed and he slowed down, responding to her silent need for slow and gentle. She felt him throbbing in his trousers, and her aching desire to consume him made her head spin. He moved Harriet's shirt up over her breasts and she awkwardly wriggled out of it. His warm and hungry mouth found her right nipple and his tongue danced over it, making her moan again. His lips found hers once more, but this time with a new sense of urgency.

"Touch me," Harriet begged. She gasped for breath, which became staggered and short in the top of her chest.

Owen obliged instantly, popping the button on her jeans and sliding his hand beneath the fabric of her pants into her warm folds that were already wet with anticipation. He still felt different, but she tried not to compare. He moved his fingers inside her in ways she had never felt before, whilst the pad of his thumb made circular motions over her sweet spot.

Harriet felt like she was brand new. She didn't know her body could respond the way it did. Owen was meticulous, soothing, and attentive. At the same time, she could feel how much he wanted her. She bucked her hips and came quickly, much quicker than she expected. But it had been over a year since anyone, even herself, had ventured into that area. It surprised her a little. A very faint chuckle followed her sweet release.

"I want you," Owen said urgently against her mouth, his breath short.

No longer able to contain the erection bulging in his trousers, he rubbed against the inside of her thigh and moaned. Harriet felt heat burning all the way into her core, and she wrestled to unbutton his jeans and shed the remainder of his clothes. She wasted little time in taking his solid form in the palm of her hand. As she moved up and down the hard length, he arched his back, tilting his head towards the ceiling.

His exposed neck was begging to be kissed; Harriet could see his pulse throbbing against the unshaven skin of his neck. She wanted to taste it and took great pleasure in running the tip of her tongue against the grains of stubble that ran down his throat. It felt rough, and he tasted as delicious as she expected. Grateful for her ongoing birth control injection which meant she didn't have to think about anything besides how instantly she fell apart once she had spread her legs and guided him inside her.

He was thicker than what she had been used to. At first,

she grimaced as he slid delicately inside her. Owen felt her tense and looked at her. She nodded, begging him to continue as she felt the pleasurable sting of unfamiliarity. He rocked gently into her. She was tight and not used to being stretched in that way, but once she stopped listening to her mind and started listening to her body, she relaxed a little.

He nuzzled at her cheek. "Are you okay?"

Harriet nodded, looking straight into his hazel eyes as he gently pushed himself fully inside her. In that moment, she consumed every inch of him, right down to his base.

"Again," she pleaded.

He pulled out and pushed back in again. He did it several times, each time more delicious than the last. Each time, his length tickled her sweet spot, and each time she wanted him more. It wasn't long before she felt herself climbing the peak again, but she wanted it to last longer; she didn't want it to be over so soon. Harriet kissed him as his mouth hung over her and he devoured her lips in the heat of the moment.

Owen slowed his rhythm and painfully pulled his lips away from her before moving her onto her side and sliding back inside her from behind. He went deeper, and it incited another moan that Harriet was sure could be heard across the bay. Harriet turned her head to his and kissed him, holding his jaw firmly in place. His free hand cupped her breast, massaging it softly as he continued to move inside her.

She took his free hand and moved it down between her legs, guiding his experienced fingers onto her clit, and helped him move them over it. He took direction well, which made her feel even more desired.

"Don't stop," Harriet gasped as she felt herself building again.

She could hear his staggered, shallow breath in her ear and his teeth grinding together as she began to tighten around him, climaxing and moaning as he huffed, clenched, and moaned as they peaked at the same time.

Her release made her dizzy, and the world around her went into slow motion. Everything fell away and all she could feel was him; their skin, hair, and bodies entwined. Harriet felt like her soul had escaped her body. And in that moment of sheer bliss, she clung to him, and it felt like nothing else in the world mattered.

Owen rolled onto his back, pulling Harriet with him. Her heart rate gradually returned to normal, but his was still racing when she laid her chin on his chest. Slowly, the room came back into focus and a steady calm resumed. Owen looked at her. She twizzled a tuft of his chest hair between her fingers. The soft, feather-like touch of her fingertips covered him in goosebumps. And then he reached out and did the thing she had been bursting for him to do all day. He tucked the loose ringlet behind her ear and spread his palm across her cheek.

THE NEXT THING HARRIET KNEW, SHE WAS BEING pulled from her heavenly slumber by an irritating sound. In the mid-morning haze of a truly satisfying evening, it sounded like a jackhammer inside her head. It took a moment for her to realise it was Owen's phone vibrating on the nightstand. He groaned, squinting, refusing to open his eyes. Harriet burrowed into the nook of his arm, feeling the heat of his body close around her. She felt peaceful in his arms.

Barely moving, he reached over and answered it. Within a matter of seconds, he threw himself out of bed, leaving Harriet in a pile of bed covers and pillows.

"I'm late," he said in a dejected tone. He pulled his shirt over his head, his jeans on, and tied his boots quickly. "We have to be in Inverness early today for the gig tonight."

Harriet jumped out of bed to throw some clothes on and pulled her hair into a clip at the nape of her neck. It all seemed to happen in a blur. Owen was flustered as he ran down the stairs, Harriet on his heels.

He was about to bolt out the door, but he stopped and spun on his heel. Pacing back to her, he threw his arms around her and pressed his lips gently into hers. She melted again, her fingers digging into the muscles of his shoulders.

"I'm so sorry to run off like this," he said with the utmost sincerity. Harriet found it impossible to be mad at him. The way his eyes dropped and his lips turned down made his face soft in a completely new way.

"It's okay," she said half-heartedly. "I understand." And strangely enough, part of her did. She knew the band came first, she knew how much it meant to him, and she knew what he was going through with Ricky and Eric. There was no denying the twinge of disappointment she felt that he couldn't stay a while longer.

He released her reluctantly and looked deep into her pearly blue eyes. Harriet was mesmerised by how a good night's sleep made the hazel in his eyes lighter, and she was quickly lost in them once again.

"Everything about yesterday was perfect," he said. "From the second I knocked on your door until now. It was a perfect day."

He pulled away as Harriet opened the back door, leaning up against the frame as he stepped down. That small step made them the same height and she rested her arms on the top of his shoulders. His eyes fixed on hers. He leaned forward, kissed her again softly and slowly, and stepped back up into the doorway, his lips never leaving hers.

He pulled her to him, pressing his hand into the small of her back. It took everything to let him go.

She nodded and smiled. "It was perfect," Harriet agreed, finally relaxing her arms and releasing him.

"Being late is totally worth it." He chuckled, resting his forehead against hers. "We'll be back tomorrow night. Can I see you then?"

Harriet nodded, and he beamed his signature Cheshire Cat smile. Without further hesitation, he had darted off up the hill and was out of sight.

The door swung closed, squeaking a little on its rusty hinges. Before Harriet had turned the latch, she heard the echo of a hundred angry voices in her head screaming, "WHAT HAVE YOU DONE?"

She froze. Her heart stopped. She crumpled to the floor, her sobs overflowing. The frenzy of guilt made her shake from her bones to her eyeballs. Even her hair follicles shook. The clammy nausea rolled down her back, across her forehead, sank its claws tight around her chest and churned in the pit of her stomach. She screamed, she laughed, and she sobbed. Over and over. All in one go as wave after wave of guilt engulfed her. Her vision clouded, she could barely breathe, the room was closing in, and her eyes felt heavy.

Angry, agitated anguish punched her in the stomach, knocking the wind out of her before building uncontrollably. There was no way of stopping it. She leaned over the sink in the utility room and emptied the contents of her stomach. And then she sat on the cold marble floor, completely numb and empty.

Gone. She felt like she was hovering over her own body, looking pitifully at the heap of broken humanity curled up on the floor.

How long she was there, was anyone's guess. The sobs subsided into silent tears that dripped from her face onto the tile floor. She caught her reflection in a paint tin and truly saw herself for the first time in months as she made the final, crippling realisation. Spending the night, sharing a bed, being held, touched, and satisfied by another man, meant this was the first day that Joe was totally gone.

"THIS DAY WAS ALWAYS GOING TO COME," SAID JULIA, her voice sounding muffled down the phone.

"I feel like I cheated on him," Harriet sobbed hysterically, struggling to catch her breath.

"You haven't cheated, Harriet. Listen to me. You have not been unfaithful. Your husband died over a year ago, and it is a natural part of the grief process to feel the way you do." Julia's tone was soft yet firm. Harriet imagined being stretched out on her couch, staring at the white foam ceiling tiles, her body rigid as she forced herself to talk and to listen.

"The hardest part is doing all the things without him. Unfortunately, one of those things is being with someone else."

She always sounded so assured and confident. Harriet envied her for it and resented herself for not having the same composure.

"Breathe through it," she said encouragingly. "I'm not going anywhere."

Julia had been her therapist for the last six months and was always at the end of the phone when needed, even on evenings and weekends. Therapy was something her parents had tried to push her into, and to start with, she defiantly refused. But six months after Joe's death, when it was pointed out she wasn't moving on, Harriet gave in and agreed to it.

For the most part, it was easier for Harriet to live in a perpetual state of sadness because it was the only thing she felt linked her to Joe. She was scared therapy would make her feel something else, and every second she spent working through her feelings brought her closer to moving past them and ultimately leaving them behind.

She pulled her breath in slowly, held it a moment, and puffed it out.

And then again.

And again.

After a few moments, she growled and lifted herself off the cool tiled floor of the utility room. Her entire body felt like lead, heavy and aching from the position she had fallen in. Dragging her exhausted carcass off the floor took strength she had to dig deep to find, but once she was back on her feet, she felt a little more composed. Keeping the phone to her ear the whole time, she heard Julia congratulating her on tiny steps and little victories.

"How am I ever supposed to meet someone else when I carry this with me? Who is going to want someone like that?" Harriet asked as she held her hand to her cold, clammy head and looked out again over the changing colour of the bay.

A storm was coming. The sky was thick, grey, and

heavy. The once clear and vibrant little masses of land on the horizon were shrouded in a cocoon of dark grey. The campers on the shore rigorously packed up their belongings and headed for the safety of their campervans as the wind whipped up a frenzy and the fat Scottish raindrops fell like pearls from the sky.

"This isn't about someone else accepting you, Harriet. It's about you accepting that you have this in your past and deciding how much it influences your future."

Harriet nodded heartily. "I know, I know."

Julia spoke sense, and suddenly the things she'd said merged with the memories of the last few days, and Harriet felt an eerie sense of calm come over her.

"We will work on this some more in our next session," Julia said. "But for now, just enjoy the moment. Enjoy your time with your new friend. And Harriet?"

"Yes?"

"You haven't done anything wrong."

"Okay." She sniffed. "Thanks, Julia. I'll see you in a few weeks."

"Goodbye, Harriet. Take care."

Harriet blinked away the remaining tears that hung from her eyelashes, closed her eyes, and put her hands on her hips.

Breathe in. Breathe out.

And she began to feel like she could do this. She felt her icy wall crumble and her mind and body filled with the lingering imprints of her time with Owen. The way his breath felt on her neck, his hands against her skin, his lips against hers. For all the guilt that was festering in the pit of her stomach, her body tingled all over at the memory of the day before.

"I did nothing wrong," she said out loud over and over again.

Walking through the kitchen and into the front room, she realised even the soles of her feet were sweaty as they stuck to the hardwood floors. Reminding herself to be delicate with herself after a panic attack, she settled into the plush orange sofa in the corner of the room and let the cushions consume her. She reached over to the wicker chest that doubled as a coffee table and pulled the scratchy tartan blanket out. Lying down, she pulled the blanket up to her chin, and within minutes, drifted off to sleep.

Chapter Eleven

Harriet slept long and deep, and while she slept, she dreamed. Dreamed of Owen, of her sister, and of Joe. Vivid, vapid dreams of colours and noise and then long-drawn-out silences where Joe stood a few inches away from her, so real she could touch him. He looked at her in stillness, his form not quite whole, a brilliant white light emanating from him. His eyes were forlorn, tired, like he hadn't slept in months. His hair was perfectly styled, in the same way it was on their wedding day, but his face was hollow and his eyes full of sadness. She tried to reach out to pull him to her, to wrap her arms around him and tell him she was trying to forgive him for leaving her, but she was frozen.

His lips moved, and he mouthed, "I'm sorry." Not in the way someone says sorry to end an argument or to bring a point to a close, but in a way that indicated it wasn't done yet. She felt as if he was trying to apologise for something that hadn't happened. It made her angry. As if he hadn't done enough already. She wanted to forgive him, for him to be at peace, but forgiveness was complicated, especially when she knew she wasn't going to get the apology she so desperately needed. At least, she hoped he was sorry for what he had put her through.

When she woke late in the afternoon, Harriet couldn't shake the feeling of there being more to come. When speaking with Aunt Ellen, she had casually said she wasn't sure Joe was at peace and the thought had festered without her knowing it.

Prompted by her imagination, Harriet felt a sudden need to speak to Louise. Her hands had dialled the number before her mind caught up.

Louise and Harriet were as close as any sisters could be when they were younger. They had their inside jokes and were always planning an adventure, musical number, or scheme to wind up their mother. One day, whilst out in the back field, Louise looked up as a military plane the most brilliant shade of red shoot across the sky above them, followed by another and another. Nine in total. Harriet felt sure this was the day she began to lose her, but she was too young to realise.

Stopping in her tracks, shielding her eyes from the sun, Harriet watched as her sister's eyes lit up, a visible spark igniting. From that moment, she was obsessed with aircraft. By the time she started secondary school, she knew the names of all sorts of planes and the day-to-day training schedule of the Red Arrows. One of her birthday parties was spent at a local air show, watching their aerial acrobatics.

It didn't come as a surprise when Louise announced she was enrolling in the RAF. She stood in the kitchen of her parents' home, aged eighteen, her thick brown hair pulled fiercely back into a tight knot on the back of her head and made her announcement. Harriet hadn't thought much of it at the time; her sister would still be living at home, and they could still be together. It was when her sister took a position in Lossiemouth just after Harriet started university that their relationship changed.

Harriet had sensed Louise was restless and would often catch her shaking her leg, staring out of the window, or losing interest in the middle of a conversation. Harriet overheard several conversations between her parents that they felt Louise was pulling away from them, shutting herself down and spending more time at work. Harriet knew her parents wanted to keep them all close, but it reached a point where she was sure Louise would lose it if she stayed in the confines of her family home any longer.

Louise left for Lossiemouth exactly eight days after Harriet had started university, less than two weeks after announcing her departure. Harriet hated it. It happened so quickly, and she was powerless to stop it. It was the first time Harriet had ever experienced any kind of loss, even though it wasn't really a loss in the conventional sense. It was more the realisation that her childhood was over. Harriet spent many a night wide awake, staring at the celling, wondering what she had done so wrong to make her sister abandon her. Eventually she accepted that her sister was on very different path to her, but by the time she made peace with it, the rift between them was too wide. Louise only visited once or twice a year from then on, and it was only when her father had a heart scare in 2019 that she spent more than two consecutive nights in the family home.

Since Joe's death, Harriet had learned who was truly there for her and who wasn't. Sadly, Louise, was one of the people who hadn't been by her side. Harriet wasn't angry.

She simply felt nothing for the sister she once couldn't live without. The clarity she had been afforded by her trip made Harriet realise she had been too busy being sad to notice that she had missed her sister.

"Harriet?" came the shocked voice at the end of the phone.

"Hi, Lou. How are you?"

"Why are you calling me?" Louise snapped.

Harriet rolled her eyes. Maybe she was wrong to think that after three months, her sister might be able to fake a shred of excitement at hearing from her younger sister.

"I'm in the highlands and thought I might come over to Lossiemouth for the day," Harriet replied. She hadn't thought about what she was going to say to Louise, and the words were out of her mouth before she could catch them. Maybe her dream was pushing her to fix some of the broken things in her life, or maybe she was simply at a point where she finally understood why her older sister had left all those years ago. Either way, she knew life was too short to not at least try.

"Really? Erm, sure, okay. I guess," Lou replied, a hint of trepidation in her tone. "Where are you?"

"I'm in Ullapool." Harriet held her breath, braced for another onslaught of questions. Her big sister had the same effect on her as her mother. "I could drive to see you, though."

"From Ullapool? Don't be daft. I can meet you halfway. Inverness? I'm off tomorrow if that works?" Her tone lightened with each word, and by the time they made plans to meet at midday, Louise sounded like she was borderline excited.

Harriet felt lighter too, but the sound of the rain hammering on the house from all angles suddenly made her jump. The air grew thick and muggy, and in a split second, the thunder rolled in.

The sky turned from white to dark grey and the horizon disappeared, and the mountains along with it. Harriet felt trapped in the house, isolated from the rest of the world. Not an unfamiliar feeling at that point in her life, but being all on her own, suddenly felt like the last place she wanted to be. There were no neighbours in the house up the hill, the bed and breakfast half a mile up the road was closed for renovations, and even the car park at the crest of the bay was empty. Harriet had somehow managed to find herself in the exact position she had wanted to be in; she was completely on her own, and in a wave of crystal clarity, she realised she didn't like it at all.

"The thing to do is keep busy until either the rain stops, or Owen comes back," she said to herself.

She occupied herself for the rest of the day and long into the night cleaning, sorting, bathing, and organising. For the first time in months, she opened her internet banking and got the shock of her life when she saw a six-figure sum in it. After Joe died, her father had taken to sorting out her life administration. Things like opening letters, looking after her finances, and sorting out Joe's estate had been beyond her. Her father had told her she had enough to never work again as Joe had taken care of her, but she was too blinded by grief to care about trivial things such as work and money.

She had no real recollection of quitting her job as a business manager for a charity, but apparently, she did. She had no recollection of picking out a casket, flowers, and reading for Joe's funeral, but she did. And she had no recollection of signing the papers releasing Joe's life insurance money, but apparently, she did. And just like that, the prospect of selling her once marital home and setting up a new place, perhaps even in a new city, or even a different country, didn't seem so impossible.

She quietly thanked Joe for being so good at that type of thing. Harriet did not for one moment think money would solve any of her problems or heal any part of her broken heart. However, she finally understood that at a time when emotions took hold, the last thing you wanted to be worried about was money.

Harriet fell asleep in the small hours of the morning. The rain dulled to a mind-numbing patter and continued to coat the house, and it was no different when she woke early the next day.

She found herself pacing a lot. The air was electric, charged with another incoming storm, and her mood was equally as unsettled. Waking early, anxiousness fluttered through her stomach. She was in two minds about whether seeing Owen again was the right thing to do. There was also a niggling feeling he wouldn't come back at all. Having convinced herself the day before that no one could possibly want her in her current state, she found that thought to be more pressing and upsetting than any other. Having done such a good job of shutting herself down, she wondered why Owen had even looked her way in the first place.

The relief she felt when the rattling at the front door came was instant, but it was noticeable from the look on Owen's face something else was going on. Sodden from head to toe, his eyes were sunken, and he bit his lips as he walked into the house without saying anything.

He padded wet footprints across the kitchen floor, droplets hanging off the hair at the top of his forehead. His denim jacket—previously light blue— was dark from the damp. His hands were shaking, and he shivered from his core. She handed him a towel and caught the back of his hand with hers—he was warm. He looked like he was about to combust from the inside out.

Owen kicked his boots off and tried to peel his jacket off his shoulders, but he seemed agitated and flustered. He wriggled, unable to rip it from his body, and when it didn't come off, he growled. Harriet turned him around and eased the jacket off his shoulders. Her hands moved over him, and she felt his muscles loosen under her fingertips. His black t-shirt was stuck to him. He managed to stand still as she peeled that layer off him too. His back erupted in goosebumps when she pressed herself against him and wrapped her arms around his waist. His skin was a mixture of cold rain and warm blood.

"What happened?" she asked cautiously.

He didn't reply.

He moved in her arms and grabbed her face, pulling her lips to his. The rain droplets fell onto her cheeks as he pushed her against the wall. She could feel every inch of him, inside and out.

"I'm sorry," he growled, stepping back.

He was all but unravelling in front of her. He sighed, he paced, he rubbed the two-day-old stubble on his chin. He looked at her, his eyes dark and exhausted. It had been a long time since she had someone silently beg her for help. Harriet took a blanket from the back of the chair and wrapped it around him. He rested his head against hers, closing his eyes, and she gently rubbed the tops of his arms.

Owen looked up and leaned in, kissing her more gently this time. Harriet held his head against hers, stroking idle circles on the back of his neck and watching as he let his eyes drift closed. Composure was a while coming, but when it did, Harriet took his hand, guiding him into the living room, where she sat him on the rug in front of the log burner. She climbed inside the blanket with him and rested her head on his shoulder as they sat quietly and watched the clouds lift. The evening sun broke through on the horizon and the room filled with warmth and dazzling orange light.

"Rough night," Owen uttered, wiping his hands down his face.

"Ricky and Eric?"

"And Adam. They were all just dicks to each other."

"What exactly is the problem?" She had heard snippets of information from Owen, and a bit from Kathryn but hadn't quite got to the bottom of the issues in the band.

"Eric thinks Ricky is an asshole. That he puts on this invincible, God-like face and behaves like he's the biggest rock star since Elvis. Ricky pushes him and dials it up just to make him angry, and it works every time. I've told Ricky to stop pushing him, but the more Eric bites, the more Ricky pushes. Don't get me wrong, Ricky is being a dick. He orders people around and he wears sunglasses inside, and sometimes someone will talk to him, and he will look right through them without even acknowledging they exist. It's infuriating and rude."

"Has he done it to you?" Harriet asked.

"No, but he has done it to Eric, and he did it to Adam last night, hence the argument. Eric will play mind games with him and is passive-aggressive, whereas Adam will speak his mind immediately. He can be just as hot-headed as Ricky at times."

"Didn't Ricky think Eric was lazy?"

"Yes, he does, and he is. Eric wants to be a musician but doesn't want to commit to the work required to actually do it." Owen sighed. "It's hard for him because Adam is a bit of a natural. It doesn't take much for him to pick something up or have a fresh idea, and Eric thinks that because they're brothers, he has the same instinct, but he doesn't." Owen laughed. "To be honest, he's not that good. He could be if he committed and practised, but he doesn't. I think this is what annoys Ricky the most. His frustration comes from a good place, despite the way it presents. He sees such potential being wasted and it doesn't sit well with him."

"So, why can't you just... I don't know, ask Eric to leave?"

"Ricky and I talked about it, but we both agreed that if Eric goes, Adam will too. Then we're totally screwed, at least for the next few months until we can find someone new and replace them both."

"Is that even possible?" Harriet found herself quite intrigued by the inner workings of a band and how it's run like a business. She asked question after question about the legalities of it all.

"Because we have contracted tour dates coming up, even if they left the band, we still have to play them. If we don't, we're in breach of contract. There's also something in our agreement about notice periods; it gets complicated with money and equipment too. Some of the amps we bought together, so they belong to the band. Our partnership agreement lets us sack someone, but the rest of us have to agree to it, and we know Adam won't agree to sacking his brother. We need them to leave of their own accord because then they forfeit their share, and we can crack on with moving forward. But they can't leave because... and round and round we go," he concluded, swirling his finger in the air.

"So, they can't leave now because you have contracts coming up. You can't find someone else because your agreement won't allow it, so you must continually spend time with people who don't want to be with each other and the melting pot of drama."

"Pretty much," Owen replied. "Part of me wishes we didn't have this album and tour coming out, then we could have dealt with this much easier. But we have at least another three months, and I suggested this time away to get us temporarily back on the same page, but neither side appears to want to reconcile." Owen leaned against Harriet and rested his head on her shoulder. "Normally, I'm so level-headed with them all. I've been around these guys for years, but last night, it just felt like I had reached my limit."

Harriet wrapped her arms around him and pulled him tight against her.

"Not to mention, they're my best friends, and it makes me so..."

"Sad?"

"Yes, but not just sad. It breaks my heart when they start going at it and I just can't seem to fix it."

Harriet felt his body heave, sucking back the emotion bubbling to the surface. "Would it be really terrible if I stayed here tonight so I don't have to deal with them?" he asked, pursing his lips and pecking her cheek.

"No. You can stay," Harriet replied. "But I'm out the door early tomorrow to see my sister." She pushed her cheek into his, inviting another kiss. "You're not running away from it, right?"

She felt him laugh in her arms. He faced her and pushed her hair back off her face. "No. I'm just taking a break. Regrouping."

Their eyes locked in what was becoming a naturally familiar and unspoken way. The look in Owen's eyes made it clear to Harriet that he wanted her as much as she wanted him. They needed each other, perhaps not for the same reasons, but for the same outcome. Harriet had already offloaded all the deepest, darkest secrets and troubles of her weary mind, and now Owen had done the same. His presence in her life was unexpected, something Harriet could not have dreamed was coming, but there he was, as if he had been there much longer than a few days.

Owen did stay the night, and they comforted each other several times throughout the evening. Any doubts Harriet had about Owen disappeared the instant he knocked on the door. She cursed herself for giving in to her insecurities and allowing them to take over, but the second they were side by side, those worries always melted away.

SHE INVITED OWEN TO STAY AT THE HOUSE THE NEXT day, but he insisted she drop him at the harbour front. He wanted to try to come up with a new approach to his dilemma before meeting the guys for lunch.

The summer sun had made its triumphant return. The morning air was still and felt nice brushing her hair. Harriet sat by Owen on the harbour wall, sipping a cup of coffee. He straddled the wall like he was riding a horse, and she sat as close to him as she could get, almost unable to control herself. Being surrounded by him was all she wanted when she was with him, and the way he looked at her pulled her to him like a magnet. Before departing, he dug his hands into her hair, crashed his lips into hers, and feverishly kissed her in a way that felt like she might never see him again. She didn't like that feeling at all, and she gulped hard to force it down her throat.

"I'll see you tonight?" she asked coyly, averting her eyes

and holding her breath. Not used to being so direct and asking for what she wanted, she made herself blush.

"You bet!" he replied as she leaned in, practically begging him to kiss her again.

———

Owen watched Harriet walk away, and out of the corner of his eye, he spotted Kathryn walking into The Seaforth. He waved at her, but she had her head down and didn't respond.

He moseyed idly around the harbour, across the park, and down by the river. His mind and body filled with the echoes of Harriet. She was like a dream, and he didn't want to wake up. Every time he thought of her skin against his, her hand on his face, or the tendril that just wouldn't behave, he smiled, and the memory seeped deeper into his skin and bones. It was an entirely new thing to be around someone who made him feel like that, but at the same time, he had to remind himself it was temporary. In no time at all, they would go their separate ways.

Suddenly, the thought of having to say goodbye to her felt like a dagger to his chest. He slumped onto a bench to take the weight off his body and his heart.

He watched the water flow through the rocks, shrouded in the canopy of rich green trees. He tossed a couple of stones in the water, making wishes to the fairies for ways to work things out with the band and to not have to say goodbye to Harriet.

His phone buzzed in his pocket, and he was marginally relieved to see Ricky's name appear.

"Stop being such a drama queen and come back to the house," Ricky barked without even saying hello.

"Good morning, Ricky. How are you?" Owen responded sarcastically.

"Seriously, dude. Stop being weird and come back."

"Weird? How am I being weird?" Owen snapped. "You guys are dicks to each other. You got us kicked out of that bar last night. I'm over it, man. I've had enough."

"We've talked about this, Owen. You know we can't do anything until after the tour. We just have to make it work until then."

Owen's blood bubbled. "The only person trying to make it work is me, Rick. In case you haven't noticed, Eric has totally checked out. He doesn't care, and you just think it's some sort of game to push his buttons every time you're in a room together. Mike has no balls and won't stand up to any of you, and Adam is bound by his loyalty to Eric, but I'm pretty sure he also hates both of you."

"That's harsh."

"Don't you dare! Don't you dare make out like any of this is my fault, and don't you dare make out I'm wrong."

Ricky fell silent.

"You need to fix it, Ricky. You're the only one who can. You need to fix it with Eric, even if all you do is find a hammer and a nail and cover up the cracks for now. You're the one who wants to be the omnipotent front man. Go and do it."

Still silence. Owen wasn't sure if the 'uh-huh' that drifted down the line was actually Ricky acknowledging his words, or if he had imagined it. Either way, Owen wanted to escape the phone call as quickly as possible and only time would tell if Ricky had truly been listening to him.

"When you've figured it out, then I'll come back," Owen concluded and hung up before Ricky had a chance to respond.

Then he got up and walked. When he stopped, he sat and, in the privacy of the trees, held his head in his hands as he granted himself permission to fall apart. In the company of the water and his purposeful solidarity, he let the tears fall, wondering how they were ever going to find a way through it.

Chapter Twelve

HARRIET FIDGETED NERVOUSLY AS SHE WAITED FOR Louise to arrive. She was already through her first cup of coffee and Louise was twenty minutes late. She was beginning to think she might have been stood up. Café Ness was built into an old dusty pink church that overlooked the river deep in the heart of Inverness. Harriet had decided sitting outside was the safest option. That way, if she and Louise yelled at each other, they could do so without it echoing into the rafters.

The air was still and warm, the trees giving a nice shade over the round picnic table as Harriet watched people walk up and down the waterfront. She debated how long she would wait before calling it quits.

A car hummed its way into the car park to the right and Louise stepped out. The door thudded shut and she made her way over to where Harriet was sitting. Harriet stood, and as Louise approached, she held out her arms. Louise stepped into them, reluctantly at first. After a second, Harriet felt her relax, the nostalgic pull bringing them back together. She wrapped her arms around Harriet, squeezing a little tighter than she was expecting.

"You look great, H," she said, sitting down.

"Thanks, Lou. You too."

The waiter, who looked more like he was attending a funeral than waiting tables, came over to take their order.

"This is unexpected," Louise said, looking her up and down and frowning.

"What?" Harriet asked defensively.

"Nothing. You just... you look different."

The last time Harriet and Louise had seen each other was before Easter, when Louise had gone back to their parents' house for a long weekend. It always felt as if Louise hated going back home. She was always quiet, awkward, and walked around with her arms folded. Harriet got the sense she felt more comfortable in her barracks with her crew.

Harriet couldn't help but notice her sister's hair was a little longer; it fell into a soft bob below her eyes and framed her heart-shaped face. She sat with her back straight, just as she had been trained to do, and lifted her cup without hunching over. Harriet did the exact opposite. She hunched over, spread her elbows across the table, and rested her head on her hand. They could not have been more different if they tried.

"I haven't behaved very well since Joe died," Harriet said, finally breaking the silence.

Louise looked at her, her brow furrowed above her soft blue eyes. "So, we're diving straight into it, are we?" she eventually replied in a defensive tone.

Harriet tensed, sitting up straighter, but avoided her sister's attacking glance. *Oh, here we go.*

But strangely, Louise took a breath and retreated before finally replying. "I didn't behave very well beforehand."

"No, you didn't," Harriet began. "But the blame doesn't lie entirely at your door. I resented you for moving away. I felt like you were abandoning me. I think I was so used to us all being together, and I naively assumed everyone was happy. It was selfish of me to think that we were all you would ever need."

She eventually looked back at her sister, who continued to sit with rigid composure to the point Harriet wondered if she was capable of human emotion anymore. Nevertheless, she continued. "But I think I understand you better now. I understand feeling suffocated. That your life wasn't yours. That you felt a barrier between what you were and the truest, most authentic version of who you wanted to be."

"Harriet, I didn't leave because of what someone did or what they didn't do." She sighed a deep, heavy sigh and leaned her elbows on the table. "You guys all take everything so personally, and it wasn't like that. I never meant it to come across as a personal vendetta or an attack. It was me needing some breathing room, to understand myself, how I felt, and who I wanted to be. I didn't feel I could do that at home anymore. I felt like I would let someone down, and when I left, I felt so guilty and selfish for a long time. I was scared you thought I was hiding or running away, but I wasn't. I guess you could say I was spreading my wings."

They both laughed.

"Did you ever actually tell Mum and Dad?" Harriet asked knowingly. She had known her sister was gay since she was fourteen, but they had never spoken about it. Louise had never officially come out and Harriet had felt it was a big secret for her to carry. She hadn't taken the time to understand how hard it must've been for Louise to hide such a big part of herself for so long.

"Not properly. I don't know if I'll ever be brave enough to tell them." A solitary tear escaped her eye and clung to her long brown eyelashes, but she swiped it away before Harriet had a chance to comment on it. "I want to, I just... I guess after all this time, it's easier to stay away than face them."

"You should tell them. All they ever wanted was for us to be happy. Have faith in them, Lou. They deserve to know, and you shouldn't feel like you must hide who you are. You deserve that peace of mind."

"Can't they just figure it out like you did?"

"They aren't wired like that, I'm afraid." Harriet tried to smile to comfort her, but she wasn't sure it was working.

"I really am sorry I upset you, Harriet. And I'm sorry I haven't been there for you after Joe."

"In all fairness, Lou, being around me hasn't been the easiest job for the last twelve months."

"You were a mess at Easter. I'm not even going to sugar-coat it. When I left, I was worried sick, but today, you look almost composed. What's changed?"

"I feel like I'm getting myself back a bit. I think a lot of it is because I've done it all once without him. Every special date, every birthday. I even lived through the day he died again. And I did run away in the middle of the night—got in my car and drove as far away as I could get, and here I am," Harriet joked, throwing her hands up.

"Bet Mum loved that," said Louise in a tone that mocked their mother.

"Mum understood."

"Bet Wendy had something to say," Louise retorted, raising her eyebrow.

Harriet hadn't shared much of the details of the fractious relationship she had with her mother-in-law over the years. She always tried to hide it from Louise, thinking she was protecting Joe, but she was sure their own mother would have offloaded some of the details to Lou from time to time. She would often rant to her mother about Wendy showing up at her house and forgetting to leave, making demands on their time, and insisting they take her places.

It always frustrated Harriet that Joe pandered to her. At times, she thought he was a total mummy's boy with no backbone. Sometimes, Harriet just went along with whatever they wanted because keeping the peace was easier than fighting a war she knew she wouldn't win. She loved Joe, despite his toxic family, but it didn't take long into their relationship before she realised how manipulative his mother could be.

"Oh, that bloody woman. I swear, I don't care what she thinks anymore. She chewed me out a few days ago and I told her to back off," said Harriet proudly.

"There's no way you were that blunt."

"Well, no, I wasn't. But I did ask her to leave me alone for a while."

"Cut her some slack, H. She lost him too."

"And that is the problem, right there," snapped Harriet. "She thinks she's the only one who did. She expects me to somehow make it all better, to carry her grief, and it's not fair." Tears welled in her eyes again, but she was more determined than ever not to give in to them.

Lou reached out across the table and grabbed her hand, squeezing her fingers hard into the palm of her hand. "Oh, H. You're right. Of course you are."

Harriet shrugged and shook her head, her flowing waves

dancing across her shoulders. Louise's eyes fixed on her, and she felt like they were finally understanding each other.

"I won't cry over this anymore, Lou. I won't. I'm done with her. I have to move forward."

"Yes, you do. H, I'm so proud of you." Louise squeezed her hand again.

"Really?"

"I wish I was as strong as you. As brave as you." Louise retrieved her hand.

"I don't feel very brave sometimes."

"You know, I tell all my friends about you. My brave baby sister, who has been through such tragedy but still gets up every day, even if all she does is sit on her bed and cry. About how she still manages to keep on existing, even though her world was turned upside down."

Harriet couldn't help but smile, and her face flushed a little, especially when she remembered the meaning of Owen 's band name. She felt a genuine connection with her sister, something she hadn't felt since they were children.

"And you know," Louise continued, "you're the only one who's ever been to see me up here. Mum and Dad never come. Ben hasn't been, and yet here you are." She raised her empty cup in a toast.

"I'm sorry I'm late." Harriet leaned over and clinked her own empty cup against her sister's.

"Better late than never."

A huge weight had been lifted, and an air of ease fell over them. They sank into silence, watching the world around them. Birds flitted through the trees, cars passed, and the river kept on flowing.

"Lou, I'm sorry I gave you a hard time when you left. It wasn't because of who you are, it was because I was terrified I would never see you again."

"I know."

"Saying goodbye is hard."

"So, stop saying it. Let's stick with 'I'll see you soon'. Goodbyes are so final. You have to always leave the door open, especially to those who want to walk through."

As Louise spoke those words, Owen crept into Harriet's mind, and she pulled her fist to her mouth to hide a smile. She briefly closed her eyes and felt the linger of the kiss he had laid upon her that morning. She had never been kissed like that and she felt it still.

Louise's eyes narrowed, and she leaned across the table into Harriet's eye line. She couldn't hide. Despite the distance between them, she knew her sister could read her like an old book.

"Tell me about him." Louise leaned back in her chair, folding her arms over her ample chest, grinning from ear to ear.

Harriet blushed, suddenly very aware how transparent she became around her big sister. She only needed prompting once and she launched into an animated recollection of tales about gigs, islands, stars, and skin. She left no detail unearthed and felt relieved talking about Owen.

Any fears she had of judgement for moving on were quelled by her sister's invitation to talk about it. Talking about Owen made him feel more real. Part of her was worried he was a figment of her imagination. But as she spoke warmly of their time together, any anxiety she had about him washed away and the reality of how she felt about him became more tangible.

As Harriet walked by her sister's side to their respective cars, she felt proud and grateful. Proud she had been brave enough to reach out. Grateful their paths had come back together, and they could move forward with a renewed sense of appreciation for each other.

Harriet clung tightly to Louise, balling her fists into the fabric of her shirt. Louise reciprocated. Harriet felt like she was pouring years of held-back hugs into one consuming embrace. She was immensely glad she had reached out, and she was even more glad to be returning to Ardmair and the man she hoped was waiting on her doorstep.

Chapter Thirteen

Harriet was mildly disappointed to not have Owen waiting when she arrived back at the cottage later that afternoon. She surmised he was off with the rest of the band and his silence meant they were finally working through their problems. She hoped they were celebrating their reunion in a bar down by the harbour.

It was only when a tentative knock came at her door just after nine o'clock that she realised something wasn't quite right.

Ricky stood at the foot of the steps, looking up at her. He was agitated, playing with his hair more than normal. Harriet was in a pair of rather skimpy pyjamas, anticipating Owen's arrival, so she pulled her robe around her to contain her modesty.

"Hi, Ricky," Harriet said curiously. She tried to read his face to figure out why he would be knocking.

"Hi," he began, a cautious edge to his voice. "Listen, I'm sorry to bother you. I know you and Owen have been, um, enjoying each other's company, but we really need our drummer back now, please." He wore a look of embarrassment and surrender. She knew instantly he didn't really want to be knocking at her door.

"He's not here," Harriet replied bluntly.

She thought Ricky had some nerve, especially with all he and Eric had been putting Owen through lately. But the look of playfulness and ambiguity he normally wore was gone, replaced by something close to worry.

"What do you mean he's not here?" he snapped back.

"Exactly that. I've been with my sister all day and not been back long." Harriet's tone was curt. She didn't much like having to justify her whereabouts to him, but it was obvious from Ricky's demeanour that panic was starting to set in.

"Well, have you seen him?"

"Not since this morning. I dropped him in town before I went to Inverness."

Ricky pulled his phone out and started scrolling.

"Have you seen him or spoken to him today?" Harriet asked.

"Not since lunchtime. He hung up on me." Ricky huffed his cheeks out, exasperated, flummoxed. His skittish energy made Harriet uneasy.

"What did you say to him?"

"Does it matter?" he bit at her.

It took everything in Harriet's power not to slam the door on him, but she remembered the state Owen had been in when he visited the night before. He practically begged to spend the night to avoid them all.

"Sorry. I didn't mean to snap," Ricky blurted out. "It's just not like him to not answer his phone or disappear."

"Have you been to look for him?"

"No. We just assumed he was here," he replied dejectedly.

Harriet knew she had to think quickly. She barely knew Ricky, and he was a bit rude. At the same time, she was exhausted from her day with her sister, which was making her more irritable than she cared to admit.

She shot Ricky a look, so he knew she was aware of the band's troubles. As much as she didn't want to know or be in the middle of it, she was because, in a roundabout way, Ricky now needed her help. She knew Owen, as well as two people who share a bed can, and she knew how deep he was, how hurt he was, and how much he had shut himself down in the past. He never gave off the vibe of someone who was reckless or would do something untoward, but there was also a possibility he had reached his limit and was drowning his sorrows in a bar or worse.

Her mind flooded with the kiss that morning and the unnerving feeling it gave her, but she didn't share those thoughts with Ricky. She quickly shut down any further thoughts of what he might have done and thought about what was most likely. She knew all too well what someone not coming home felt like, but she also rationalised the chances of it happening again were slim to none.

Momentarily abandoning Ricky on the doorstep, she darted around the house to retrieve some clothes. Once again, she was in a position where she was forced to do the right thing. Even if it wasn't her problem, someone needed her help, and as a pathological people-pleaser, she sprang into action. All but running to her car, she shouted Ricky to join her as Eric and Adam came running down the hill.

"Is he here?" Adam asked. Ricky shook his head.

"Get in," Harriet commanded. "We'll drive into town and figure out where he might have gone."

No one argued with her. Perhaps what these boys needed was the firm hand of a woman to tell them to cut the shit given they seemed incapable of arriving at that conclusion on their own.

"We could try The Seaforth," Eric suggested. They all agreed that was a good place to start.

"What about your friend's place?" Harriet suggested. They all looked puzzled. She rolled her eyes, trying to remember the name of the person he had stayed with. "The one whose sister works in the pub."

"Oh, Elliott," Ricky jumped in. "Yes. Can you drop me at his house? It's on the way into town."

"Sure," Harriet replied, following his directions to the house where Owen had hidden away for all those months.

Ricky swiftly jumped out. "I'll meet you back in town," he bellowed as he jumped the wall at the front of the property.

Harriet wondered how he managed to run in skin-tight chinos and a fur coat that came past his knees, but surprisingly, he managed it. A few minutes later, she let Eric and Adam out near the ferry terminal, and she drove around the side streets alone, seeing if she could spot Owen's tall frame in the shadows of the narrow streets.

Harriet drove slowly, sometimes at the frustration of other drivers who seemed more eager to reach their destination than she was. Ricky had told her that Owen was in the park when he spoke to him earlier, but Harriet concluded that watching children running around laughing was not somewhere he would have lingered for long. She drove past the venue where the gig was earlier in the week, but that was in darkness.

Suddenly, it came to her, and she pulled a U-turn. Her tyres screeched as she took off towards the outskirts of town. Wherever you go in Scotland, if there is a body of water and a nice mountain to look at, there is more than likely a bench to sit and admire it. Sure enough, on the edge of the banks behind the old rowing boat that had been turned into a flower bed was a bench overlooking the bay. On that bench was a familiar silhouette.

Harriet abandoned her car on West Terrace and ran the short distance to the bench. She was instantly relieved to find Owen as well as he was when she left him that morning. Silently, she approached and slumped down next to him.

"You found me," he said. He had the same air when he stepped off stage. The same wild, wide-eyed energy that gave off all the mixed signals.

"The boys are worried sick. They're racing around town looking for you," Harriet replied, unimpressed with the situation.

"I told Ricky to come and find me when they had sorted themselves out," he replied. "But I think there may have been some flaws in my plan. I guess going radio silent didn't have quite the impact I was hoping for." He dropped his head and leaned forward on his knees.

"They thought you were with me," Harriet replied, undoing her coat and feeling a little flushed after her brief jog. She wanted to be mad at him, but she understood wanting to run away and be alone.

"It's the easier explanation. Heaven forbid they take some responsibility and own up to what they've been doing. All they really know about you is that we've been spending time together." He sighed, standing up, pacing the grass verge. "They don't know how much I've offloaded to you."

"Do you think they would be upset?"

"Probably. Ricky is really precious about this type of stuff."

"You should talk to them. Tell them how difficult things have been and the toll it's taking on you."

Owen shook his head. "I've tried." His normally glistening hazel eyes were dull and tired.

"Have you, though?" Harriet couldn't hold back how exasperating the situation was. From the outside looking in, she could see their difficulty communicating was making the situation a thousand times worse.

"No, I haven't. I've been weak and pathetic, just like I've always been."

"That's not what I meant."

"Yes, it is. That's what everyone thinks of me. Poor push-over Owen, who can't stand up for himself. Who holds on to things he should let go of, but doesn't, because he's so scared of being alone."

And there it was, the thing Harriet had been dreading the most. The mirror of herself in someone else. Someone who felt just as she did, who was as lost as she was. She didn't know if she was strong enough to pull herself out of her own hole of self-pity, never mind someone else.

Harriet felt dejected. Had Owen seen shades of himself in her too? Was their time together a fleeting moment of serendipity? Perhaps all she had been, was a distraction from his band drama.

Owen's eyes fixed on her as she stood.

"Why have you been spending time with me, Owen?"

He didn't reply, which made Harriet's heart race. A rush of embarrassment spread up her cheeks. She looked desperately into his eyes, searching for a shred of something that told her he cared about her. If he hated himself for being weak, how could he feel anything differently for Harriet? Perhaps she had got it all wrong, misread everything about him.

"So, I've been a good distraction at least," she said sarcastically.

"What? No, of course not, that's not how I feel about you at all." Owen jumped forward, taking her hands in his.

Her heart beat faster against her chest. Of all the things she was expecting when she returned from Inverness, this was the last thing she thought would happen.

Owen released her hands as she stepped away. "I can't do this," she said, turning her face towards the shadows. He dipped his head towards her, but she looked away, determined not to let their eyes meet. She was certain, one brooding look and she would crumble, and she couldn't bare him looking at her when all she could see was herself in his eyes.

"You should call Ricky and let him know you're okay." Harriet moved her bag onto her shoulder to fish for her keys. Owen nodded and pulled his phone out to text Ricky.

"I'm gonna go," Harriet announced.

Owen grabbed her arm gently before she could walk away. She looked up at him. His hazel eyes bore right into her, apologetic, confused, and kind. Her brows rose as her lips drooped and her shoulders sagged.

"It's fine, Owen," she said, brushing him off.

She knew getting the band back together was the most important thing. More important than her bruised feelings. She had become the master of protecting herself, and although she had grown fond of him, she wasn't about to let herself fall head over heels for someone she had only known a few days, even if he was the best surprise the universe had given her in a long time. "Your boys need you," she continued, "and what you have going on is way more important than me."

She didn't give him a chance to respond, and he made

no attempt to follow her. As she drove away, she spotted the other three band members walking towards the bench and felt a small satisfaction that she had at least managed to get them back together.

The drive back was longer than Harriet remembered. She realised Owen was trying to protect himself. He had been hurt so badly in the past and his band was his safety net, and he now felt like he was losing it.

She hated how every vulnerability she felt was suddenly staring back at her. She hated how much he loathed himself for not feeling like he was strong enough. More than anything, she hated that she wasn't strong enough to fight for someone as incredible as Owen.

Deep down, she had hoped this would be more than a holiday fling, but the likelihood of anything continuing beyond the week was very slim. Their time together was coming to an end, and perhaps it was easier for her to think she was a distraction from the band stuff rather than having the difficult talk about how she was dreading saying see you later. The thought of not seeing him again made her heart heavy.

Chapter Fourteen

HARRIET RESIGNED HERSELF TO SPENDING THE following day cleaning the cottage, ready for her departure. She had also resigned herself to not seeing Owen again, something which gnawed at her. She was putting a barrier back up. She wasn't about to give in to those types of feelings when she had something more pressing on her mind.

She wanted to see the sunrise on the bay. She wanted to take the box out of the boot of her car and leave a piece of Joe in the highlands. They had not been afforded the chance to see the west coast together in the way she had seen it over the past week, and she wanted to make sure a piece of him would always be there. Joe may have been a career man in his adult years, but the free-spirited guy she fell in love with was the one she wanted to honour.

She dressed swiftly, poured coffee into her travel mug, and set off towards the bay as the stars began to fade. The car park was quiet; only a few campervans had stayed overnight and she was able to easily locate a parking space away from anyone else.

The crisp air of dawn bit her cheeks and rustled her hair, whipping it beneath her chin. Slowly, she made her way onto the pebble beach towards the low tide. Fragments of light had begun to illuminate Ben Mór in the distance. The water was still and clear, almost like a sheet of ice had formed. Nothing disturbed the water or the silence. Even the birds were still quiet.

As the water got closer, the small slap of the sea touching the rocks intermittently intruded on her quiet thoughts. After a few minutes of idling towards the tip of the bay, she found a flat pebble and sat down. Taking in the sea air once more, she breathed and felt herself relax in her moment of solitude.

She pulled the box from her handbag and sat it next to her, willing Joe to make his presence known. She waited patiently for a sign.

But nothing came.

She stifled a laugh.

"You never were one for early mornings," she said, looking down at the box beside her.

Vivid images of the last few days flooded her mind as she made a conscious effort to commit them to memory. The first memories of happiness since Joe had gone.

She sighed again.

"I forgive you, Joe," she whispered, picking up the box and passing it back and forth between her hands. "I forgive you for leaving me."

And she did forgive him. She had to. She knew she had to forgive him and make peace with the apology she was never going to get from him. Deep down, she knew he was sorry, and it was important to acknowledge that feeling and let it pass through her.

The bay came to life as the sun rose above the hills

behind her and the colours changed from grey to blue and green. The water sparkled as the summer sun rose slowly in the sky, and Harriet felt at peace, or at least as much peace as she was capable of in that moment. She closed her eyes, the warm embrace of the sun settling upon her, and she leaned herself into a further feeling of stillness.

Owen fleetingly crossed her mind. She pulled her lips together and rolled her neck. The nerves in her body fired waves of heat as she recalled their time together, the way his arms held her, and how his hands felt moving softly across her skin. Her bottom lip fell open, and she gasped as she remembered the way his breath had delicately fallen at the nape of her neck.

Harriet shook herself back to reality, taking a moment to check she was still alone on the shore. She found herself passing the box between her hands once more, and she eventually opened it. The soft grey ashes stared up at her, encased in a plastic bag within the box. Joe's ashes had been split so that Harriet had some and so did his parents. The agreement was made that they could do with them as they wished with no influence or judgement.

Although Wendy had more than enough to say on the subject at the time, Harriet knew what she wanted to do with hers. She wanted to set him free far away from the chasm of grief they all lived in. Harriet stared at the box some more, willing herself to open it. Until that point, she hadn't thought about the logistics of scattering ashes. She didn't know if she should tip them out or grab a handful.

She began to panic. Her breath caught in her chest. Hands shaking, tunnel vision, she tried to breathe in. Her vision blurred. She could feel the void taking over and she shut her eyes, waiting for it to consume her.

But then it stopped. She felt a warmth on her shoulder,

like a hot water bottle had been placed softly against her skin. It seeped through her clothes and into her muscles. She was scared. She didn't dare open her eyes to look. *'It's all right. Breathe,'* came a familiar voice from behind her. She squeezed her eyes shut but obeyed, sucking cool air between her gritted teeth.

Her heartbeat slowed, and her head felt stable again. *'It's time,'* the voice continued.

Harriet, still unable to open her eyes, felt the warmth move to her hand, and she looked down to find she had opened the plastic within the box.

She pushed herself up to her feet, all the time holding it firmly in her right hand. She read out loud the inscription on the lid of the box.

"Feel my breath across your cheek when the summer winds blow strong.

Feel me wrap you in my arms when the winter nights grow long.

Watch me dance with shooting stars across the velvet sky.

Hold me tight but let me go, and remember, we were more than just goodbye."

It was strange. Harriet hadn't held much stock in those words when the box was given to her, but something about her reading them, running her hands across the embossed print, and saying them aloud resonated with her. She couldn't remember where they had come from, how she had picked them, or why they were there, but in that moment, they felt right.

As she softly uttered the words between gasps and tears, a breeze picked up and she titled the box to its side, releasing the ash from within. Her hand shook as she watched the powdered dust rise above her and drift off into the sky.

She stood watching the wisps of grey dance with the breeze, spreading out in all directions. Her eyes darted back and forth as she clung to the final glimpses of them floating away, merging with the earth and disappearing into nothingness.

And when she could no longer strain her eyes to see it, she slumped back down. Her body heavy and aching, she cried a release of tears until there was nothing left inside her head but air. Like a statue, she sat in a trance, unmoving, unwavering, unfeeling, numb. For so long, she had wished for time to stand still, and it finally felt like it had.

Hours went by; Harriet felt like she was dreaming, staring out across the water. It was only when the hustle and bustle of a lunchtime swimming group splashed into the ripples of the rising tide that she began to acknowledge anything going on around her. She hadn't meant to lose track of time, but also, she had nowhere else to be.

Her stomach growled involuntarily, indicating she had neglected it for long enough and it was time to eat. Part of her didn't want to leave. She knew leaving that spot meant leaving the final pieces of Joe. Committing what was left of him to the safety and peace of the Scottish air was the final step on his journey. She had longed for it to be over for such a long time she was surprised at her reluctance to follow through with it. There was safety in staying sad, and she knew it took more bravery than she ever thought she had to move forward.

She permitted herself a few more moments to dwell before engaging the muscles in her legs and forcing herself to her feet. A feeling of pride overcame her. Not always the bravest of souls, she let herself experience it and committed

it to herself. Joe would be proud too. At least, she hoped he
would.

Not wanting to be alone with her thoughts, Harriet
decided lunch in The Seaforth would do quite nicely. Part
of her wondered if she might bump into Owen or at least
have a chance to thank Kathryn for being so nice to her
during her stay. So, she made her way back to her car and
once again began the journey into Ullapool.

She arrived at The Seaforth ahead of the lunchtime
rush and was seated in what had quickly become her
favourite table near the window. Harriet unwrapped her
jacket, draping it over the back of the chair. Kathryn
instantly spotted her across the room and offered a friendly
wave as she disappeared through the swinging doors into
the kitchen.

Harriet sat, her hands in prayer position as she looked
out across the harbour. The small seaside town was quieter
than usual. The hustle and bustle had descended into a
quiet lull.

Once she had ordered her food, Harriet returned to
staring out of the window. Every time the light changed, the
landscape looked different, and she was quietly enjoying
watching a family of ducks bobbing up and down on the
water when Kathryn inserted herself into the picture,
slumping down in the chair opposite.

"Good afternoon to you, fine lady," said Kathryn in an
all too quirky voice.

"And to you, m'lady," Harriet responded in tone with
her companion.

"How's it going?"

"Pretty good," Harriet lied.

Kathryn leaned back in the chair, pulling the straw to
her mouth, and downing a large slurp of her drink.

"So," she began, placing her glass on the dark wooden table. "You and Owen?"

Harriet almost spat her drink out. She managed to catch it just in time and suck it back in through her teeth.

"What do you mean?" Harriet asked, lying again.

"I saw you." Kathryn went on. "Sitting on the harbour wall yesterday morning."

Harriet blushed and looked down at her lap and back out the window. All the while she could feel Kathryn's inquisitive eyes fixed on her as she sat grinning from ear to ear.

"Oh," replied Harriet, hiding her smile behind her clenched fist, which rested on her chin.

"I see a lot in this place, but I tell ya, I have never seen anyone kiss someone like he kissed you yesterday." Kathryn smiled. Oh, how Harriet wished she would stop.

Harriet was floored by Kathryn's astute awareness, but thinking back to the night of the gig, she remembered just how much Kathryn knew about the band. Harriet hadn't been at the root of gossip since senior school and fought to hide her embarrassment. It made her uneasy and vulnerable. Kathryn, seemingly unable to judge the situation, kept talking.

"He's such a great guy and you seem real nice too. I really hope it works out for you guys. I mean, after the whole mess with Tess, it must be nice for him to have someone finally."

Harriet leaned over and steadied Kathryn's hand firmly against the table. "I need you to stop," she said in a low voice.

Kathryn stared at her, her green eyes piercing, confused, and agitated. Harriet silently begged her to rein it in, but

Kathryn was now consumed by the notion of what she perceived to be a budding romance.

"Oh, I do love a good love story, and how serendipitous of you two to meet on holiday and fall for each other. It's like a movie." She squealed like an excitable child.

"Kathryn, stop!" Harriet said, more firmly than before.

She looked at her and squinted like she was in pain. "I need you to stop, and I need you to listen. Can you do that for me?"

Kathryn nodded.

"You are so lovely, and you see the world in such a beautiful way, but I have to tell you, it's not like that, I'm afraid."

Kathryn stared forward, lips sealed and eyes wide open. Shock and confusion shrouded her.

"Whatever vision you have of my and Owen's story is wrong. It's not a poetic love story and it's nothing like a movie." She sighed, trying to carefully pick her words, to be honest but keep Kathryn's innocent view of the world intact. "It is an understanding we have of each other."

Kathryn looked at her, even more puzzled.

"Kathryn, I'm not here on holiday. I'm not a lonely female traveller seeking companionship on my gap year, like most people assume. I'm here because I am trying so very hard to fix myself."

Kathryn's eyes narrowed into a sympathetic pout. Falling back into her chair, she silenced herself, much to Harriet's relief.

Taking yet another deep breath, Harriet began.

"About a year ago, my husband, my Joe... he died. Very suddenly and very tragically. And Owen. Oh, God, Owen." Her voice shook. "His story is equally as crushing. Some of it you know, some of it you don't. And what he has going on at the moment is a total mess. But one thing I can tell you is that we are not destined to be together. We are not a beautiful story waiting to be told. We are two broken people who happened to be exactly what each other needed for a very brief moment in time. I'm going home tomorrow, and he is leaving the day after. I'm ninety-nine percent sure that we will never see each other again. "

Kathryn paused a moment longer, removing her hand from her gaping mouth.

Harriet knew people like Kathryn. Her father was very similar, seeing the world in black and white, struggling to accommodate any shades of grey.

Harriet watched her cogs turning, the way her face contorted as she processed things. She couldn't make her understand how two people could be together, sleep together, spend time together, and then never see each other again.

"I'm sorry," Kathryn said, lifting her head. "I don't understand."

Harriet reached over the table, taking Kathryn's slender, pale hand into hers. She smiled softly, appreciating wholeheartedly that she was at least trying to.

"Let me give you some advice," Harriet said warmly. "You don't have to understand or even agree with what other people do. Most of the world's problems can be solved by people just being left alone to do their own thing without question or judgement."

"I'm not judging you," Kathryn blurted out.

"I know, honey."

Kathryn's eyes were fixed on her.

"So, how does this type of thing happen? I mean, how did you and Owen end up... you know."

Harriet smiled and dropped her head, blushing slightly. "I guess the universe has a weird sense of humour."

In unison, they both burst into hysterics, laughing uncontrollably at the ludicrous, confusing, and weird situation they had found themselves in.

Harriet had warmed to Kathryn even more and thanked her for her time and attention during her stay. They exchanged numbers and agreed to stay in touch. Kathryn returned to work, chewing her lip, her head clearly spinning as she tried to process Harriet's revelations.

Harriet departed the restaurant and made her way back to her car. She sat for a moment gripping her steering wheel, and a sense of sadness came over her. The reality of leaving, going back to her lonely corner of the world and having to face things once again made her stomach churn. For all the strange situations she had found herself in during her time in Scotland, she had felt little pieces of herself come back, and she was scared returning to real life would scatter them again.

And then, poetically, she thought of Owen.

Chapter Fifteen

It didn't take long for Harriet to clean the cottage and pack her car up. She had neatly lined up her clothes for the journey back the following morning and she took the time to meander around the house, taking one last opportunity to touch the surfaces and admire the quirks of her temporary home. Once again, she was captivated by the sunset. She sat quietly in the wicker chair in the conservatory, watching the sky turn a million shades of orange as the sun sank into the ocean.

Owen was on her mind. She had tried to fight it, but he kept coming back. She wasn't feeling great about how they had left it the night before, and although she felt quite sure nothing would come of their time together, she didn't like the thought of leaving things on bad terms. He had been the first person she had properly opened up to since Joe died, and he was the first person she had trusted enough to give her body to since her late husband. Maybe she should have been thanking him rather than pushing him away, but it was too late for that now. She was leaving in the morning, and if he truly wanted to see her, he would have knocked on the door.

Time ticked by and Harriet dozed in the chair. She was jolted awake by her phone vibrating against the wooden windowsill, and she was surprised to see Ricky had texted her. She had forgotten she had given him her number the night before.

Ricky: Are you coming for drinks or not?

Harriet: Drinks?

Ricky: Last night drinks at our place. I assumed Owen invited you."

Owen had not invited her, but it didn't matter. She had been looking for an excuse to see him one last time and was dressed and out the door in a matter of minutes. When she arrived at the house at the top of the hill, Ricky was waiting at the door, and he wrapped his arms around her like a long-lost friend.

"Thank you for your help last night." He beamed, squeezing her tighter than she had been hugged in her life. He was a little intoxicated but in the way where you love everything and tell everyone they are your best friend. She welcomed the appreciation and reciprocated the embrace.

"Are you guys okay now?" she asked warmly, hiding how much she truly knew, but enough for Ricky to know she cared. He nodded and pursed his lips, indicating they were perhaps in the calm at the eye of the storm. The atmosphere was light and cheerful for the time being, so she didn't press further.

Harriet glanced around the room. Eric and Adam were on the veranda talking quietly. Mike was sitting on the couch next to someone Harriet didn't recognise, but as soon as Kathryn clocked her, she was ambushed into another hug.

"You're here," Kathryn squealed as she thrust a drink into Harriet's hand.

"I'm here," Harriet replied, taking a large gulp.

Kathryn took her by the arm and led her into the corner of the open-plan kitchen. "I'm sorry about earlier," Kathryn said. "I didn't mean to blindside you."

Harriet leaned back against the granite counter, forcing her body to relax. Old habits die hard, and she reminded herself that she was not in a hostile environment. "It's okay."

"I've been thinking about you all day," Kathryn went on. "I can't imagine what it's like to lose someone like that."

Harriet looked her up and down; her slender physique was wrapped in a brown floral dress. She exuded such an air of confidence it was hard to imagine her being anything but flawless.

"It is tough," Harriet admitted, realising that Owen wasn't the only person she had let her guard down around. She sighed, trying to lean into the openness her present company demanded. "I like being here with you guys because you let me tell my story on my own terms and in my own time. It's hard back home because it's all people see when they look at me. Being here, I feel more like myself again."

"I get that," Kathryn replied. "I had a hard time at university and the people I saw every day didn't seem to understand me."

Harriet remembered Owen mentioning that Kathryn had a breakdown, but it was never elaborated on. She understood how people needed to vent on their own terms, though. She nodded and encouraged Kathryn to continue.

"I've always been so sure of everything. Of who I am and how the world is supposed to be. Being outside of here, away from home, I realised how wrong I was. It was like being slapped in the face by reality and I didn't know how to handle it. My mum and dad didn't prepare me very well for that."

Harriet nodded again as she slurped her drink.

"Maybe that's why the thing you said about you and Owen floored me so much. I've always had that solid parental unit. That forever pairing to fall back on, and it can be hard for me to grasp that not everyone lives like that."

"It's not your fault how you were raised," Harriet replied sympathetically. "My parents were the same. They still are a bit."

"Yeah?" Kathryn smiled appreciatively.

"My sister is in her mid-thirties and still hasn't come out to them because she's terrified they won't know how to handle it."

"That's rough."

"Yeah, but she makes it harder for herself by not being honest, and she doesn't give them enough credit. I keep telling her that she can't help how Mum and Dad are. They did the best they were able to do, but she has to be accountable for the things she felt were lacking in her upbringing and try to remedy them now."

"That's good advice," Kathryn replied as she polished off her drink. "We'll stay in touch, right?"

"Of course." Harriet needed new people in her life and Kathryn was a very welcome addition.

"Do you want another?" Kathryn asked as she poured a can out into her glass.

"No, thanks," Harriet replied. "I think I'll go find Owen." She squeezed Kathryn's shoulder and headed back into the main room, glancing around.

"Where's Owen?" she asked Ricky, who was in deep conversation with Eric over the stereo system.

Seeing them in a temporary ceasefire warmed her heart. She had developed quite an affection for the wellbeing of these guys, and she hoped with every fibre of her being they could survive the next few months. One of Harriet's turning points had been reconnecting with the complex and vivid lives of other people. Knowing that the world kept turning and other people had their own real problems took her out of herself and stopped her being so inwardly focused.

Ricky didn't reply, he simply pointed towards the stairs.

Harriet's heart pounded in her chest as she ascended the dark oak stairs. She slid her hand up the curved banister and peered into the rooms where the doors were open. One was closed at the far end of the corridor, and she approached nervously. Gently tapping on the door, she didn't know what to expect as she stood under the dim light of the aging bulb, waiting for a reply.

"Come in," invited the voice from beyond. The handle creaked, and she stepped over the threshold. She shut the door behind her, pressing her back up against it. There was a double bed to her left and a small table with a lit lamp next to it. The sheets were neatly pressed and folded across the top of the mattress. The far wall had a faux fireplace, and a TV hung above on the wall. A chest of drawers with clothes spilling out of it finished the internals of the room. Owen sat on the deep window ledge, his legs stretched out as he looked out across the bay.

"I saw you coming," he said quietly without looking. "I saw you walk up to the hill, and I thought to myself that you are perhaps the most beautiful thing I have ever seen in my life."

He pulled his fist to his mouth and huffed out a long,

protracted breath. "I know how it all looked," he said, breaking the silence. "I was feeling particularly sorry for myself last night."

Harriet shuffled and looked at her feet. "Me too," she admitted, "I see a lot of myself in you."

She scurried awkwardly to the foot of the bed and sat down, not wanting to wait for an invite.

Owen didn't move. His white T-shirt was pulled tight across his chest and arms, and Harriet watched as his chest rose and fell. She was scared; not in the way she had been when the police knocked on her door the night Joe died, or when the hearse pulled up outside their home. Nor like when she returned to the empty echoes of their once vibrant home. She feared herself. Feared letting herself feel anything for anyone else. In that moment, as she watched the light of the full moon illuminate the perfect features of Owen's face, she was scared of not ever seeing him again.

"You are the first person who's truly seen me since Joe died," she whispered hesitantly. "You're the first person I felt safe around, who I could be myself with. I never thought I would be able to let myself open up like I have when I've been around you this last week." She stood up and took a couple of steps towards him as he slowly turned his head to look at her. "Owen, you aren't a distraction from the mess. You showed me there can be something after it."

He didn't reply. He just looked at her, his eyes piercing hers. After a few moments of continued silence, she dejectedly sat back down.

"Are you really ninety-nine percent sure we'll never see each other again?" he asked, his voice cracking.

Harriet jerked her head up. His eyes were locked on her. "Kathryn," she muttered under her breath. "She saw us on the harbour front the other day, and when I saw her at the pub, she bombarded me with questions. I guess I felt backed into a corner." Owen frowned. "She has no idea about me. Or you, for that matter. She talks with such innocence about couples and people. Yes, I said that to her, and I know I shouldn't have, but I did, and I regret it, so..." She trailed off.

Owen watched her intently. She felt like she was once again starting to come apart at the seams. Whether it was the wobble in her voice or the way she pulled her arms around herself, but something she did made Owen sit up.

"And why would you want to see me again? I'm a total mess," she concluded, dropping her head into her hands and lowering herself back. She sat perfectly still on the mattress, churning with embarrassment and vulnerability. Hearing herself say words like that out loud solidified her belief that she was broken beyond repair.

"No, you're not," Owen said as he climbed down off the windowsill and knelt in front of her. "You've had a rough time, but you are so much more than what has happened to you."

Harriet sat up, not expecting him to be as close as he was. She felt his warmth and understanding.

"You are kind and funny, you're easy to talk to, and you listen without judgement. You don't try to fix things like everyone else does, and you have this way about you that makes me want to bare my entire soul." He gently rubbed her legs as a smile lit up his face. "The boys adore you and you seem to get this band rubbish. The thought of not seeing you again after we leave here makes me sad. And it's been making me sad all day. I know I should have told the fellas what was going on between us and I have now, I promise. And I promise I'll be stronger and stand up for myself better."

Harriet took his hands in hers, her eyes brimming with happy tears.

"You and I," Owen began, "I think…"

"Are just what each other needs right now," Harriet interjected, knowing what he was going to say before the words fell out of his mouth.

He nodded in agreement, gently lifting her chin with his index finger. The way he stroked her chin with his thumb sent shivers all the way down to her toes.

"But the practicalities? We live at opposite ends of the country and you're going on tour. I have to go home and sort out the mess that is my life."

"Hey, forget the practicalities. Forget the what-ifs of tomorrow, next week, next month. Answer me this, Harriet. At this moment in time, what do you want?"

She looked deep into his eyes and rested her hand gently against the light dusting of stubble on his cheek, taking a thoughtful pause before replying. "I want you."

He leaped forward instantly, crashing his lips into hers. The motion pinned her to the bed as his weight bore down on top of her. He kissed her fiercely and she reciprocated, pulling his shoulders and arms, wanting the comfort of his body pressed against hers. Every part of her burned for him and it was only a matter of moments until their naked bodies were interlocked and the once smooth bed sheets were a messy pile on the floor.

They lay in peaceful, satisfied silence as the moonlight shone in through the open curtains. Harriet's flushed body was warm and supple against Owen's firm chest. He wrapped his arms around her as she rested her head on him, determined she wasn't going to let them part the following morning without him knowing she wanted him. They could figure out a way for it to happen.

"So, I'm thinking that if I put your name on the guest lists for the tour, you can just drop in when you get a chance?" He kissed the top of her head whilst she closed her eyes, listening to his heart thudding away beneath his chest.

"That sounds like a plan," she replied wearily as she drifted off into a deep sleep.

———————

HARRIET WOKE EARLY; THE OPEN CURTAINS LET THE light flood in, rousing her to life way before she intended. She slipped quietly out of bed, leaving Owen curled up on a pile of linen sheets. She took a moment to admire his bare chest, the curve of his muscles, and the peaceful look he wore whilst he slept.

Harriet tiptoed out, clutching her shoes and bag tight to her chest. She softly padded down the stairs into the emptiness.

"Sneaking off so soon," came a voice from the easy chair in the corner.

Ricky's voice startled her, and she almost jumped out of her skin. He stood up and approached her, a frown burrowed into his normally porcelain forehead.

"Owen's still asleep. I'm just going to square things up at the cottage," she replied, smiling, trying to dispel whatever tension Ricky was bringing between them.

"Huh," he huffed, half nodding.

"Listen," he said quietly as he leaned in close to her. Harriet stopped in her tracks, turning to face him properly. "Do not break his heart." He held his finger up to her, commanding her attention. "Please. Do not break his heart," he repeated, giving her a look that touched her deeply.

Harriet felt sure Ricky knew the burden he had put on

Owen, and perhaps playing the role of protective brother was easing some of his guilt. Either way, Harriet knew what he meant. Ricky flicked his hair in his trademark way before wandering out onto the veranda to take in the morning air.

Harriet knew what Owen had been through and she knew how intensely he and Ricky looked out for one another, even if they did fight like an old married couple. It had taken a lot recently for Harriet to realise there was more going on around her than what was racing through her own mind. And whilst she was nervous about letting someone new in, she understood the same applied to Owen.

AFTER A QUICK SWEEP THROUGH THE HOUSE, HARRIET locked the door and deposited the key back in the lockbox. She took a moment to walk the exterior path and say her farewells to the heather and the clouds, the mountains, and the ocean, to the piece of Joe she had left here. She welcomed the pieces of herself that had returned and the new friends she had made. When she rounded the corner back to the car, Owen was leaning against it with his hands extended towards her.

She reached for him, and he pulled her close, kissing her softly. "Not leaving without saying goodbye, are you?" he said, stroking her cheek.

She shook her head. "We don't say goodbye anymore in my family, we say see you later."

"Oh yeah?" he replied, cradling her face, pulling her lips to his once more.

"Goodbye is too final," she said as he released her.

"Well, in that case..." He chuckled. "I'll see you later."

She stood on her tiptoes and threw her arms around

him. Owen picked her up off the ground, burying his face in her hair. Resting her forehead against his as his arms held her firmly against him, she whispered, "I'll see you later."

Harriet didn't want to let him go. She watched him waving in the rear-view mirror as she drove up the hill, and when he disappeared from sight, a fresh wave of sadness came over her.

———

OWEN RETREATED TO HIS OWN DWELLING AND WAS greeted by the embrace of his best friend. No words were needed. They knew each other so well and had been each other's comfort for many different things over the years. Owen knew this time was different. He felt different, like something had come alive inside him. Something that had lay dormant since his heart was crushed all those years ago.

Chapter Sixteen

It wasn't the physical act of driving away from Ardmair that made Harriet's heart ache, it was the sense of what she was leaving behind. Focusing hard, she tried to stay in the warmth and mindset of how Owen made her feel. But with every mountain that turned into an all too familiar pokey hill, every sun-kissed lake that turned into a grim asphalt puddle, the little pieces of herself she had felt coming back felt fainter. She felt a million miles away from the person she was whilst she was in Scotland. She knew she had to hold onto those feelings, but fear gripped her, and Harriet wondered if she would ever be completely whole again.

"That's the price we pay for knowing and caring about people in different corners of the world," Jess said over a glass of rose wine one night after she'd returned. "We are never fully in one place."

"When did you get so wise? Harriet laughed as she glanced around her house knowingly. The pale grey walls, the clutter, the drawn curtains... she felt nothing for the walls surrounding her. "This isn't my home anymore," she conceded. "It's as good as the box they carried Joe away in."

"That's pretty bleak," Jess retorted, with an upward inflection, tossing the playing cards for Harriet to shuffle. Harriet caught her friend's eyes as she shot her a look of disapproval. Perhaps it was bleak, but it was also true, and if her time away had taught her nothing else, it was that she was not going to lie about how she felt anymore.

"Is it really, though? What am I doing here besides holding on to something that isn't coming back?"

The two friends polished off the wine and abandoned the game of cards. Jess pushed the deck to one side and shot Harriet an intrusive sideways glance, like she knew what she was about to say. Harriet had never hidden herself from Jess, until Joe died, and she hid from everyone. She trusted her completely. She was probably the only person who truly knew how broken she was after Joe died and the only person she didn't need to explain it to. They had been friends for so long they knew what the other was thinking. Having never held anything back, Harriet wasn't about to start now.

"This house, this town, it's full of him. His memory, his echoes, and his absence. What am I doing staying here besides constantly punishing myself?"

Jess nodded in agreement. Fluttering her pale eyelashes, she yawned and stretched her slender arms above her head. "I guess you'll never move on if you never move out," she concluded.

"Exactly," Harriet replied, opening another bottle.

More Than Goodbye

THE DAYS AFTER RETURNING FROM ARDMAIR BLED into weeks, and before Harriet knew it, a month had passed. She spent the first few days catching up with her parents and attended two counselling sessions. Julia commented how well she was doing, and Harriet noticed that even her parents breathed a sigh of relief. She had finally turned a corner and was coming out the other side of her grief. She spoke with Owen most days, mostly to catch up. The sound of his voice, excited to hear from her, continued to light her up. He was getting ready for the tour and constantly reminded her she was very welcome to one, two, or all of the stops along the way.

Harriet had stopped seeing and sensing Joe around her since she scattered his ashes on the bay, but she still couldn't shake the niggling feeling there was something she had missed. It had started as a passing comment when she spoke with Aunt Ellen, but the more she thought about it, the more it festered until one day she found herself rummaging through her wardrobe, trying to remember where she had stashed the boxes of Joe's things.

Two different estate agents had been to value the house, and she was moving things around to prepare for photographs being taken. Her time in Scotland had given her the clarity and determination she needed to follow through on her ideas. Her once happy marital home was going on the market; she had decided it was time for a new family to live there and fill it full of the love and memories a house like hers deserved.

After the house was sold, she thought she would travel a little. Just in the UK to start with, but she had sown the seeds of a trip overseas with her best friend for the following year. Jess jumped into ferocious planning mode, but not before commenting she had been at a loss for what else she could do to help Harriet, and she was glad to finally start plotting adventures again.

Harriet spent days poring over boxes, and it was only when the items marked 'Joe' materialised at the back of the guest room wardrobe that she threw herself into delving into him again. It had been difficult for her to look at his things after he passed. His clothes, backpacks, anything that still carried a piece of him held memories, so she had thrown everything into boxes. She'd hidden them away where she wouldn't have to be reminded that the only thing left of her husband was a handful of boxes with his stuff in them.

She was still ignoring the calls from his mother. Wendy hadn't rung again whilst she was away, but now she knew Harriet was back, she had taken to calling in the evening once the bottle of gin she devoured during the afternoon had seeped into her properly. Her messages grew more bitter and nastier as the weeks went by. Harriet couldn't face her—not yet.

She was becoming more and more consumed with trying to figure out what she or her father might have missed when settling Joe's affairs. She didn't remember much, so she spoke to her father about what happened in the aftermath of Joe's death. She probed, asking if he had spotted anything unusual or untoward that he felt Harriet should know. Her father couldn't bring anything to mind.

He had kept all the files Harriet had given him, everything from insurance paperwork to bank statements, police reports from the accident, and everything else she had thrown his way. She was thankful for his organisation and inability to throw anything out as she sat with papers spread across the kitchen table.

Harriet spent hours going through each piece of paper

meticulously. With nothing but stubborn determination, she had convinced herself she was going to find something, but after several days of searching, she could only laugh at herself and her pointless task. Finally giving up, she began scooping everything into a pile ready to place back into the cardboard box at her feet, when one of Joe's bank statements caught her eye.

For the most part, they had always shared their money. Everything was in joint names, which was one of the reasons she found things so difficult and shut herself down after he passed, but she remembered him opening an account in his name only for his business expenses. She went through the transactions from the months before he died. Initially, nothing seemed out of the ordinary. Obvious travel expenses, meals out, and gold passes for his golf club, but on a second look, she spotted a direct debit for a mobile phone. She couldn't remember him having two phones and she noticed the payments had started a couple of months before he died.

Rummaging in the box further, she pulled out the clear bag which held the personal items the police had retrieved from the scene of the accident. She hadn't touched them at all since they were given to her the night of the crash.

His beige leather wallet still had cash, his bank cards, and his driver's licence in it. She ran her fingers over his picture as tears welled in her eyes. Even now, she sometimes struggled to believe she was looking at the face of someone who was no longer alive.

She kept digging. A packet of gum, some keys, and sure enough, two mobile phones sat at the bottom of the bag. She recognised the one he carried with him, but the other was unfamiliar. Hunting through one of the kitchen drawers, she pulled out a bunch of chargers and eventually connected one that fit to the foreign handset. She waited for it to power up, chewing her fingers as it came to life.

It pinged constantly as the apps loaded. Five minutes of constant chimes made her head hurt, and she rested it on the counter whilst the phone caught up. When the sound finally stopped, she picked it up. There were over a hundred unread text messages. All it took was for Harriet to read the first one before she fell to the floor under the weight of her discovery.

I miss you.

Harriet held the phone in her shaking hands. She knew that once she started reading the messages, there was no going back. She knew whatever she uncovered would never be able to be reburied. She sat for a while on the cool, tiled floor, going back and forth on whether she really wanted to uncover these secrets.

Eventually, she concluded that she wouldn't be able to let it go, and finding out the truth now was better than a lifetime of never knowing. She knew, deep in the pit of her stomach she had missed something, so she took a deep breath and began to scroll. The message chain went on and she read each one, right back to the beginning, and sat into the small hours of the morning going over the exchange. She paced for hours reading and re-reading the messages before she fell asleep on the couch with the phone in her hand.

The next morning, Harriet sprang to life in a panic. The estate agent was arriving at nine o'clock and there was still a pile of papers and boxes all over the kitchen. She busied herself arranging the house, opening the curtains and windows. She set a vase of flowers on the kitchen windowsill and a bowl of vibrant fruit in just the right place, exactly as the estate agent had advised. She didn't have time to give the messages a second thought. Once the estate agent and the lovely couple he was showing around had left, she flicked the kettle on and retrieved the ominous device from the kitchen drawer where she had stashed it in a rush.

She read the messages again. Some could have been interpreted as pleasantries between friends:

Good morning, how are you?

I hope you get that case sorted today.

Harriet had deduced the person Joe was messaging was someone he worked with at the law firm. The number didn't have a name attached to it and she didn't see one in any of the messages, but as it was the only number that had ever contacted the device, she soon realised what was really going on. It was the more recent messages that cemented her suspicions.

Last night was incredible.

Can't wait to see you again.

I can't stop thinking about you.

It was the ones just before Joe died that caused Harriet the most concern.

We need to talk about this. I can't do this.

The ones after it were more subdued.

I miss you. I can't believe you're gone.

Harriet called Jess for reinforcement, just like she always had, and she was so grateful that Jess came running. Until recently, Harriet hadn't realised how stubborn she had been in holding onto her grief and how much of the burden Jess had taken on. She had looked after her parents, listened to Harriet berate her mother-in-law, and sat by her side as she fell apart night after night.

Since she returned from Scotland, Harriet had been determined to change her behaviour and take responsibility for herself. Jess knew every detail about Owen, Aunt Ellen, and the band she was suddenly smitten with.

So, when Harriet called her in floods of tears, it felt like a step backwards. She had come so far and felt like she was being catapulted back in time.

"What's going on?" Jess asked as she barged through the front door. Harriet was slumped over the kitchen island with the phone in her hand. She said nothing but tossed it to Jess, who caught it with one hand.

"Joe was having an affair," Harriet said, choking back the tears.

Jess's green eyes widened, and she raised her hand to cover her heart-shaped lips. As she waded through the messages, Harriet looked on, watching her becoming more and more shocked. Her creamy skin lost all its colour, a look of disgust crumpled her face.

"That absolute pig," Jess said. Harriet watched Jess's face wrinkle as she got to the more intimate and graphic messages. Eventually, she threw the phone across the counter and wrapped her arms around Harriet.

The anger Harriet felt was like nothing she had experienced before. Her entire body shook with rage. She wrestled against Jess's arms, trying to pull away, but her best friend held her firm, tensing her arms, keeping Harriet tucked tightly into her. Harriet could not believe she was in a situation where, once again, Joe had pulled the rug from under her.

Almost poetically, her phone rang, vibrating against the worktop. "Wendy" appeared in the caller window, and that was enough to tip Harriet over the edge.

"That bloody woman," she screeched, reaching for her phone and rejecting the call. "It's borderline harassment."

She manoeuvred out of Jess's arms and they both leaned against the kitchen counter. Jess rubbed her back and Harriet closed her eyes, swaying.

"It's not, love," Jess replied. "Despite what you've just found out, she is still suffering like you were." Harriet folded her arms, defiantly refusing to agree. "Listen, H, you have to remember that you are the only link to her only son, and she feels like she's losing you too."

Harriet rolled her eyes, dropping her arms, knowing Jess was right. She had always had a wonderful way with words; her late father had told her she had the soul of a poet.

"What the hell am I going to do?" Harriet sniffed, searching her friend's eyes for an answer.

"We should call that number," Jess blurted out.

"Oh, I don't know about that." Harriet's head was already pounding, and the thought of finding out who the mystery person was at the end of those messages was almost too much for her to bear.

"You have to," Jess went on. "This has been eating away at you for weeks, and you didn't come this far to give up. Don't you want to know?"

Harriet hesitated and let her mind run through every outcome.

"Call it from your phone," she agreed reluctantly.

Jess dialled the number and put the phone on speaker so they could both hear.

Waiting for someone to answer felt like eternity, but then a woman's voice echoed down the line. "Bridget, Nelson, and Cook. This is Marie speaking. How can I help?" Harriet recognised the name of the firm as the one Joe worked for. His father, Arthur Cook, had practised law all his life and Joe joined the family business straight out of university.

Jess fumbled for the phone and pressed it to her ear. Harriet was terrified by what she might say but also curious to see how it would unfold. "Hi. Marie. My name is Angela

Rice. Your services have been recommended by a friend of mine."

"Hello, Angela. It's great to hear from you. What in particular are you needing assistance with?"

Harriet was floored by how quickly Jess could think on her feet and her reply. "I need help with my late mother's estate; she passed away quite recently and I'm not sure what to do."

"Oh, I am sorry for your loss, Angela. I can help you sort things out. Let me see. I have an appointment available on Friday morning at eleven. Does that work for you?"

"Yes, that's great. Thanks very much."

"Bring all your mum's paperwork and we can go through it together. I'll tell you what we need to do and what to expect throughout the process."

"Uh huh," Jess replied, faking a very believable cry. "Thank you." And she hung up.

Harriet was flummoxed, her mind racing a million miles an hour. "Oh my God, Jess! What have you done?"

Jess appeared quite pleased with herself, smirking at Harriet. Her wide green eyes sparkled with a hint of mischief. "I've got you an appointment with this woman. You have until Friday to decide if you want to go." Her matter-of-fact tone didn't leave Harriet much room for protest, so she retreated silently, going over things in her head.

After half an hour spent drinking cups of tea and Joe-bashing, Jess left, leaving Harriet to consider her next move. She now knew for certain Joe had been having an affair and she knew the name of the person he had been sleeping with behind her back. Forcing her mind to think back to the weeks and months before the accident, she tried to see if she could pinpoint any tell-tale signs of his infidelity.

All the pieces seemed to fall into place. The late nights at the office, the increase in business trips, the distance that had grown between them that Harriet blamed herself for. She had admitted to Owen that things with Joe were less than perfect before he died, but this was the last thing she expected to uncover. She felt naïve and stupid for not seeing how far off course things were. She had forgiven Joe for leaving her, but how was she ever going to move on from this?

Joe had always worked late, so his arriving home after seven in the evening wasn't anything that would cause her any concern. They were sharing a bed, like any normal couple who had been together a while. Whilst they weren't exactly ripping each other's clothes off at every opportunity, they were loving and affectionate when the situation called for it.

Harriet had always thought they had a lovely, normal life. But now she knew how blinkered she was by the fact he was dead. She wouldn't allow herself to think ill of someone who couldn't defend themselves or explain their actions, but the proof was in her hand. He had been unfaithful—not just once, but repeatedly—and he had been carrying on a relationship of some description with another woman.

Harriet didn't know what she might do or say once Friday rolled around, but she was sure that if she wasn't ready then, at some point in the future, she would want some answers, and she owed it to herself to get them.

Her phone rang again. Harriet answered straight away. "Hi, Wendy. I'm coming over."

HARRIET APPROACHED THE WEATHERED TERRACE IN the centre of Lincoln, and her heart sank. Wendy sat with the curtains closed most of the day, and the house stank of stale cigarettes and damp. It was no surprise Harriet hadn't stepped foot in the door since before Joe died; she hated coming here.

Joe had badgered his mother for years to get the place squared up, but she refused to listen to anyone. Wendy claimed her bad back prevented her from completing the simplest household chores and his father, Arthur, had given up trying, residing mainly in his smoke-free, well-kept office most evenings.

Harriet had always wondered how a high-end lawyer lived like he did, and the penny started to drop. Thank God Harriet had regained some clarity, as it gave her the headspace she needed to see the things that had always been there. Walking down the front path, she realised Arthur spent his weekends at the golf course or the country club. His business trips became more frequent and lasted longer each time. Once, he came home and didn't try to hide the smear of lipstick on his collar. He was a man who wanted to have his cake and eat it too. Sometimes Joe would go with him—perhaps it was his father who had encouraged him to have the best of both worlds; a dutiful wife at home and a mistress to play with whenever he felt like it.

The thought made Harriet sick to her stomach. She clung to the fabric of her mustard-coloured cardigan, pulling it around the frame that had filled out a little. Since she returned from Scotland she had started looking after herself a little better. It was long overdue, but it was all part of her journey.

Her heart ached for Wendy, despite how much her calls irked Harriet. Wendy had lost her son and had an estranged husband who treated her like garbage. No wonder she kept reaching out to Harriet. She had no one else.

Harriet knocked lightly on the door, pulling her collar up. She braced herself for the cool chill that ran through the house. Wendy opened the door and her bottom lip quivered. A short woman, with dishevelled grey thinning hair stood before her. A pair of glasses perched at the end of Wendy's nose, and the lines in her face showed every moment of a life half lived.

She was a foot shorter than Harriet and stood on her tiptoes to unexpectedly pull Harriet down to her level. Wendy wasn't quite able to wrap her arms all the way around her as she forced her across the threshold. Harriet, shell-shocked, reciprocated the embrace as best she could. Still unsure as to what she might say to Wendy about her recent revelations, or if she was even going to mention them at all, Harriet released herself from the embrace. She knew it was wrong to keep ignoring her and had begun to feel guilty about it. She looked into Wendy's eyes, trying to get a read on her. Harriet thought she almost looked relieved she was there. She was a strange woman at the best of times, but the wild energy she exuded put Harriet's defences up. And sensing a whirlwind of pent-up emotions bubbling beneath the surface, she wasn't surprised when her stance shifted.

"Where the hell have you been?" she huffed as she ushered Harriet down the dank corridor and into the sitting room. Harriet's pending arrival looked to have prompted a flurry of activity. The curtains had been drawn back and a window cracked open. The cool breeze drifted in, bringing with it the first hint of autumn as it moved the nets and gave a small reprieve from the smoky smell that generally hung in the air. In the past, Harriet would always jump straight in the shower after visiting her in-laws. Today would be no exception.

"I've been on holiday, Wendy," Harriet replied, sitting down on the small pouffe next to the large front window.

"You could have told me you were going," Wendy said sharply.

"I am sorry I left so quickly, but I needed to get away for a bit."

"You can't just leave without telling anyone," she snapped, sitting back in her battered chair.

"Yes, Wendy. I can. I'm a grown woman and I can do exactly as I please."

Wendy folded her arms and pursed her withered lips. She didn't speak, choosing to sit in a childish huff that filled the room with strained silence.

Harriet looked around. Photographs of Joe through the years adorned every wall. The place hadn't seen a lick of fresh paint in over a decade. One of Joe's old suit jackets was tucked under the coffee table alongside an empty box of tissues. A half-drunk bottle of gin was hidden behind a fake green plant beside the fireplace, and recently dislodged photo albums hung precariously from the shelves of the bookcase. It was abundantly clear Wendy was drowning in her grief.

Harriet moved the pouffe and sat in front of Wendy, wrestling her hand into hers. Wendy's posture softened and her lip trembled. "I miss my boy." She coughed, and her tears fell like rain from her weary eyes.

Harriet said nothing; she sat and held her hand, her heart aching at the despair she saw in the frail old lady falling apart in front of her. Anger at Arthur for letting it get this bad coursed through her. As much as the old lady aggravated her, she did not wish the torment of the prison she had made for herself.

When she had calmed a little and wiped her face, she looked hopelessly at Harriet, her eyes begging her for help.

"Wendy," Harriet uttered softly. "Wendy, are you listening to me?" The old lady nodded. "No one is coming to save you. You have to start saving yourself."

Wendy frowned, deepening the lines in the middle of her forehead. Harriet had rehearsed what she would say to Wendy, and before she knew it, the words were falling of her mouth, purposeful, firm, and clear.

"Joe isn't going to walk through the door. I can barely hold myself together, and I know Arthur is neither use nor ornament." Harriet rubbed the translucent skin on the back of Wendy's fragile hand. "I will help you get some help, Wendy, but you have to want it. Do you hear me?"

Wendy nodded.

Harriet offered to make her an appointment with Julia for the following week and to take her and bring her home, but Wendy remained reluctant. They sat a while longer, Harriet making small talk about her trip to Scotland. She was careful to divulge only cosmetic details, nothing about Owen. She knew how fragile Wendy was having now taken the time to sit with her, and although she didn't much like lying, omitting certain details was in everyone's best interest.

She studied the face of the broken woman before her and carefully chose her next words. "Wendy, we can't keep going on like this. You can't keep going on like this." Wendy opened her mouth to try and interject, but Harriet put her hand up. "Please, let me finish. You can't stay here, locked in your grief. He wouldn't want that for you. You have to go back out into the world and start living."

Wendy stared blankly at Harriet, her eyes red and still brimming with tears.

"We can't live in a world where all Joe did was die. If you step outside, you'll feel his echoes every day. When you walk into a shop and his favourite song comes on, or the smell of his aftershave drifts through the air from a stranger. When someone remembers something about him and shares it. Wendy, we loved Joe, and we miss him, but he didn't just die, he also lived."

Harriet was trying hard to be delicate but also firm and concise. She wasn't used to speaking that way to Wendy. For all the time they had known each other, Harriet had been a timid, compliant daughter-in-law. She hoped a little honesty would jolt Wendy back to reality and she would realise the world was moving on without her.

"You know, we were told we likely wouldn't be able to have children." Wendy leaned back in her chair, pulling her hands from Harriet's. "When we found out we were expecting Joe, it felt like he was our little miracle." She closed her eyes. "He was everything to us."

"I know," Harriet replied, watching her fidget. She knew this was going to be uncomfortable but didn't realise what the physical manifestation of the awkwardness would be like.

"I know you're right, Harriet. I do. I just, I'm scared that if I feel something else, he will disappear."

Harriet's heart ached for her; she knew exactly how she felt and was surprised to hear Wendy felt the same way she did. "Letting ourselves drown in sadness stops us from remembering all the good times, and boy, we had some really good times. We hold them dear, but we have to move forward."

"Are you wanting to move forward?" Wendy asked.

"Honestly, Wendy, I don't really know what I want. But I know what I don't want, and I don't want this for me or for you. I want to be able to speak his name without breaking down. I want to be able to drive home and not expect him to walk through the door, but more than anything, I don't want to be on my own, and you shouldn't want me to either. I feel like the right thing for me to do is honour the relationship you and I should have, but I cannot do that unless you try. I can't go on like this."

Harriet stood up and reached out her hands to Wendy, hoping she would take them, agreeing with her, but she didn't. She sat with her eyes closed in stubborn defiance.

Harriet rolled her eyes as she placed her hands on her hips. "I'll leave you to it, Wendy. Please think about what I've said."

Wendy didn't reply. She looked straight through Harriet, clearly off in her own world.

"In the meantime, I need you to stop burning my phone up and leaving me awful messages."

She was totally zoned out. Harriet bent down to her eye level, forcing Wendy to look at her properly. "Do you hear me? I need you to stop." Harriet was firm in her tone, her face stern with her request.

Wendy nodded as any remaining shred of emotion drained from her face and Harriet swiftly left. Uncertainty nestled in the pit of her stomach. She wasn't sure if she felt any better for confronting Wendy, but as she drove home, she concluded she didn't feel any worse.

Now the only task before her was determining if she was brave enough to face the woman Joe had been sleeping with behind her back.

A brief conversation with Owen lifted her spirits in the evening. She missed him more than she expected and was disappointed she hadn't made it to any of his tour dates. She hadn't told him about revelations concerning Joe, scared it would frighten him off. As the days of the tour went on, she noticed the growing defeat in Owen's voice, the raised voices in the background, and the feeling he was also hanging by a thread. Harriet knew the only way back to Owen was to put the Joe mess to bed.

Chapter Seventeen

Friday morning arrived. Harriet dressed early, having spent longer than required picking a suitably confrontational outfit. She was pacing her kitchen when Jess walked in before heading for work.

"I see the sign has gone up," Jess remarked as she helped herself to the coffee pot percolating in the corner.

"Yeah. I accepted an offer yesterday."

Jess, in her pencil skirt suit and slicked-back hair, looked fierce as ever, and Harriet didn't envy anyone who crossed her path. "Are you going to that meeting?"

Harriet nodded. "But I do keep asking myself what good could possibly come of it." She sighed. "I know Joe was cheating. Do I really need the details?"

Jess reached for her friend's hand and squeezed it gently. "If nothing else, love, you need to tell her off. Look her in the eyes and tell her what she did was wrong. Carrying on with a married man. Whatever next?"

Harriet envied how Jess always saw the world in black and white, without any shade of grey. She looked forward to the day she could have her and Kathryn in the same room. Chalk and cheese in some respects, but so similar in others.

Jess had always been more practical than emotional. Always good in a crisis and the one who took charge of plans. Harriet wanted to be her friend from the moment she met her. She was fixing a problem with the computer system in the university library and didn't falter for a moment. That was the kind of composure Harriet strived for.

"Plus, isn't there a part of you that's just a little curious as to what she's like?" Jess went on.

"Yeah, I suppose."

Harriet knew deep down Jess was right. She had carried the weight of Joe's grief like any loyal wife would, and now it felt like it was all for nothing. Harriet would never be able to thank Jess enough for standing by her side through it all. Even now, she knew she could count on her best friend to have her back.

"Let me know how it goes," Jess said before leaving Harriet to her thoughts.

⸻

Harriet sat in the waiting room of the solicitors, nervously fiddling with her handbag strap, and tapping her toe against the leg of the wooden chair. Aware she was disrupting the teenage receptionist, she soon stopped.

For a split second, she wondered if anyone would recognise her. In all the time she was with Joe, he had worked at his family firm, and they were regulars on the safari supper circuit. Harriet pulled her hair around her face and kept her eyes focused on the floor to conceal herself.

"You can go through, Miss Rice. Marie is just finishing a conference call, but she'll be right with you," said the fresh-faced timid girl as she peered over the top of her computer monitor. She pointed towards the door to Harriet's left before looking back down at her screen, scrabbling with papers that made her look busier than she likely was.

Harriet entered the airy office and sat down with her back facing the door. The room was clinical white, with ferns and greenery scattered around in opulent pots and vases. Certificates in dark wooden frames embellished the long wall and the desk she was seated at was flooded with light from the two windows that faced out onto the street.

Marie Nelson, read the name plate at the front of the desk; a brass triangular block presented her to her clients before they had even entered the room.

Harriet felt out of her depth and her heart was racing. She was about to get up and bolt for the door when a pair of stilettos clicked against the marble floor outside and the door opened.

Marie entered the room wearing a light grey skirt suit. Her blonde hair was pulled into a tight bun, and when she sat down and took Harriet in, all the colour from her peachy skin drained from her face.

"Harriet!" She gasped, adjusting her jacket, smoothing it down against her narrow waist. "What a surprise," she remarked, attempting to smile.

"You know who I am?" Harriet asked, extraordinarily calmer than she was expecting.

"Of course," Marie replied. "I worked with Joe. It was hard not to know about you."

Harriet could feel her blood boiling and instantly wanted to reach over the desk and punch her, but she remained steadfast in her determination to say her piece.

"It's funny, he never mentioned you."

"Oh, really?" she replied, tapping her computer keys unnecessarily rapidly. Harriet was expecting to be greeted by unabashed confidence, but the lack of eye contact and fumbling fingers made it obvious Marie was nervous.

"I thought you'd be, I dunno, more."

"What does that mean?" Marie's back seemed to stiffen suddenly as her eyes fixed with laser focus on her computer. "It's a shame what happened to Joe. He was a nice guy," Marie went on, still yet to look at Harriet properly. "I am sorry for your loss." She glanced at Harriet out of the corner of her eye.

"I didn't know anything about you until a few days ago," Harriet said, sucking in a breath between her clenched teeth. "But tell me, just how long were you sleeping with my husband?"

Marie paused, her long fingers with perfectly manicured nails froze on the keyboard and she sucked her bottom lip under her pearly white teeth.

Before either woman had a chance to speak again, the receptionist burst into the room. "Marie, I'm sorry to interrupt, but Anthony's nursery is on the phone. They think he has chicken pox and asked if you can go and get him straight away."

Marie stood up quickly, whilst Harriet sat flustered and infuriated by the interruption. Harriet watched her, studied her as she wasted no time collecting her personal belongings.

"I'm sorry, I have to go," Marie mumbled, bolting out the door quicker than a heartbeat.

Harriet had the woman who had turned her husband's eye in her sights, and in an instant, she was gone. All the adrenalin in her veins surged and she stood up to follow her. More than anything now, Harriet wanted answers, and she was determined to get them. The wind was taken from her sails when she caught the eye of the receptionist and asked, "Who is Anthony?"

"Marie's son," replied the girl dismissively.

"Son?" Harriet replied, sitting back down in the chair she first sat in. Part of her hoped the ground beneath her chair would open up and swallow her whole. The colour drained from her face, her hands shaking.

The receptionist cleared her throat, rousing Harriet from her perplexed shell. Harriet shot out the door and into the bustling high street. The sting of the autumn breeze cut her face and she pulled her coat up around her ears. People walked by her, gently brushing against her in slow motion. Harriet walked back to her car like she was wading through glue.

All the way home, she went over this new revelation in her mind. The child was in nursery, so less than four years old. But how old was he? There was no way he could be Joe's son, could he? The messages had only started between him and Marie a couple of months before he died, but they could have been seeing each other long before that. Harriet couldn't bring herself to think about the possibility of Joe having a child with someone else and concluded it was very unlikely that Anthony was his.

She arrived home a few minutes before the folks who were buying her house arrived for a second look. The rest of the afternoon was spent wearing a fake smile and exchanging pleasantries with the people probably already mentally moving themselves in. She had already begun packing and apologised profusely for the clutter scattered about the rooms.

The couple was persistent and relentless with their questions. When was the boiler last serviced? What were the neighbours like? And Harriet's personal favourite, "I know you said your husband died but just so we are absolutely clear, he didn't die in the house, did he?"

By the time they left and Harriet found a moment to pause for breath, she felt drained. All she wanted was for Owen to wrap his arms around her. She let her eyes close for a moment and the warm feeling comforted her, but she was jolted back to reality by tapping at her front door.

She threw the door open without checking who was there and was surprised to see a less-than-perfect-looking Marie on her doorstep. The smudge of mascara under one eye and the loose threads of hair that had escaped the perfect knot in the back of her head made Harriet's insides flip. She had clearly gotten under this woman's skin.

"What do you want?" Harriet snapped.

"I think we need to talk," Marie replied, once again adjusting her jacket.

Harriet hesitated a moment, not sure if inviting the woman into her house was a good idea. It also crossed her mind that Marie may have been in her house before. Harriet pushed that though aside as curiosity and anger bubbled in the pit of her stomach. One way or another, she felt she deserved the truth.

She opened the door fully and motioned for Marie to come inside. Marie sat in the single armchair whilst Harriet perched on the edge of the couch like an animal stalking its prey. Tension filled the room.

"Well, go on then," Harriet said, unable to take the quiet anymore.

"I've been wanting to reach out to you for a while, I just wasn't sure how to do it," Marie began shuffling nervously. She pulled her slender calves together and cupped her hands onto her lap.

"How long had you been sleeping with Joe before he died?"

"Not long," she said. "A few months maybe. It happened sort of by accident."

Harriet was instantly raging. "How the hell does sleeping with a married man happen by accident?"

"It started as harmless banter at work. You know how it is."

"No. No, I don't. Please explain." Harriet was determined she would not show this woman a shred of understanding or give anything remotely resembling an easy ride.

"Jokes, playful comments, flirting," Marie went on, adjusting her winged glasses. "Then we had that business trip to Newcastle. We both had too much to drink, and we spent the night together."

Harriet cringed, screwing her face up. It took everything she had to suppress her gag reflex.

"We both said it was a mistake and a one-time thing, but there was tension between us. It lingered in the office, and after a few weeks, it happened again." She sighed. "Joe always said he felt so guilty because you hadn't done anything wrong, but he couldn't help himself. Neither of us could. It spiralled quickly, and I fell for him hard."

Harriet froze, struggling to comprehend the words she was hearing.

"And, the night of his accident, we had gotten into a huge fight."

Harriet stood up and started pacing the floor. "So,

you're the reason he was late home. You're the reason he was on that stretch of road at that time of night."

"Yes, it was my fault he was late. I was begging him to stay and talk, but he was determined he was coming home to you."

Harriet's mind flashed back to the night of the accident. She had prepared a nice meal for them, opened a bottle of wine, and even lit some candles to set the mood for her hard-working husband. It had all been on the table at seven o'clock, ready for him to dive into the moment he walked in the door. But seven had turned into eight and then nine. At nine-thirty, the red and blue flashing lights lit up her kitchen and there were two police officers at her door telling her that Joe's car had spun off at a blind corner and hit a tree. He had died on impact and there was nothing anyone could have done. They stayed a while whilst Harriet's and Joe's parents arrived, said they were sorry, and left. Any reports Harriet had read since about people being supported by specially trained officers made her laugh.

A single tear had accidentally leaked from her eye and she batted it away as she stood over the woman who was ruining what was left of her marriage.

"What exactly were you arguing about?" Harriet asked.

Marie said nothing, she simply handed Harriet her phone. Staring back at her was a dark-haired blue-eyed boy, not even a year old, who had the same jawline and slightly crooked nose as Joe. She gasped and dropped the phone, pulling her hands to her mouth and crumbling to the floor.

"I had only just done a test that night, so I wasn't very far along. I told Joe and he freaked out and left me."

Harriet rocked back and forth, sweat making her hair stick to her face. She pushed it back with her hands. "That's Anthony," she said through gritted teeth.

"Yes. I named him after my late father."

Harriet's head buzzed, electricity pushing through her veins. Her fingers and toes tingled and a massive surge of adrenaline overcame her. She pounced up, making Marie gasp.

"Get out," Harriet said in a volume only bats would have heard. Marie remained seated. "Get out," she repeated, this time even louder, but Marie still didn't move.

Harriet jumped forward, grabbed Marie by the sleeve of her impeccably pressed jacket, and yanked her out of the chair. "GET OUT!" she screamed at the top of her lungs, throwing her out the front door and watching her stumble in her perfect heels.

"Harriet, please. I'm sorry. I'm so sorry. I never wanted you to find out like this."

Harriet marched up to her. "You had my husband's child. You slept with a married man and it's your fault he's dead," Harriet snarled at the strange woman. "I hope you can live with yourself, you washed up, dressed down, classless skank."

Marie burst into tears and scrambled into her car, leaving Harriet raging on her doorstep. One of the neighbours had stuck their head out to see what the commotion was but quickly retreated when Harriet glared at them. She watched Marie's silver BMW tear down the street, then she slumped down the door frame and onto the cold concrete doorstep. She tried several times to push herself up and back inside, but no matter how hard she tried, couldn't bring herself to re-enter the house.

All she could do was sit on the threshold of the cold stone porch, staring into the distance. Her mind bent, her head throbbed, and her eyes burned. The door slammed shut with a strong gust of wind. Checking she had her keys, she got up and pounded off into the darkness.

She walked, and she sat, and she wept. And then when she was done, she walked, she sat, and she wept. She wept for all the things that happened and for all the things that hadn't. She wept for the past and the present, for how stupid she felt and how sad she had been. She wept for the time she had lost buried in grief for a man that now felt like a stranger. She wept for her mother-in-law, for the innocent way she looked at her son and for how she was ever going to find the words to once again break her heart.

Everything she knew, everything she was, and everything she thought she shared with Joe was gone, lost to a secret life of wandering eyes, wandering hands, and a wandering heart. There was now a piece of Joe left in the world, and her heart ached because it didn't belong to her.

The darkness gave her the shadow she craved to push it all out. All the feelings she'd tucked away in her heart—all the regret, the guilt, the helplessness. The love she once felt for Joe now frittered away into nothingness and all she felt was empty.

Harriet felt like she had left her body and time was nothing more than an illusion. It was when the sky over the football field was illuminating with the golden promise of early morning sun that she returned to herself. She watched it delicately touch the drops of dew hanging from the overgrown grass. It hit her face as it rose above the pine trees and she wondered how she could have been so stupid, so naïve to have wasted so much precious time on someone who wasn't worthy of it.

Harriet had nowhere to go but home. The mist hung low to the ground, slowly melting away as the autumn sun pierced the veil, bursting through the clouds as it settled delicately on her cool, rosy cheeks. As the door clicked shut behind her, Harriet knew there was only one place in the world she wanted to be.

Chapter Eighteen

"I'll kill him," Ricky bellowed down the long breeze-blocked corridor. Owen was pushing against him, his arms wrapped around his body as the singer struggled against him to get to Eric, who was walking in the opposite direction with his middle finger up in the air. The air was damp, sweaty, and brimming with tension.

"No, you won't," Owen said as he struggled to keep hold of his friend. "We have to get through tonight and then it's over."

Ricky growled through grinding teeth, grunted, and eventually relented. Owen let him go, slowly releasing his grip, tentative and cautious, ready to restrain him again if he decided to pounce. The pair stood dressed ready to perform. Clean-cut trousers, open-necked shirts, yet enough stubble and messy hair between them to pass as the rockstars they were trying desperately to become.

Eric had all but checked out of being involved with the band, doing the bare minimum required of him. He attended pre-gig meetings to discuss setlists and lighting cues, but that was all. He hadn't spoken to them outside of logistical matters since the first date of the tour when he had overheard Ricky telling Owen he had found someone to replace him at the end of the year.

Adam had sided with his brother as expected. He had given his notice to leave the band at the end of the tour, making things a little less hostile between him and the rest of the guys. Things with Eric continued to escalate, and Owen wished he would just officially quit. However, with Adam in his notice period, it meant the remaining members could kick Eric out with no objection or legal ramifications.

Owen was completely exhausted. Living on the road was trying enough—a different city each night, a different hotel room most nights, and there had been a couple of nights where they had slept in the bus sandwiched between their equipment. On top of that, keeping Eric and Ricky from ripping each other's heads off and the deep aching he felt in the pit of his stomach every time he thought about Harriet had drained his battery to critically low levels.

He was ready to go home, ready to go back to the comfort of his pokey little room in his shared house back in London. He was ready to go back to teaching his students and time away from the boys whose pockets he was tired of living in. Ricky, Adam, and Eric shared the house with him, but when they weren't on the road, Adam and Eric only used it as a crash pad and Ricky would spend a couple of nights a week with his on-again-off-again girlfriend, Leah.

Owen had been against bringing her on tour, but Ricky had insisted she would make a good band photographer and they wouldn't have to pay her. Their tour bus was already pretty full, what with the band, their equipment, and two roadies, who also helped out with merchandise. Squeezing Leah in had been a struggle but one Owen had concluded would be worthwhile, especially if it kept Ricky a little more level-headed.

For the most part, it worked. She had talked Ricky off the edge of the cliff several times and there was finally a light at the end of the tunnel as the tour drew to a close. Emotions were bubbling hot beneath the surface, and it was only a matter of time before something, or someone, blew. Owen was tired of holding it together, and as he sat in the stairwell of another beaten-up club, he found himself scrolling through his phone looking at pictures of Scotland, pictures of Harriet, and pictures of them together.

They had spoken most days since leaving Ardmair, but he hadn't seen her and had pined for her from the moment they parted. He knew she had a lot going on and, from their conversations, he knew they were both holding back, not wanting to add to their stress levels. He felt guilty he wasn't there for her in the ways he had promised himself he would be. More than anything, he missed her, and he was bursting to see her. As the tour rolled on and her name remained unchecked on the guest list, he knew it was becoming less and less of a possibility.

"HARRIET COOK, GUEST OF OWEN WHITLOCK. HE'S IN the band Whelven," she said to the doorman of the Nottingham club where the band was playing that night. The tall, butch man in a bright yellow jacket checked his clipboard, smiled warmly, and opened the door, granting her entry.

The autumn air was crisp and had whipped her hair across her face. She was grateful for a minute to adjust herself, but the moment of solitude was interrupted by

Owen crashing into her. He wrapped his arms around her and picked her up off the floor.

"You're here!" He beamed as he buried his face in her hair and squeezed her so tight, she felt she might pop. She wrapped her arms and legs around him and squeezed back just as hard, relief washing over her as they stood embracing in the middle of the entrance foyer.

"Don't let me go," she whispered into the nape of his neck.

"I can't believe you came." Owen's voice shook a little, his arms tightening even more around her. Prying herself away from him was like pulling Velcro apart, but Harriet's self-consciousness got the better of her and she released him.

"I'm so sorry it took me so long," Harriet replied, grasping his hands in hers and falling back into his chest for another hug.

"Come with me." He took her by the hand and ushered her into the stairwell. The stone steps echoed and there was more than a hint of damp in the air, but Harriet didn't care. She sat right up against him on the steps and took his hands into hers.

"Is this where you've been hiding from the rest of them?"

He nodded and smiled, taking a moment to take her in. He blinked repeatedly. Harriet couldn't do anything but stare at him. She felt like she was dreaming and about to wake up.

Her hair was pulled back with half of it draped around her oval face. The soft waves rolled off her shoulder, and Owen, with his shaking hand, reached over and tucked one behind her ear. She held his gaze, concerned by how tired he looked. He was a little pale and a few pounds lighter than last she saw him.

"Are you alright?" she asked, inching closer to him.

He shook his head. "No, not really. I'm ready to go home, for this to be over."

Harriet squeezed his hand sympathetically. "You can tell me, it's okay."

"Adam has quit. He's leaving at the end of the tour. We found someone to replace Eric, but he hasn't officially quit yet. We've told him after tonight he's done."

"And Ricky?"

"He and Eric are about ready to kill each other. Eric has checked out and Ricky is fighting him at every opportunity. I had to physically restrain him earlier. Ricky was going to floor him."

"Jeez, that's intense. And what about you?" She leaned over a little to pull his eyes level with hers.

"I'm fried and I'm sad," he responded quietly. Harriet put her hand on the back of his neck, gently stroking his chin with her thumb. He nuzzled into her touch and leaned in to rest on her shoulder. He closed his eyes and breathed out, his warm breath rolling across the skin on her chest.

"God, I missed you," he said quietly, barely whispering. She delicately moved her fingers over the soft skin at the back of his neck, ushering the tension out of him.

"What's been going on with you?" he asked, sitting back up.

Harriet wasn't sure where to start, so she settled on blurting it all out in one breath. "I sold my house, I found out Joe had been having an affair which involves an illegitimate child, and I told my mother-in-law she's a mess and needs therapy."

Owen looked at her in shock. They burst into fits of

hysterical laughter that left her out of breath, her sides hurting, and her mouth sore. Harriet hadn't felt so relieved by a belly-laugh in all her life.

"Jesus Christ, we're both a total mess, aren't we?" Owen said as he struggled to catch his breath.

Harriet had all but given up and was howling so loud it echoed all the way up to the rafters of the old building.

"Yeah, we are," she replied, grabbing his hand. "But let's be a mess together."

Their eyes met and Harriet felt instantly lighter. She had a new sense of purpose and composure. Gone was the fragile girl who ventured to Scotland; she was now a woman who knew what she wanted. Her energy seemed to invigorate him. The colour returned to his cheeks and a smile reached his eyes. He leaned in, his breath dancing across her lips.

"Five minutes till doors," Ricky shouted, peering through the crack in the double doors at the bottom of the stairs. "Oh, hey, Harriet."

Springing to his feet, Owen took Harriet's hand, and they followed Ricky back into the entrance foyer through a long dark corridor that led to the dressing rooms backstage. Halfway down, Harriet paused and jerked Owen backwards. Glancing around to make sure no one was looking, she pushed him against the wall and kissed him, snaked her fingers into the hair at the back of his head, and pulled his lips to hers.

Taken by surprise, it took a moment for him to respond, but when he did, he grabbed her hair and kissed her back, slowly and decisively. "Oh, so we're doing that are we?" he uttered cheekily. "I wasn't sure."

"Yes, we are," Harriet replied, standing on her tiptoes and blowing softly on his lips. He grabbed her again and spun her around. Pressing his body against hers, he pinned her to the wall. "You'll stay with me tonight, right?" He was very forthright and made no attempt to hide the way his body responded.

Harriet pushed her hips into his, pulling his lips to hers. She wanted him so badly she felt she might crumble. "Damn right I will."

Owen found her a half-decent spot in the shadows at the back of the stage to watch the show and bid her a temporary farewell to go and meet the rest of the band. Harriet was swiftly joined by a tall, slender girl with flowing auburn hair and a camera hanging around her neck.

"You must be Harriet," she said, sitting down on the equipment box next to her.

"That's me." Her tone was sweet and overly friendly.

"I'm Leah." She extended her hand. "Nice to meet you. Owen's told me all about you."

Harriet raised her eyebrows and smirked. "All good things, I hope?"

Leah nodded. "Oh, God, yes." She flashed her an all-knowing look, the type that passes between two people who have known each other a lifetime, not just a few minutes.

They both chuckled, and Harriet knew in an instant they were going to be firm friends. The lights dimmed and the smoke machine filled the stage with mist.

"That's my cue," Leah said, jumping to her feet.

Harriet was glad of the good view and not being squashed into the crowd. At a guess. it was three times bigger than the one she had been part of in Ullapool. She bopped and sang along to the songs she knew, happily swept up by the energy of the room.

She watched Leah dart in and out of people, angling her camera in all sorts of ways, craning to get the perfect action shot. Every so often, Owen would glance Harriet's way and wink at her, which made the butterflies in her stomach flutter excitedly. She couldn't keep her eyes off him—he was captivating. The way he moved, closed his eyes when he sang, licked his lips, and smiled, sent wave after wave of burning desire surging through her.

Ricky led the band and the crowd effortlessly through the set. He steered them to the top of the notes that touched deep in your soul, to the valleys of the whispers, intensely filled with deep, harrowing, and relatable prose. He was a puppet master, and the crowd was his willing subject.

It was hard not to notice the frustrated looks he threw at Eric whenever he noticed him doing nothing on stage. Eric wore sunglasses and a beanie hat, with small tufts of blonde hair poking out of the bottom, framing his face. He wore clothes that looked like they hadn't seen a washing machine or an iron in weeks. He stood in the same spot and didn't move an inch for the entire show. Even Adam nudging him didn't shake his resolve.

By the time the band finished and exited stage right, Ricky was steaming mad. Before anyone could stop him, Ricky had pinned Eric against the wall. His forearm pushed against his throat. Eric said nothing, just looked down at him with a troublesome smirk across his face.

The rest of the band and the roadies rushed to separate them. Arms, legs, bodies, and a sea of black, moving masses rolled past into the corridors. Finally, the two former friends and bandmates were ushered into separate rooms. Leah slid past too, hot on their heels. Harriet, although invested, felt best to stay out of it and she made her way outside the back door to catch some fresh air.

No sooner had she exited the venue, Eric threw the far door open, and Leah was chasing after him. The ground was damp from an earlier downpour, the uneven surface of the Nottingham street glistening under the lights at the back of the club. Leah almost lost her footing as she followed the disgruntled keyboard player.

"Please, Eric. Don't do this," Harriet heard her say.

Turning, she saw Eric as he approached their tour bus. He flung the side door open and pulled his bag out, rummaging quickly through it frantic and swift; he appeared to be collecting his belongings. His keyboard was stowed in the carry case secured to his back. He slammed the door with such force the sound reverberated back and forth between the deep red bricks of the alleyway they were parked in.

"Give me the damn keys, Eric," Leah begged, holding out her hand.

"Why should I?" he bellowed back, holding the keys high above his head. The nasty, almost evil curl of his lips earlier had taken up permanent residence on his unshaven, disgruntled face. His eyes were hollow, empty, and callous.

"You can't just leave us here in the middle of nowhere," she argued back.

Harriet walked towards them, sensing the desperation in her new friend's voice.

"What's going on?" Harriet asked as she cautiously approached. She was wary of inserting herself into a volatile situation, but she also wasn't about to let Leah square up alone to a guy who had a good foot and a half on her.

"The bus is in his name, and he says he's going to take off and leave us all here."

"What?" Harriet barked. "You can't do that."

"Just watch me," he said, clearly taunting them. He pulled a packet of cigarettes out of his back pocket with his free hand and took great delight in sparking it up and blowing smoke in Leah's direction.

Before Harriet could blink, Leah had pounced, jumping on his back in an attempt to get the keys out of his hand. He wrestled against her, spinning back and forth to try and shake her off. With one mistimed backwards elbow, he caught her right in the bridge of the nose and she fell to the floor with blood streaming down her face. Before Harriet had time to react, Ricky burst through the back door, followed by Owen, Mike, and Adam, just in time to see Leah hit the ground. She burst into tears and screamed as the blood began pooling in her hands under her nose.

Ricky didn't hesitate. In one swift motion, he was in front of Eric and his fist connected with his jaw. Eric fell back into the bus before Ricky retracted and hit him again in the side of his face. Adam put himself in the middle of them which stopped Ricky recoiling for a third blow. Owen pulled Ricky back by his waist, but he broke free and managed one more blow to Eric's mouth, splitting his lip wide open.

"You guys can all go fuck yourself," Eric shouted, spitting blood on the floor. He threw the van keys at Ricky, clearly aiming for his face. Eric squared up again, but instead of jumping back in, he growled and slunk off, defeated. His thick boots splashed the water clean out of the puddles as he stormed off into the dark alleyway.

Harriet now stood in the middle of them all and watched them in their stalemate, her heart racing in anticipation of what might happen next.

Adam pulled his lips into a tight line, threw his guitar and backpack on his back, and disappeared into the darkness after his brother.

Harriet stripped her white shirt off, dropping to her

knees in front of Leah. "Keep looking at me," she said, motioning her eyes to lock on her. She mopped the blood out of the young girl's hands and pinched her nose to stem the bleeding. "Keep breathing. You're doing great," Harriet reassured her. Harriet's bare shoulders were exposed to the bracing, damp wind but she felt nothing besides a need to take control. Jess would have been proud.

Removing a hair tie from her wrist, she pulled Leah's hair back, securing it at the base of her neck before gently leaning her forward. Harriet took the shirt from her shaking hand, catching the droplets that oozed from her nasal passage in her linen shirt.

Leah was crying. She closed her eyes, breathing shallow, panicked breaths as Harriet reassured her she was all right. "Crying will make the pain worse. Try to take a couple of breaths."

Harriet watched her puff her cheeks out and breathe deeply. In no time, the tears stopped, and the blood began to dry in patches around her mouth. She sat in the middle of the alleyway as the others crowded around her. They huffed and puffed, Ricky in particular, trying to offer suggestions, wearing a guilty badge of honour.

Harriet couldn't take it.

"Would you lot back off," she shouted, standing up. "Mike, go and get me some water and some towels or something. Owen, for the love of God, would you get him away from us for a minute and let me get her cleaned up."

Everyone obeyed her command. Harriet didn't care if she upset them. She was more concerned about the poor girl who had ended up in the crossfire of their chaos.

"Take a couple of deep breaths and look at me," she said to Leah. She retrieved the discarded shirt from the floor and pulled it back to her face.

Mike quickly returned with water and towels, and Harriet set to gently wiping down Leah's face and hands.

"There, good as new," Harriet said reassuringly as she closely inspected the damage. Leah's nose was still perfectly straight, thankfully, but it was a little swollen. It was likely to swell more giving her two puffy and gloriously black eyes.

"Can you see straight?" Harriet asked. "Any double or blurred vision?" Leah shook her head. "Do you feel dizzy or sick?" Again, she shook her head. "Do you think you can stand up?" Leah nodded, the motion making her grimace in pain. Harriet stood up and put her arms under Leah, helping her to her feet.

"Thank you," Leah said softly, taking a moment to compose herself. Once she was on her feet, Ricky was immediately by her side and his big arms wrapped around her while he apologised repeatedly.

Harriet stood back and wiped her forehead with the back of her hand. Beads of sweat had stuck to her hair. Her edgy energy retreated and she felt a chill run through her. Owen approached with a fresh towel in his hand and a warm and grateful look in his eyes. He covered it in water and held Harriet's hands, cleaning the stripes of Leah's blood off them. The look of adoration in his eyes cut deep into her. Harriet had surprised herself with how she instinctively knew what to do and how she was able to command a group of the most chaotic musicians. Shivering and wrapping her arms around herself caught Owen's attention and he draped his denim jacket over her shoulders.

"What are we going to do?" Mike asked, collecting the empty bottles and dirty towels and throwing them into the van.

"What do you mean?" asked Owen, his gaze momentarily pulled away from Harriet.

"The hotel was booked in his name on his credit card and the petty cash tin was in his bag," Mike replied, pulling at the long hair of his beard. "Do you think he'll come back?"

"He'd better not," said Ricky as he and Leah walked arm-in-arm to re-join the rest of the group.

"What are the chances of us getting a hotel with a secure lock-up at midnight on a Thursday?" Mike asked, slumping up against the bus and pouring water down his throat.

"Pretty slim, I reckon," Ricky replied. He looked down at Leah, her eyes getting bigger by the minute.

"You guys can come and stay with me," Harriet suggested.

"Really?" Owen replied.

"What?" Ricky asked.

"I have enough room for all of you and you can park your van on my drive. It's only a forty-minute drive from here."

"Oh my God, you absolute hero," Ricky said, releasing Leah and wrapping his arms around Harriet.

"Please tell me you have a working shower?" chimed Leah, seemingly unfazed by her recent altercation.

"Uh-huh, and fresh towels," Harriet replied, laughing and tossing another blood-stained towel into the bus.

"Lead the way," Ricky said, bouncing the keys between his hands and sliding into the driver's seat. He was still wearing the sweat-soaked shirt he had worn on stage.

"You wanna ride with me?" Harriet asked Owen. He smiled and looked for an approving nod from the rest of the band. Ricky flicked his head, giving him his seal of approval, and Owen beamed. He jogged to catch up with Harriet, who was already unlocking her car. He grabbed her and spun her around, kissing her like she was the most important person in the whole world. In that moment, she felt like she was.

Chapter Nineteen

HARRIET WATCHED RICKY SLOWLY REVERSE THE VAN safely into her driveway. Owen stood beside her with his hands in his pockets, gently knocking into her and smiling. He had a cheeky glint in his eyes, and she felt every nerve in her body come alive as she pressed tenderly against him. The two tag-along roadies, whose names Harriet hadn't learned, Ricky, Mike, and Leah all piled out of the bus, knocking over a large ceramic pot, tipping soil and bedding plants everywhere.

"Sorry," Mike said, attempting to pick it up and rearrange it.

"Just leave it," Harriet replied, keenly aware of the commotion and her nosy neighbours. She rattled the keys in the door and pushed it ajar.

Upon opening the door, the empty nothingness hit her all over again. That was until she turned the lights on and the party behind her made their way in. They took no time at all making themselves at home. Shoes, jackets, backpacks, instruments, and everything in between soon littered the entrance porch and kitchen floor. Bodies lay weary across her couch, chairs, and soft ruffled carpets. As strange as it was, their being there breathed new life into the empty walls. Leah headed straight for the downstairs bathroom, yet Owen lingered a moment on the front step.

"Are you coming?" Harriet asked, reaching her hand out to him.

"Wasn't expecting to see the inside of your house tonight, that's for sure," Owen replied, linking his fingers into hers and following her inside.

"You're lucky it's still here. Another few weeks and it'll be someone else's."

Most of Harriet's house was packed into boxes to be donated or to go into storage. She still didn't have a plan as to what she was going to do after the sale completed, so had decided to put all her earthly belongings into storage and stay with Jess. The plan was fluid. Harriet felt like she was waiting for the right opportunity to present itself as to what her next move would be.

Leah came back through the archway. The soft skin under her eyes had puffed up into two faint purple circles and she squinted under the spotlights of Harriet's black and white kitchen.

Harriet rummaged in the corner cupboard and pulled out some ibuprofen. Leah received them gratefully, along with the bag of frozen peas Harriet dug out from the depths of her freezer. "Towels are in the cupboard under the sink in the downstairs bathroom," she said. "I figured you and Ricky could take the bedroom downstairs and I'll chuck the rest of them upstairs."

Leah wrapped her arms around Harriet. "Thank you so much. You have no idea how much this means to us."

Harriet squeezed her back. If nothing else, she was happy to have made a new friend. Ricky and Owen were talking quietly near the front door, being extra cautious to not allow anyone to overhear them. Mike and the roadies—Lee and Jason—had crashed, barely able to keep their eyes open. The dulled voices faded, and for a brief moment, silence fell.

"You guys want some food?" Harriet asked, opening her snack cupboard. She looked at the time on her watch, determining they wouldn't be able to get a takeaway at this small hour of the morning. No one replied. Owen came and stood behind her and wrapped his arms around her waist. She could feel him waning. His grip was soft and tired, and he rested his head on her shoulder.

Harriet went over and kicked Mike's foot, startling him back awake. "Follow me, folks. I'll show you where you can sleep."

The boys followed her up the stairs. Mike took the spare double room, grateful for a big bed to spread his stocky, six-foot frame on. Lee and Jason took the twin box room at the back of the house, seemingly not caring where they slept, simply grateful for a soft pillow and central heating.

Harriet passed Ricky in the downstairs corridor. He thanked her again for letting them stay and retired to the room where Leah was already showered and snoozing.

Owen remained in the front room. He had removed his hoodie, denim jacket, and shoes. He sat on the floor against the armchair, enjoying a moment of quiet. Harriet slid into the chair behind him, and he smiled as she squeezed her legs around him. He tilted his head, resting against Harriet's knee. His gaze fixed far beyond the TV he was glaring at. She couldn't help herself, she just had to reach out and touch him. Since the moment she had laid eyes on him earlier in the evening, she hadn't even attempted to keep her eyes, or her hands, off him. She sensed his unease, frustration, and need for comfort. Something about the way he silently begged for reassurance created a magnetism she could not resist.

Delicately, she stretched her hand and let her fingertips touch the back of his neck. He flinched, then relaxed, closed his eyes, and practically purred. Softly and slowly, she moved her fingers up and down his neck. His head dropped further to the side and the tension in his shoulders began to melt away.

"Don't stop," he said.

She leaned forward, landing her lips at his collarbone, once, twice, and more. Her breath travelled down his neck, laying light kisses intermittently on his pebbled skin. She moved her other hand over his chin, lingering her index finger just below his lips as his mouth fell open and his head dropped backwards against her shoulder.

"Rough day at the office?" Harriet uttered, caressing his throat and collarbone, before gently sliding her hand down the front of his shirt. Her breath landed gently across his cheek.

"Something like that," he replied, barely above a whisper.

"Tell me what to do to help you," she asked, knowing full well what his response would be.

Her hands moved over his skin a few seconds longer and then he replied, "Take me to bed."

It was more of a request than a command. She made sure her warm breath moved slowly against his cheek as she breathed him in. Her hand lingered on his chest as she reminded herself of the valleys of his toned chest. Before she devoured him on her front room floor, she stood, took his hand, and led him up the stairs. She hadn't slept in the bed she had shared with Joe since finding out about Marie, and she felt no guilt whatsoever about inviting a new man into her new bed.

Tired and weary, he slumped onto the edge of the bed, looking up at her. Harriet bent over him, lifting his lips to hers as she straddled him. His hands made light work of her shirt, and she revelled in every second he had his hands on her. He spread his fingers wide across her back, pulling her close against him. It was even better than she remembered. He went hard the second her hungry lips touched the soft spot between his neck and shoulder.

Harriet pushed him back, ushering his jeans off, releasing the hard, pulsating cock beneath them. She watched his eyes roll back in his head as she slid down onto him, guided him inside her, and rocked back and forth. She delighted as every movement drew him deeper whilst she kissed him relentlessly until neither of them could breathe.

He flipped her over, remaining inside her, and slowly moved his hand down her throat, over the crest of her breast, towards her hips and under her butt cheek. He pulled her closer, digging his fingertips into her as he moved hard and fast, in and out.

When she arched her back at the beginning of her climax, he kissed her neck at the base of her throat, and she groaned so loudly she was sure the whole house heard her. She clung to him, tightening around him as he thrust again, reaching his own release. He growled in the back of his throat and fell onto her, panting like an animal. He clung to her like his life depended on it, and she relished the warmth and weight of his skin against hers.

Harriet lay still in blissful satisfaction, watching Owen try to keep himself awake next to her. He rubbed his eyes and shook his head. She knew he was spent in every way a man could be. She too was physically exhausted, emotionally drained, but satisfied beyond comprehension. She pulled the bed covers up over herself. "Come here," she said, stretching her arm out.

Owen lay in the nook of her shoulder and wrapped himself around her, winding every limb into hers. Before Harriet could protest that she needed more room to sleep, his breath settled into a quiet rhythm; he had drifted off and she didn't have the heart to wake him. She managed to turn the lamp off at her bedside table and rested her head against him, slowly letting her eyes fall shut and the sleep consume her.

———

THE NEXT MORNING, HARRIET STOOD IN THE CORNER of the kitchen, her brown hair piled up on top of her head, and she was wearing just a skimpy pair of shorts and a soft pink vest top. She hadn't heard Owen approach quietly from behind.

The moment he snaked his arms around her waist, delicately running his fingertips across the bare skin of her stomach, her mouth fell open. Falling into his chest, she reached up and ran her fingers along the stubble of his chin.

"Here you are looking like that," he whispered, kissing her neck." It's very distracting."

He moved his hand along the elastic at the top of her shorts, teasing her with kisses and light touches. "Mmm, come back to bed," he said as he nibbled her ear.

Harriet didn't need a second invitation. She took Owen's hand and ran back upstairs, coffee cups in hand. The drinks went cold on the nightstand as they fell into another pit of passion and desire, skin, and pleasure.

It was only when Owen emerged from beneath the

sheets, he saw he had three missed calls from Eric. Sitting on the edge of the bed, he looked at his phone as Harriet wrapped her arms around his shoulders and rubbed her face against his.

"Where do you think you're going?" she asked playfully, trying to tease him back to bed.

Owen sighed. "Sorry. I have to sort things out with Eric." He swiped right and held the phone to his ear.

"Owen?" came the voice at the end of the line.

"Eric, are you okay?" Owen asked.

Harriet could tell he wasn't really that mad at Eric. There was no anger in his voice. She could see why things like this fell to Owen to take care of.

"Like you care," came the brash response.

Harriet couldn't help but listen. Owen wasn't hiding the conversation. If he had wanted some privacy, he would have left the room.

"Of course I care," Owen said, raising his voice.

"Whatever. Listen, I don't even wanna get into it anymore. After last night, you guys can go fuck yourselves. This is me quitting."

Owen's back tensed and he sat up straight. "I thought as much." Harriet stroked the bare skin on his back.

"And after last night's fiasco, you can forget any sort of notice period and me doing any more dates with you guys."

"Fair enough," Owen said, rubbing his forehead.

"And if you can stay away from the house today, I'd appreciate it. Gives me chance to move my stuff out without seeing Ricky."

"You're leaving the house too?" Owen gasped.

"You really think I'm staying after all this?" Eric growled before he paused. "It's not you, mate. It's Ricky. That guy has lost his mind. Just, please, keep him away from the house today. I really don't want to get into it again with him."

"You know you made a right mess of Leah's face last night," Owen continued.

"Yeah, not feeling great about that, but she shouldn't have jumped on me."

"You're twice her size. It's not on. You should apologise at least."

"Not a chance, mate." Before any further exchange could be had, the line went dead.

"Fucking prick!" Owen hissed, standing up. He threw his clothes on and left the room.

Harriet swiftly dressed and followed him downstairs. Everyone else was up and had helped themselves to the coffee pot and the contents of Harriet's kitchen. The counters were strewn with crumbs, coffee grounds, wrappers, and everything else they had managed to get their hands on. She didn't mind in the slightest. It had been over a year since she had a house full of people and a mess to clean. She quickly busied herself wiping the counters and filling the dishwasher.

"Has anyone heard from Eric?" Mike asked.

"Yeah, I have," Owen replied, sitting on the couch next to Jason.

"What did he say?" Ricky asked as he gently ushered Leah up. She had been sprawled across his knee in the chair. Despite two deep purple puffy eyes and a rosy, red nose, she still looked like a Grecian goddess.

"He quit. He and Adam are moving out, and he asked if we can stay away from the house until tomorrow," Owen said quickly as if ripping off a well-worn plaster. "Also, he's not sorry about Leah's face and he thinks you've lost your mind." He pointed at Ricky.

"What are we supposed to do, then? We have to go home. We have to take this equipment back and return the bus," Mike chimed in.

Harriet could see the group becoming more unglued. It was one thing to have nowhere to stay for a night, but it was quite another to be told you can't go home. She felt bad for them all, and as much as her hard-wood floors and hot water might suffer, she felt little other choice. "Why don't you take a hit, pay the fine for returning the bus a day late, and stay here for another night?"

Silence fell across the group.

"No. We can't impose another night," Lee said instantly. "But thank you anyway."

Owen looked at Harriet and then at Ricky, who seemed remarkably peaceful and comfortable. Leah had closed her eyes and was enjoying Ricky's fingers combing gently through her hair. It was almost like they weren't even paying attention.

"You aren't imposing. I kinda like having you here," Harriet replied, refilling the coffee pot.

She liked how the house felt as if it stretched with the life that was buzzing inside it. Like it had finally exhaled after holding its breath for so long. A house like this needed to be full of people, laughter, and noise, not hibernating for months on end.

From the look on his face, she could tell Owen wanted to stay, but she knew the decision didn't rest solely with him. She felt her stomach turn at the thought of him having to leave so soon. No one made any waves towards answering her and she felt stupid for saying anything. Averting her embarrassed face to hide her flushed cheeks, she opened a cupboard door to disappear into.

"Harriet." Owen said, regaining her attention. She turned to face him. "We'll stay another night."

Harriet gave him a goofy smile and nodded. "Good!"

Relieved, she made a fresh round of drinks and set the tray down on the table in the middle of the room.

Owen had claimed the easy chair, and when she walked by, he reached for her hand and pulled her onto his lap. She manoeuvred to put her arm around his shoulder, and he looked up at her. "Thank you," he said softly.

She pushed her lips to his ear and whispered, "You really think I'm gonna let you go that quickly?"

She giggled and reached over. Grabbing her cup, she took great delight in watching him watch her. Not normally one for public displays of affection, she was surprised how little self-restraint she suddenly had as she let him kiss her cheek.

No one could deny how they gravitated towards each other. She caught Leah and Ricky smiling at them. Harriet had found the last twelve hours to be nothing short of a whirlwind. An eye-opening, unusual whirlwind where she had stepped so far out of her comfort zone, she knew she could never go back. Everything from going to a gig on her own to having a house full of people was a million miles away from the girl who had greeted the sunrise with a heavy heart and a face full of tears just a few weeks before.

Chapter Twenty

A COMFORTABLE STILLNESS HAD SETTLED AND everyone had relaxed into every available space across Harriet's living room. Harriet sat in Owen's lap and dozed happily with his arms circled around her, his fingers gently stroking her arm.

Mike had been fighting with the TV remote for a while, frustrated he couldn't get it to work properly so he could watch the football match kicking off at one o'clock. Harriet couldn't remember the last time she had watched TV and was hopeless when it came to configuring electronics; that had always been Joe's department. Mike had given in and was waiting for her streaming services to load up. When the users came up on screen, he blurted out, "Harriet, who's Joe?"

Harriet had totally forgotten he had his own profile, and she reached over and grabbed the remote from Mike. "He's my ex-husband," she replied, tinkering with the settings. "Can you take that profile off?"

He fumbled around for a few minutes and the spurious

profile vanished from the screen. "Sorry." Mike rubbed his hand through his beard awkwardly.

"Not your fault," Harriet said as she watched him delete Joe's profile. Everyone was looking at her as she perched on the edge of Owen's knees. She felt their eyes probing her, plainly wanting to know the story. Owen sat back saying nothing, but he offered her a gentle squeeze on the back of her shoulder, telling her it was okay to tell them.

"He was a cheating ratbag who slept around and had a child with someone else," she said quickly. She waited for the eyes of curiosity to turn into the eyes of judgement and braced herself for that all too familiar feeling of pity. But it didn't come.

"That's bullshit," said Lee, barely flinching at the revelation.

"What a dick," chimed Ricky in agreement.

Harriet sucked in her breath and went on, "and then he had the audacity to die, leaving me to uncover all his little secrets."

"What?" Lee growled, sitting up and leaning forward. "He died?"

Harriet nodded.

"And you had no idea about any of it?"

She shook her head. "When I went to Scotland, it was just after the anniversary of his death, and I was still grieving hard. But since then, all his skeletons have come falling out of the closet."

She caught Leah's eyes, which were whirling in a mixture of shock and sympathy. Ricky pursed his lips and frowned, and Harriet immediately looked to Owen for reassurance.

"It's okay," he mouthed at her, pulling her back into his lap.

Harriet felt a little relieved at telling them; she knew they had been trying to figure her out, especially Ricky. The curious glances he had given her, although not intrusive, were obvious, and she had been waiting for the right time to tell the pack what had happened. She knew how protective Ricky was of Owen and it was one of those things she felt inappropriate to bring up in everyday conversation. It felt like the right time, and she bravely spoke of the details of the tragic night Joe died and the things that had come to light in recent weeks.

"I really did want to come see you guys on tour and I was starting to get worried I wouldn't make it at all. When I finally stopped and collected my thoughts, I realised the only thing I wanted was to wrap my arms around this guy and hang out with you lot again." She jabbed Owen in the ribs and threw the remote back to Mike.

"So, there you have it," she said, polishing off her coffee. "That is my sad little story." She caught Ricky's eye. "Feel free to use it in a song one day."

He laughed, and eventually, so did she. Harriet knew there wasn't anything she could do to change the situation, but having these boys, Owen, and Leah around her, she finally felt like she was pushing through the other side of it.

As she settled back into the comfort of Owen's arms, her mind drifted back to Marie and the child she had shown her. The picture of that child was engrained into her mind, and she recalled it often. She was still flabbergasted by how much he looked like Joe, with his jet-black hair and stubby nose.

The vibration of her phone on the kitchen counter caught her attention and she jumped quickly out of Owen's lap. When she saw who was calling, she stepped out the front door, not wanting her new friends to hear what her likely drunk mother-in-law was about to spew at her.

Harriet paced the pavement at the front of her house. The mess of the plant pot still needed cleaning up and the bus, in the light of day, looked enormous in her driveway.

"What exactly do you think you're doing?" barked the scowling voice down the phone.

Harriet sighed. "What do you mean, Wendy?"

"Arthur drove past the house this morning and he said there was a sold sign outside."

"That's right. I've sold the house," Harriet said with gritted teeth.

"You can't do that, you silly girl. You can't sell Joe's home."

"Yes, I can. It's not his anymore. It's mine, and I don't want to stay here."

"Good God, it's like you're trying to erase him completely. How dare you?"

"I'll do exactly as I please. Besides, it has absolutely nothing to do with you," Harriet bit back, trying hard not to let it get to her.

"And Arthur said he'd seen a huge bus and people, mostly blokes he didn't know pouring in and out of the house. Why have you got a house full of blokes? You can't be moving out already. What the hell is going on?"

"Oh my God, Wendy! What I'm doing in MY house, with MY friends is nothing to do with you."

"They aren't your friends, Harriet. Are you so lonely you'll latch on to anyone? Who knows what you've all been getting up to in that house, in the bed you shared with Joe."

"STOP! For the love of God, shut up," Harriet begged, flummoxed as to why she was still entertaining the conversation.

"Carrying on with every Tom, Dick, and Harry whilst your husband is still warm in the ground."

"Your son was a cheating, deceitful, lying bastard, and I'm glad he's dead," Harriet blurted out.

Shocked at her admission, she hung up the phone and threw it across the road. She watched it shatter into a thousand tiny pieces as her legs gave way beneath her and she fell to the floor.

The world drew in. Her breath got stuck in her throat. Tears fell. Her pulse pounded so loud in her ears she went deaf. She scraped her hands into her hair. Sweat soaked her back, her chest, and her head. This must be what suffocating felt like, she thought, as another failed attempt to breathe made her throat dry and chest ache.

Panic set in. She tried again. Nothing worked. Panic multiplied. Rocking back and forth, her eyes slammed shut.

Reaching out her arm, Harriet tried to grasp something, anything, to ground her, to bring her back. Her arm hit a solid object. What was it? She balled her fist into it, gripping with all her might and turning her knuckles white.

Something pined her hand, forcing it still. She gasped, forcing air into her lungs and stopped rocking. Somehow, she caught a breath, and an oxygen rush filled her head, making her dizzy. The mist in front of her eyes pulsed. Her vision narrowed. Her heavy head hung between her legs, but she heard a faint voice.

"I got you," it said, softly at first, but then a little louder. "It's okay. I got you." The grip on her hand became firmer, and she felt warmth at her side.

Air slipped slowly down her throat and her body convulsed as she pushed it back out. Jagged and raw, it stung, but she did it.

"I got you." The voice was clearer this time.

She blinked, tears stinging her eyes. They stopped, and she shook them away. The jackhammer in her head dulled and her skin went cold as the sweat evaporated. She looked up. Owen sat beside her. Her hand rested against his chest and his arm was on her shoulder. He looked down at her still shaking form, leaning in.

"I got you," he said once more. The walls caved in. Her eyes went black, and she fell into his arms.

HARRIET WOKE LATE IN THE AFTERNOON, UNSURE HOW she made it into the bed she was sharing with Owen. Her hair was matted to her face, and she felt sticky from head to toe. She lay for a moment trying to piece things together. It took a while, but in a wave, it came flooding back.

She hadn't had a panic attack since returning from Ardmair. This one had come so out of the blue she hadn't remembered any of the things Julia had told her to do when she felt one taking hold. She felt fresh embarrassment at falling apart in front of Owen and the rest of her new friends, and she rolled over into the pillows, groaning.

The door creaked a little on its hinges as Leah peeked into the room. Her smile was as flawless as ever despite the swelling in her nose being at its worst. It had forced her eyes to close a little, but she didn't seem bothered by it. She entered the room and sat on the bed, pulling strands of hair off Harriet's face.

"Why don't you go get a shower and I'll fix your hair for you," she said.

"Where is everyone?" Harriet asked, sitting up, holding her hand to the side of her aching head.

"They're all downstairs. Owen and Ricky carried you to bed."

"Oh, God." Harriet's face fell into the palm of her hands.

"Hey," Leah said softly. "You're fine. You've seen us at our absolute worst these last couple of days. The least we can do is take care of you too."

Harriet looked up at her, willing herself not to cry again.

"We got you," Leah finished, pushing the hair behind Harriet's ears.

Once Harriet had showered, she sat perfectly still as Leah rearranged the matted mess on top of her head. Harriet felt intense trepidation at showing her face to everyone again, but she knew she had to be brave enough to re-join her friends downstairs. She only hoped they had been able to fend for themselves, hadn't wrecked her house or run for the hills, terrified of the crazy woman whose house they were staying in.

She took a deep breath as she approached them. They sat around, enjoying the beers she had forgotten were in the fridge and eating takeout they had acquired from somewhere.

"There she is," Ricky sang, making everyone laugh.

No one said anything. No one made a big deal. No one looked at her with pity or judgement. They simply thrust a plate full of food at her and welcomed her back like nothing had happened. Owen sidled up to her, smoother than caramel, and rested his hand on her hip and his forehead against hers, whispering again, "I got you."

"Thank you," Harriet replied, still feeling fragile, achy, and a little uncomfortable, but more than anything, she felt grateful. The feeling of safety and acceptance had been something she had severely missed, but she knew that with these people, she could be her true self, panic attacks and all.

———

"Stay," Harriet said as she lay on top of Owen later that night. He ruffled her hair and pulled it behind her ear as she looked up at him. "I don't want you to go."

The hour was late, the rest of the house was silent, and Harriet had been determined to bleed every last waking moment of time with Owen before he left the following morning. She surprised herself with her recent panic attack and even more so with her swift recovery. She felt she had Leah to thank for that.

He held her face in his hand; feeling his skin against hers was something she knew she would never be able to get enough of.

"God, I want to. I really do," he replied. "But we have to get this bus home and all of our equipment needs servicing before we go back into the studio next month."

Harriet knew it was a long shot asking him to stay longer, but she also knew she would kick herself if she didn't at least ask.

"Come back with us?" Owen asked, his eyes lighting up.

Harriet crawled up to him, straddled him, and kissed him softly. "You and I both know there isn't enough room in that bus for anyone else." She giggled, cupping his face and drawing his mouth to hers.

"Well, come anyway. Pack up here and just come to London," he replied, flipping her over and pressing her firmly into the bed.

"I have to tie up some loose ends here," Harriet replied.

"Tie them up then," Owen continued as he kissed her neck. "Tie them up quickly and come to London."

He pulled back, his breath warm against Harriet's lips. She looked into his glistening Hazel eyes and smiled.

"You don't belong here anymore," he said. "You belong with me."

Chapter Twenty-One

Harriet wasn't sure what reception she would be met with as she lingered in the car park at the back of Marie's office. She hadn't seen the woman since she manhandled her out of her house and blamed her for Joe's death. Harriet knew deep down what she had said was wrong, even if there was a small part of her that believed it.

She had always known what to say to get right under someone's skin. It had been the case ever since she was eight years old and had been off sick from school with tonsilitis. She had seen one of the popular girls' mums letting a man, who definitely wasn't her father, into the house at noon and not leave until mid-afternoon. Harriet's mother had warned her that her ability to observe didn't give her the right to gossip and that knowledge could be a powerful and dangerous thing when misused.

She had wanted Marie to feel as rotten to the core as she had done this last year, and in a moment of clarity as she bid Owen farewell, she realised that raising a child alone couldn't be easy, even more so when you were likely to have to lie about its origins. Harriet didn't believe she owed

Marie anything besides a half-baked apology, but she did think Marie owed her, and that was why she forced herself to wait.

"What are you doing here?" Marie barked, looking flustered from what had likely been a very long day. Harriet knew Fridays for solicitors were stressful. Harriet only lingered a split second on Marie's loose strands of hair hanging out and that she didn't seem to care that her jacket was misaligned.

"Just a minute of your time," Harriet said as Marie pushed past her to her car. "Please." Harriet placed her hand on the woman's forearm, less aggressively than the last time they have been in each other's company.

"You have one minute," Marie insisted, throwing her bag into the back seat.

"I shouldn't have said it was your fault Joe died," Harriet uttered.

Marie's exterior softened a little. "No, you shouldn't." She shut the car door and folded her arms towards Harriet. "You think I haven't been down that road? All I did was blame myself for months. Even after Anthony was born, I still blamed myself."

Harriet didn't know how to respond. She felt strangely happy the woman had suffered, but the empath in her felt nothing but sympathy.

"Do you have any idea how difficult it is for me?" Marie asked. "Raising a child who looks just like him, having to lie to my parents and friends about his father. What do you think gets you labelled more of a slut? A one-night stand or sleeping with a married man?"

Harriet shrugged. "Frankly, that isn't my problem. But believe it or not, I get it. I don't want to get it, but I do."

Marie chewed her rose-tinted lip and looked off in the

opposite direction. Harriet's understanding seemed to bounce off her, and as the tension built, she went to climb into her car. "If there's nothing else, I have to go."

"Wait, there is," Harriet said quickly. "Look, I didn't come here to talk to you about me. I came to talk to you about Joe's mum, Wendy."

"What about her?" Marie asked, raising an inquisitive eyebrow.

"Since Joe died, she hasn't coped very well. She's been worse than me. Probably worse than you."

Marie nodded. Harriet was surprised to see her acknowledging someone else's suffering. Perhaps there was more to this woman than Harriet allowed herself to believe. She shook that thought out of her head.

"I don't know if this is even possible, but would you be willing to meet her with Anthony?" Harriet asked, finally looking into the eyes of the woman who had turned her late husband's head. Her piercing blue eyes were momentarily captivating.

Marie paused, pulled her fingers to her lips, and chewed the end of her thumbnail. Harriet found it out of character, and she had to stifle a laugh.

"I'll need to think about it," Marie replied, hopping into her car and driving away.

That was the best Harriet could have wished for.

———

IT TOOK LESS THAN TWENTY-FOUR HOURS FOR MARIE to agree to take Anthony to meet Wendy and Arthur in the park. It was the first time Harriet had seen Wendy outside the confines of her house in months. She was a far cry from the empty shell of the woman she was when Harriet last saw her. Her hair was brushed, her clothes were ironed, and she wore on her face something closely resembling a smile. Harriet felt that in itself was a massive victory. She had agreed to make the introductions, but after that, she would be on her way.

It was an unusually warm and dry October day. The park was bursting with life. Children squealed with delight as they kicked piles of leaves. Mums pushed their little ones on swings, nattering away. The large trees surrounding the park were awash with every fiery colour of the season. Harriet liked to think Joe was watching over the moment from wherever he was.

Harriet's stomach nearly fell out of her when she locked eyes with the familiar, innocent eyes of the child who was a living double of his father. The silent, timid child with pensive eyes, just like Joe's, clung to his mother, who cradled him with the same love and affection Harriet was familiar with.

Introductions were made under the big oak tree as promised. Harriet wrestled with sorrow, relief, and jealousy when she saw Wendy take the child in her arms. Her face lit up like a beacon at sea. Harriet wouldn't have been surprised if it was the first time Wendy had smiled since Joe died. Besides Joe's funeral, it was the first time she had seen Arthur at all. Perhaps this would be a turning point for them. For all of them. She walked away, a weight lifted.

Harriet climbed back into the car where Jess was sitting with the engine ticking over. She was grateful for her best friend's ongoing moral support and didn't decline when she offered to drive her. The two sat and watched the interaction between the newly formed family for a few more minutes before Harriet insisted it was time to go.

When they pulled up at Harriet's parents' house, Jess reached over, taking Harriet's clammy hand into hers.

"You know you didn't have to do that," she said. "You don't owe any of them anything."

"I know." Harriet sighed. Not just an ordinary sigh, but a deep, easing sigh as she finally let go of all the trauma, guilt, and sadness she had carried for the last eighteen months. "But it was the right thing to do."

"Harriet, I don't say this enough, but I really am so proud of you. What you've been through, how you've coped, and how you've somehow managed to come back from it is nothing short of remarkable. And that, what you just did for those people..." Jess trailed off, biting her lip to supress the tremble. "What you just did, giving Wendy a piece of her son back, giving Marie a new support network —you had absolutely nothing to gain from it, yet you did it anyway. It's the most selfless act of kindness I'll ever see in my life."

Harriet welled up and squeezed her friend's hand.

"You deserve so much love and so much happiness," Jess concluded, and Harriet wrapped her arms around her, squeezing her as tight as she possibly could.

"Just one more thing to do and then I'm out of here." Harriet beamed, excitement brimming in her voice.

She sprang from the car, took her friend's arm, and burst through her parents' front door. After a preamble of hugs, pleasantries, and generic comments, Harriet uttered, "Sit down. I have some things I need to tell you."

She went through every intricate detail of the last couple of months. Harriet knew she had kept her parents at arm's length since her trip to Scotland. She had wanted to rebuild herself on her own and was grateful for the space they had given her to do so. She also hadn't wanted to burden them with the revelations about Joe, especially when she wasn't sure what the outcome was going to be.

Harriet's mother tended to overstep her mark and interfere, which, more often than not, caused more trouble than it was worth. Her father had always been quite reasonable and level-headed, but even he had his limits, and Harriet wasn't sure if infidelity and a child out of wedlock might be his tipping point.

"So, what's next?" her mother asked, as she dried her hands on her floral apron and leaned against the kitchen counter. Her stance screamed, *'fess up or you're getting a whooping.*

Harriet placed her house keys on the kitchen counter and slid them to her mother. "Can you see the estate agent gets these ready for completion in a couple of weeks? The house is empty."

"Empty?" Her mother's shock was tangible; Harriet recognised her unease and took her hand to comfort her.

"Everything is in storage until I decide what to do." She turned to Ben and threw her car keys at him. "Yo, Benny," she said. "Don't wreck it."

"You're giving me your car?" he replied before bolting out the door. He had only passed his test a few months ago and had often complained that he hated sharing his mother's pokey lime green car. Harriet's mother couldn't form the words to object, but her look said it all. She clung to her daughter. Her mother's shaking hands tightened around hers.

The day had been a mash-up of awkwardness, trepidation, and revelations. Harriet was almost spent and was itching to leave. The truth was no one in her mixed-up circle was to blame for Joe dying; they didn't ask to be in these bizarre and confusing situations. The paths these people had taken were a result of a choice Joe had made, and now they were left in the wake, trying to paddle through it.

"Where are you itching to get off to?" her father asked, giving Harriet his all-knowing glance. The one that he gave her as a child instantly made her tell the truth.

"I'm going to London to stay with Owen and the band for a little bit," Harriet replied.

"You're really going to take off like that?"

"Yes, Dad. I am. I can't stay here and risk bumping into them playing happy families. I can't stay here in a house that has no life, no soul, and no memory in it. I can't stay here and be constantly reminded of everything every time I turn a corner."

He nodded, pulling his furry brows together, at least trying to understand. Her mother was smiling, a small tear in her eye. Harriet understood how hard it had been to watch her fall apart since Joe died, and it would likely take them some time to adjust to the new version of herself she was trying to build.

"More than anything, I want to be with Owen. I want to start my new chapter, not sit here rereading the old ones. No amount of going over what's happened is going to change it. It's time to turn the page."

Harriet hugged her parents and as she stepped back outside, wrapped her arms round her younger brother as she bid him a temporary farewell. As they stood on the threshold of their front door, Harriet took a mental picture, reminding herself this was not goodbye but see you later.

"Get in the car, you little rebel," Jess said, hiking her oversized suitcase into the boot of her car.

Harriet felt like things had finally come full circle. She had been in a no-win situation, yet she still felt like she had won. She was now in a place in her life where the plan was to not have a plan. She was excited to go to London to be with Owen. She was optimistic and open to whatever opportunities and possibilities the future might throw at her. But if it all went wrong, she knew she could always come home, to the warmth and safety of her parents and family.

THE TRAIN CLATTERED INTO KINGS CROSS, BRAKES screeching and echoing around the high glassed ceilings of the old station. The main concourse had been adapted to look like an airport terminal, but the history of the building still managed to cling on for dear life.

The rain and sleet had begun to pour, and the biting wind whipping off the river Thames brought a nasty sting with it. Steam bounced off the pavements and buildings. Harriet power walked from the end of the platform, her suitcase wheels clattering behind her.

Her heart skipped a beat when she saw Owen waiting for her, a beaming smile on his face and his hands stretched out towards her. She ran at him, abandoned her suitcase, and leapt into his waiting arms.

Pulling him close, she wrapped her arms and legs around him and he held her tight against his body. He smelled like rain and denim, just like he did in Scotland.

Her body moulded against his, like it was made to be close to him. She was so relieved to be there she didn't ever want to let him go.

His smile thawed her nerves. Harriet didn't dare admit she was half expecting him not to be there. She was still struggling with someone wanting her in any capacity, let alone in the capacity Owen had desired her since they met. She ran her fingers along the light dusting of stubble on his jaw and kissed him softly.

He took her suitcase and wrapped his arm around her, leading her towards the steps down to the tube station.

"Jesus, how long are you staying for?" he asked cheekily when they reached the bottom of the steps. He adjusted himself, bent over, and stood up to Harriet looking into his eyes and chewing her lip playfully.

She took a step towards him, totally oblivious to the bustling crowds around them. "I dunno. How long do you want me for?" she asked, breathing him in.

His breath was warm and soft against her lips. Her skin tingled when he traced her jaw with his fingertips. He lit her up from the inside out. He reached for her waist, pulling her snugly against him. He kissed her softly as he whispered, "Permanently, endlessly, repeatedly."

THE END

Acknowledgments

Oh my, where do I start?

This story feels like it's been brewing for years. What started as a romance, soon turned into one woman's story about grief, growth, and gratitude. It went from writing about a band to writing about rebuilding, being brave, and rediscovering life.

I spent a lot of time researching how people cope with loss. To those who have fearlessly shared their stories online and in person – thank you for your bravery. Everyone deals with things differently and I am especially moved by those who have lived their stories out loud, baring their souls for the whole world to see. I couldn't have written it without you. I hope you all find peace and healing.

On that note, if the subjects in this story trigger anything for anyone, please get help, please reach out to someone, and please don't be on your own. Grief is a ball that never changes in size and our lives grow around it. Sometimes the ball touches the sides, and the shock and sadness all come flooding back. Be gentle. I see you. You are not alone.

To Mat – My rock, my constant, my anchor, my home, my best friend, and the love of my life – This is what I was doing instead of making you that sandwich. We never stopped fighting and we never gave up. We have a lovely life and not a day goes by that I am not thankful for it. I love you.

To Jensen and Brianna – Being your Mum has taught me more about love than I ever thought possible. You are the light of my life. I am so proud of you both and I can't wait to see what's around the corner.

Mum and Dad – Thank you for trusting me to make my own decisions after giving me the wisdom and confidence to do so. For all the teasing and all the banter, watching you grow old disgracefully is a genuine pleasure.

Rob – My big little brother. Who would have thought proofreading was yet another thing you were good at. I swear you could fall in a pile of crap and come out smelling like roses. I've known you all your life and you still surprise me. Music was the heartbeat of our childhood, and I am truly blessed to have spent it with you. I am so proud of the person you have become.

My extended family – Joel, Gemma and Chris – When the wind doesn't blow my way, you always help me adjust my sails. There isn't much we haven't all been through together. Thank you for always having my back, for cheering me on, for making me laugh. I love you guys with every fibre of my being.

Dee – My truest, dearest friend. My sounding board, compass and lighthouse. My fiercest cheerleader, agony aunt, voice of reason and a constant source of hilarity.

Sarah – You once said, "You can't write this shit." Ha, yeah, I can! Thank you for coming on the silly adventures with me. Thank you for being what I needed when I didn't know I needed it.

My wayward sisters – Ama (Melts!), Lucy, Nova, Sandy, Ness, Ellie, Hayle, Louise and Lorraine. You guys showed me, without any doubt, that family doesn't end with blood. We have seen each other at our worst and celebrated at our best. Thank you for the countless hours we have spent laughing in the gutter, for the understanding and open arms you have always shown. You guys know the deepest darkest secrets of my soul and I am forever grateful of a safe, judgement free space to keep them.

My Alpha Team – Lucy, Alison and the marvellous Tori. Alison — the first person to read this book. Your comments were so helpful and helped shape the story. Lucy, thank you for being brutally honest and telling me what worked and what didn't. Tori, Tori, Tori—my number one Alpha. Thank you for always being there to pick up my messages, for replying before I spiralled and for your gentle kindness. I mean it when I say, I could not have done this without you. I don't think I'll ever be able to put into words how grateful I am for everything you have done for me.

My Beta Team is the best!

Kathryn – I promised I'd name a character after you and I'm sorry about the braces line.

Claire – My day isn't complete until I've spoken to you. Thank you for giving me the best line and the best chuckle during the editing process – "If I hated it, I'd tell you, but I'd be really nice about it."

Simon – someone said having a bloke beta read was brave, but it needed a male perspective and I'm grateful for yours.

Hayley – a self-branded bookworm. You were the first person outside of my inner circle to read this book and I appreciate your insight so much.

In a world where we are all busy, building a business, raising kids, renovating houses and everything in between, you guys took the time to help me make this story the best it can be. Thank you all for your honesty, your feedback, your time and for your lovely comments. I love you guys!

ELJ – What the actual f**k would I do without you?

Seriously...what the f**k? I know I'm not the first person to say that and I doubt I'll be the last. In one way or another, over the past three years, we have been on a journey together. Just so you know, you are now totally stuck with me.

My writer friends – Julie Thorpe and Claire Bentley—for sharing your knowledge, answering my questions, pointing me in the right direction and your abundance of warmth. It is something I will be forever grateful for.

Karen Sanders – I was so scared when I handed my book over to you and you were straight on the phone steering me in the right direction. Your patience, guidance, and gentle coaching made the process so much easier than I expected it would be. I had to dig deep for that second round of edits but you were there cheering me on. Thank you.

Thanks, Mich, for proofreading so quickly. Your lovely comments made my day.

I once read a quote that said we are a mosaic of all the things we love, and I fully believe this is true. Huge love to all the TV shows, films, books, bands and songs that inspire me every day.

To Scotland – my roots, my heritage, my bloodline, my spiritual home. Every time the light changes, you show me something new and I am constantly open to and grateful for a new perspective.

Most of all, thank you to you, the one reading this. Thank you for supporting an aspiring author, it means the absolute world to me. And if I may, a word of advice; write your truth and live it, unwaveringly and unapologetically. Do not ever be afraid of loving the silly things that make your weird little heart happy.

Until next time...
Rox

About the Author

Rox Blackburn was born with songs in her heart and stories to tell.

By day, and sometimes evening, she is a mortgage broker, and when she's not doing that, she's ferrying her kids to the endless number of activities they take part in.

Her favourite hobbies include listening to the same song on repeat for days on end, buying books she promises herself she will read and laughing with her husband at how old they feel, despite not being.

Any downtime is spent dreaming up stories, gazing longingly at Scottish sunsets and rolling mountains and planning her next adventure, convention, gig or shenanigan.

Find Rox Blackburn on social media:

Facebook – Rox Blackburn – Author

Instagram – roxblackburnauthor

Twitter - @AuthorRox

Hive - @roxauthor

Follow Rox Blackburn on Spotify where you will find the soundtrack to this book and maybe some others.

Playlist

Track listings for this book are under the playlist 'More Than Goodbye'. It is recommended to listen in the order displayed whilst reading the book.

'Pieces' – Rob Thomas
'Lost' – The Goo Good Dolls
'Runaway Run' – Hanson
'Fat Bottomed Girls' – Queen
'Numb' – Linkin Park
'Ghost of Days Gone By' – Alterbridge
'The Boys of Summer' - The Ataris
'Call Me' – Shinedown
'Broken' – Seether ft Amy Lee
'Give Me Love' – Ed Sheeran
'Run To The Water' – Live
'Photograph' – Ed Sheeran
'Far Side of the World' – Tidelines
'Kids' – Deaf Havana
'Free Fallin'' – Tom Petty
'Brother' – NeedToBreathe ft Gavin DeGraw
'Watch The Stars' – Tidelines

Playlist

'*Light Me Up*' – Ingrid Michaelson
'*Crash and Burn*' – Savage Garden
'*We Will Stand*' – Tidelines
'*Run Baby Run*' – Boston Levi
'*More Than Goodbye*' – Fatal Charm
'*Down for the Ride*' – Slaves ft Jessie Abbey
'*Wild Is The Wind*' – Bon Jovi
'*Goodbye to You*' – Michelle Branch
'*What About Us*' – Pink
'*The Dreams We Never Lost*' – Tidelines
'*Closer*' – The Chainsmokers ft. Halsey
'*Bad Life*' – Sigrid & Bring Me The Horizon
'*Slow It Down*' – The Goo Goo Dolls
'*Follow You Follow Me*' – Genesis
'*Say*' – John Mayer
'*Where The Dandelions Roar*' – The People The Poet
'*Home*' – Blue October
'*I Want You*' – Bon Jovi
'*More Than Goodbye*' – Ted Poley

Printed in Great Britain
by Amazon